SEVEN THOUSAND FEET
ABOVE THE PACIFIC . . .

The scientist came back to consciousness to find himself propped up against a hard, cold surface that vibrated slightly. Looking up, he saw the commander of Earth-based forces standing over him and realized that he was almost certainly going to die within the next few minutes.

"I trust that you are not too uncomfortable to answer a few questions for me." Diana smiled. "We know that you have been working on a new form of the red dust bacteria. I want its exact genetic composition."

Slowly, he shook his head. "I don't know anything to tell you."

Diana turned to a large Visitor shock trooper standing nearby. "Do we have a crivit with us?"

"No, Commander."

"A pity. I guess the sharks will have to do."

Other V books from Pinnacle

V
EAST COAST CRISIS
THE PURSUIT OF DIANA
THE CHICAGO CONVERSION
THE FLORIDA PROJECT
PRISONERS AND PAWNS
THE ALIEN SWORDMASTER
THE CRIVIT EXPERIMENT
THE NEW ENGLAND RESISTANCE

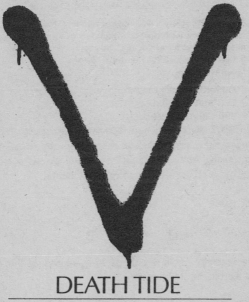

DEATH TIDE

A. C. Crispin and Deborah A. Marshall

PINNACLE BOOKS NEW YORK

V: DEATH TIDE

Copyright © 1985 by Warner Bros. Inc.

An original Pinnacle Books edition, published for the first time anywhere.

First printing/July 1985

ISBN: 0-523-42469-8
Can. ISBN: 0-523-43443-X

Printed in the United States of America

PINNACLE BOOKS, INC.
1430 Broadway
New York, New York 10018

9   8   7   6   5   4   3   2   1

For Gary Hannaford and Howard Weinstein, two talented gentlemen, friends, and all-round great human beings. Thanks for being there from the beginning.

ACKNOWLEDGMENTS

For understanding, love, advice, assistance, psychological counseling, and other forms of hand holding, the authors wish to publicly and fondly thank the following:

• Pixie Lamppu—who helped from the beginning.
• The producers, cast, and crew of *V*—who made this real to us.
• Harriet P. McDougal and Robert Jordan—who edited.
• Charles O. Thomas—who was always there.
• The Whileaway Writers' Co-op—for the best in friendship and writing help this side of Sirius.
• Margellina's—who helped keep body as well as soul together.
• Randy and Jason Crispin—for sharing room and board.
• Warren Norwood—who gave practical tips for success.
• The (056) gang (Al, Betty, Bil, Charlie, Don, Gail, Gwen, Jerry, Jim, Kip, Ron, Susan, and Wanda—and honorary members Judith, Shirley, and Rosemary)—who consistently cut through the red tape.
• Nena R. Marshall and Josephine G. Marshall.
• Everyone else who loves us. (You all know who you are!)

AUTHORS' NOTES

Ann C. Crispin is one of the world's finest human beings.

Okay, I've said the most important thing I'm going to, here in the introduction to my first book. If you want to skip on ahead into the story, fine by me.

For the rest of you, I'll tell the short tale of how this book came to be.

It began over eight years ago, when I met Ann at a Star Trek convention in New York City. We discovered we both shared a passion for writing and other things besides one of the best TV shows that ever was—and we lived within an hour of one another in the Washington, D.C. area.

Ann and I swapped ideas for stories over the few years—then she demonstrated how the pros do it, by sitting down and writing (and rewriting five times) *Yesterday's Son*.

Last September Ann and I vacationed in Los Angeles. Because of her success with *V*, we got to visit the set in Hollywood and meet the cast, crew, and producers of the TV series, even watch a couple of scenes being filmed. Two days later, while cruising around Catalina Island on a tour boat and listening to the lecture on how bladder kelp grows a foot a day in these waters, I stared down into the Pacific, nudged Ann and said, "Supposing the Visitors threatened our ecology by something they were doing to the seaweed? And furthermore . . ."

Ann, sunning herself on a bench, opened one eye, said something profound like, "Huh."

I smiled, thinking I had amused her for a moment. Then she said after a while, "Not only that, but I think . . ." We both played the game for several hours that hot, sun-dappled day on Catalina.

Then Ann called me up the day after our vacation and suggested we collaborate on a TV script proposal. We talked, I wrote, and Ann revised. We both have the same kind of computer/word processors (Morrow), so it was easy meeting for dinner and disk-swapping.

Ann mentioned our project to her editor, Harriet McDougal, who said if we wanted to expand the proposal into a book, then she would buy it.

Ann had to repeat this to me several times, in easy, two-syllable words, before I understood that it was possible to sell one's first novel before ever having written it.

And here's where Ann proved she was not only a terrific writer and friend, but a fine collaborator and teacher. Expanding our basic premise, we worked out the plot together. Then Ann suggested I handle the first draft. Her matter-of-fact acceptance that I could rise to the challenge and meet a tight deadline helped me learn a lot of things that are also proving useful as I write my own novel. Among the best of these is Rule Number One of writing: More than talent or inspiration, it's hard work, folks. (Rule Number Two is, it's worth every minute.)

I hope you enjoy reading this a fraction as much as I enjoyed writing it with Ann. I have only a few more parting words of advice. *Don't* send any *V* ideas you may have to Ann, me, or the publishers. Pinnacle is the only publisher with the copyright to publish *V* books, and they are only buying books from professional writers and on an individual basis. Any unsolicited manuscripts must be returned unopened. If you want to be a writer, set your story in a universe of your own making.

To my collaborator and best friend, thanks. I love you, Ann. To the rest of you, take the advice that Visitor parents give their children: Never accept mice from strangers.

Enjoy!

—Debby Marshall
December 1984

Hello again. Writing this book has been fun, though the usual rush-rush. You all know about working mothers and how hard it is to schedule a career around small children. At least when you're a writer, you have the freedom to set your own hours (although frequently those hours are from ten P.M. to two A.M., when the house is—finally!—quiet).

Writing a book with my buddy Debby while trying to complete another by myself (*Sylvester*, a spring 1985 TOR release) has been a real challenge, but one I wouldn't have missed for the world. Debby is a terrific friend, and her enthusiasm, warmth, and sense of fun make her a joy to be around. She's no slouch as a writer, either. You'll be seeing her name on printed pages again, I feel sure.

At this point, I've been privileged to collaborate on three books with other professional writers, and I find it one way to alleviate (but not eliminate) the inevitable solitude that is the essence of writing. There's no way around it—in order to produce a book, you *must* sit down and write it. And then, in many cases, rewrite it. And rewrite . . .

But in collaborations, there is someone else who cares, someone to whom this book matters as much as it does to you. And that's why I've done a number of them. Sharing a book with a friend is a good way to deepen and strengthen a friendship.

If you don't kill each other first!

Seriously, I want to thank Debby for the experience—and for the fun. I hope you enjoy *V: Death Tide* as much as we did!

Yours in lizardry,
Ann C. Crispin
December 1984

DEATH TIDE

Chapter 1

Current Events

The helicopter swooped low, then banked over the Pacific Ocean, its shadow a dark blotch sliding over the improbable blue of the Catalina waters. In its passenger seat, Dr. Juliet Parrish frowned, reached into her purse for a couple of Maalox, and chewed reflectively.

From this height, the indigo swaths marking the seaweed beds below appeared unchanged. Julie narrowed her eyes against the brilliant sparkle of the early afternoon sun as she peered down at them, hoping fervently that the kelp would look as healthy under a microscope.

"The camp's down there." A buzzing voice sounded in her headphones and she turned to look at the pilot, Mac, a friendly, gum-chewing redhead as he pointed to a tiny deserted cove on the leeward side of the island. "Y'can make out the cook shed and tents even though they've been camouflaged—if you know where to look. See the shadows near the ironwood trees?"

Almost deserted, Juliet mentally corrected as she made out five tents and a battered little plywood hut huddled around the charred remnants of a campfire. As the Science Frontiers chopper nosed toward the sand, its blades slicing the hundred-plus summer air, a blond young man in swim trunks came out of one of the tents and waved, then disappeared back inside.

"That's Andrew Halpern, Doc," Mac commented, circling down for a landing on the flat stretch of sand. "No, wait till I shut her down," he cautioned as the young scientist began unbuckling her seat harness. "This baby kicks up a lotta dust."

1

Julie sat back against the seat, looking out at the sun-bright beach.

"Andrew Halpern," she murmured. "I've heard of him. Nathan Bates hired him right out of school."

"Yeah," Mac said, busy with switches. "He's like you, Doc. Young and smart. But there's a big difference. *He* never lets you forget it."

"Is he a biochemist too?"

"Nope. A botanist. And he thinks he's the greatest gift to women since unrationed panty hose. Has a real thing for blondes. You'd better watch yourself."

Juliet nodded absently as she slid out of the chopper, glad when the dying *whupa-whupa* of its blades stopped and the wave sounds became audible again. She stood for a moment looking up the cove, shading her eyes against the glare, which was strong even through her prescription sunglasses, feeling the heat settle over her body like a muffling blanket. Turning, she scanned the horizon for the faint smudge of the Los Angeles smog, but the heat had burned the sky clear of everything except pale blueness. Even the giant Visitor Mother Ship hovering a mile or so over the city looked dwarfed, insignificant.

Julie took a deep breath, feeling some of the tension that was her constant companion these days ebb away like the tide at her feet. Far out to sea a silver arc marked a dolphin's passage, and she smiled at its beauty. Despite the heat, the sea air was fresh against her face, a marked difference from her laboratory at Science Frontiers.

She pushed a hand through her shoulder-length hair, trying to remember the last time that she'd gone to the beach with nothing more than a good time and a tan in mind. It had been at least two years ago, before the Visitors arrived. An eternity ago—an eternity of experience, if not years.

Two years ago Juliet Parrish had been a fourth-year medical student at UCLA, eagerly pursuing her sideline interest in research biochemistry. "What were you doing when the Visitors arrived?" was still a standard social question, much the way "Where were you the day John Kennedy was shot?" had been over twenty years earlier.

Julie vividly remembered her own day. She had just completed tests on a small white mouse she'd kiddingly dubbed Algernon. verifying that a formula she had helped develop might speed the healing process in injuries. She had still been glowing in the warmth of rare praise from her mentor, Dr. Rudolph Metz, when Dr. Benjamin Taylor had rushed in to turn on the lab's TV set, and Dan Rather's face had filled the screen, telling them that giant UFOs—*UFOs!*—had been sighted all over the world. Then the picture was there, confirming the newsman's impossible words—a huge silver vessel, saucer shaped like in those old fifties movies, hovering over San Francisco, dwarfing the Bay and the Golden Gate Bridge—and Rather was saying that identical craft, estimated at five miles or more in diameter, had appeared over fifty or more major cities, among them Paris, New York, Geneva, Rome, Buenos Aires, Tokyo—and Los Angeles.

The Visitors had looked reassuringly human, although their voices had a strange resonance about them, as though electronically multitracked. John, their supreme commander, had promised to share their vast scientific knowledge with humanity in exchange for assistance in manufacturing a chemical they said was desperately needed to save their dying planet. Julie's excitement (she had wanted to ask them about their DNA and physiology, for starters) had turned to disappointment and frustration as the weeks passed and the promised scientific seminars had been repeatedly postponed with vague and disquieting excuses.

Then Ruth Barnes, their lab assistant, didn't come in to work one morning. Other disappearances in the scientific community were followed by the nightmarish escalation of events. Accusations arose, along with trumped-up charges that scientists were forming a conspiracy against the Visitors and were withholding important discoveries from the public, and a shocked and angry outcry against the scientific community grew. When Dr. Metz was arrested, Julie had left her increasingly distant stockbroker lover, Denny, to go underground and lead a handful of people determined to fight the growing and insidious threat of the Visitors.

The threat became hideous reality when they discovered the real reasons behind the Visitors' journey to Earth—the aliens were stealing Earth's water for transport back to their barren home world circling Sirius. Pure, liquid water, it seemed, was a rare quantity in this portion of the Milky Way. By taking over the Earth, the aliens were fulfilling a master plan to strip the planet of its water and food resources. Beneath their outwardly human masks, the Visitors were reptilian, requiring live or freshly killed meat. Including human meat.

Julie turned away from the *whoosh-boom* of the beach and began slogging toward the camp. Sweat gathered in her armpits, made her cotton blouse cling lovingly to her midsection. She was fleetingly glad that she'd worn a skirt instead of slacks. Hot sand cascaded over her sandals, gritting between her unstockinged toes, until she was tempted to go barefoot, but the heat radiating off the beach argued against it. Even with her polarized sunglasses, the glare was making her dizzy. Her thoughts wandered again to the past.

From the beginning of the resistance efforts to unseat the Visitors' ever-tightening grip on the city, Juliet had emerged as the group's leader. She still didn't know how it had happened—always, it seemed, decisions had had to be made, and she'd been the only one willing or able to make them. Their tiny cadre had grown into a trained fighting unit, and Julie, a medical student who'd never even touched a weapon, had before long found herself knowing as much about the care and use of guns—including the Visitor laserguns—as she knew about anatomy.

Leadership—she'd hated it, every minute. The sleepless nights of worry, people looking to her for answers she didn't have, planning raids where people died, plotting ways to destroy life instead of preserving it. For a long time she'd been too preoccupied coping with the crushing responsibility, the problems of simple survival to worry much about herself or the emptiness inside her when she remembered Benny. Ben Taylor had died in her arms, and Julie herself bore a livid seam across her hip that still pained her in damp weather. And they were just the first scars. . . .

The only good thing to come out of those early days of the Visitor occupation was Michael Donovan. The former freelance cameraman had been the first to discover the true nature of the aliens and, with his Vietnam experience in reconnaissance and piloting, had become one of their most valuable resources against the Visitors. Julie grinned wryly as she picked her way over the stony ground bordering the beach, remembering.

When she had first met Donovan, she had been annoyed at herself for finding him attractive. His green eyes and handsome Irish features notwithstanding, he'd been a reckless, driven loner, cynical and hard-shelled, who made no secret of the fact that he was more interested in getting his son, Sean, back from the clutches of the Visitors than with actively helping the resistance. At first Juliet had wrestled with herself over recruiting him—his obsession over his son's imprisonment in the Mother Ship made him a security risk.

As the months wore on, though, Mike had come to serve a larger cause than himself—and he and Julie had learned to care for each other. Thanks to a hideous, artificially-induced Visitor/human pregnancy the Visitor leader, Diana, had implanted in a teenage girl, Robin Maxwell, Juliet and her research team had discovered a bacteria deadly to the reptilian Visitors. V-Day had come with the release of thousands of balloons into the atmosphere, spreading the red dust of the bacteria and sending the Visitors back into space, minus thousand of casualties and their hold on Earth.

Life had gone back to normal again following the Visitors' defeat. Julie had been able to complete a Ph.D. in biochemistry at UCLA and join the staff of Science Frontiers, a prestigious research laboratory headed by the wealthy and powerful Nathan Bates.

And then Nature played a cruel trick. The red bacteria, which had settled harmlessly into the ecosystem of Earth, turned out to require a dormant period of coolness in order to reproduce. A year after the Visitors left, it had vanished from all regions below the frost belt. The hated saucer shapes of the Visitor Mother Ships, thought to be banished forever from the skies of Earth, had reappeared over Los Angeles and other cities in the warmer climates. They had been hiding behind the moon, trying to find an antidote against the red toxin, waiting. . . .

Nathan Bates, founder of Science Frontiers and Julie's boss, had bargained with Diana, the leader of the aliens, to keep Los Angeles a free zone where both Visitors and humans could mingle. The situation reminded Juliet of the Casablanca depicted in her favorite Bogart film. The majority of the world's tropic and subtropic zones weren't so lucky; there, the aliens held complete sway.

Julie's ongoing work consisted of mutating the red dust bacteria, trying to coax a strain into adapting to hot climates. This Catalina variant had showed the most promise to date, flourishing in the bladder kelp surrounding the island in the month since they had introduced it. If this form of bacteria could also be genetically altered to be happy in a land-based environment as well . . .

This could be it, she thought, frowning a little as she felt another twinge in her stomach. *Or it could turn into an ecological disaster on a huge scale.* Footsteps sounded behind her.

"You okay?" Mac asked as he peered down at her, his homely, craggy face full of concern.

"Yeah, fine," she said. Actually, she'd been queasy and subject to nausea for the last couple of days. She wasn't sure whether it was a stress reaction, or possibly some allergy to the substances she was working with. *Occupational hazard in my line of work,* she thought.

"Well, I'm due back to take Mr. Bates to the ranch for the long Fourth of July weekend," the pilot said. "Just have them send a message on the radiophone when you want to be picked up, okay?"

"Sure," Julie said, giving him a cheerful wave, but she couldn't help feeling a little abandoned as she watched the chopper beat its way into the air again.

"Hi!" Juliet jumped to find that the blond young man she had seen from the air was behind her, grinning pleasantly. She looked up into his tanned, regular features and smiled back.

Something about Halpern's lithe, well-muscled body and easy grin reminded her of Mike Donovan. Julie found herself eyeing him appreciatively and thought wryly it had been *much* too long since she and Mike had had any time to themselves— nearly two weeks since their last encounter. And making it on the couch in the deserted underground headquarters beneath the Club Creole definitely didn't qualify as the most romantic and relaxing of interludes. When would they ever get any real time alone again?

Shading her eyes against the sun with one hand, she looked up at him. "Hi, I'm Juliet Parrish. You must be Dr. Halpern."

"You're our resident seaweed expert," he said, extending his hand.

'Yeah," she replied. "I'm trying. Actually, I've contacted the group in Hawaii to see if we can't get a real marine biologist up here. We need one."

He held up a dripping stalk of ropy kelp. "We're having a special today. Three bunches for a dollar."

"About the only thing in California now that isn't rationed."

"Yeah, well, I knew you'd want the most up-to-date specimens. Come on in, Julie." He led the way into the largest of the tents. After the brightness outside, the darkness seemed close and almost total. Blinking, Julie took her regular glasses out of her bag and after a minute could make out the hulking outlines of microscopes, lab tables, tubs, and incubators. The air inside the tent smelled of sweat, agar, and the ever-present fishy reek of the kelp.

Three people rose from camp stools as she approached. "Drs. Amelia Anderson, Juan Perez, and Bill Kendall," Halpern indicated each in turn. "This is Dr. Juliet Parrish."

After murmured greetings, Perez, a short, stocky Hispanic, pointed to a pan steaming on a kerosene stove. "You miss lunch, Dr. Parrish? Join us, please."

"Spécialité du maison," said Halpern, grinning as he reached for a paper plate. "Pork and beans with fresh sea trout, which I caught this morning."

Julie's stomach lurched as the fried fish assaulted her nostrils. "Uh . . . no, thanks. Maybe later."

Sitting with her back against the brick wall of the alley, Maggie Blodgett watched Chris Faber carefully manufacture a bomb and tried to ignore the stink of the garbage spilling out of the ancient green dumpster beside them. The big man whistled softly between his teeth as he spliced two tiny wires together, then looped them around a screw. For the umpteenth time, she marveled at how such large hands could do such delicate work. "How long did it take you to learn that?" she asked.

"When you're working with Ham Tyler, nothing takes long to learn." Chris shifted his gum from one side of his mouth to the other. Shading his eyes, he shifted his position to peer cautiously around the dumpster at the ancient Ford Fairlane they'd towed over that morning to block the mouth of the alley. "With him, you either catch on fast or you're dead."

She nodded in agreement. Since the Visitors had landed, that was a pretty fair summary all around. Maggie herself had learned a lot after joining the resistance two years ago—how to shoot an M-16 or a lasergun with equal skill, how to infiltrate Visitor enclaves, how to obtain vital information using whatever means proved necessary. Blodgett frowned, remembering the weeks when she'd deliberately set herself to attract the infamous Daniel Bernstein, the human turncoat who had become the leader of the Visitor Friends group, sleeping with him to glean the facts that had helped lead to the aliens' initial defeat.

She'd also learned about the anguish of loss. First Sam, her pilot husband, had been killed when the Visitors declared martial law, crushing the few military groups that had dared fight back, then she'd lost Brad McIntyre, an ex-cop and fellow resistance fighter who had become her lover. They'd made plans one night to marry, daring to hope there would be a tomorrow, then he had died two hours later in an explosion the resistance had set in a hydroelectric plant. He had covered their escape as he lay trapped, his leg shattered. Maggie's throat tightened, remembering the way Chris had scooped her up and dragged her away, shrieking and struggling.

"So where are you from?"

"Huh?" Maggie blinked as Chris's voice broke into the silence of her memories. "Oh. Encino. And you?"

"Baton Rouge, Louisiana." Hoisting his lasergun to his shoulder, he sighted along its barrel. "I liked the West Coast beaches better, so I made L.A. my home base between missions. Damn! Sure don't like the way this power pack's reading. Hope this raid works, or we'll be stuck trying to fire these babies with Duracells."

"Yeah." Maggie glanced nervously at the reading on her own laser pistol. All of the Visitor technology—their guns, their ships, their communications devices—was powered by the palm-sized energy cells that apparently contained atomic batteries. No one was sure precisely how they worked, because the few attempts to open the small metallic cases had proved disastrous for the curious—as well as anyone within a one-block radius. The power in each small cassette was enough to drive their captured skyfighters for over a year. But now they had only a handful of the packs left—hence this broad-daylight raid on the expected Visitor supply vehicle.

Chris had evidently observed her anxious frown. "Scared?"

"A little."

"Good. I don't trust a partner who isn't a little scared. Makes me think he or she knows something I don't. Want some gum?"

"Sure."

"It's Juicyfruit." Reaching into the pocket of his ever-present camouflage jacket, Chris pulled out a crumpled yellow packet and handed her a stick.

"God, I haven't had this in years." She chewed gratefully, glad for something to do with her tongue besides constantly running it along the dryness of her mouth and lips. "How'd you get hold of this?"

He grinned. "I never reveal my sources."

Maggie indicated the power reading on her laser pistol. "Mine's in even worse shape than yours. Think I ought to chance stopping them with this?" She tapped the .38 Police Special tucked into the waistband of her jeans. Specially modified to use the Teflon-coated shells that were their best projectile ammo against the Visitor armor, the .38 nevertheless lacked the power to kill or disable except at point-blank range.

Chris shook his head. "Uh-uh. There ought to be at least a coupla jolts left, and you're a good enough shot that you won't need more."

Maggie grinned, genuinely touched by the compliment. "Thanks."

They settled into a companionable silence, waiting.

The Visitors' own laserguns had proven to be the most effective weapon against their body armor. Unfortunately, the weapons and a couple of Visitor shuttlecraft the resistance now possessed had proved easier to steal than the small energy cells that powered them. They'd gotten the tip on this shipment from a resistance member who had managed to eavesdrop on a conversation outside the L.A. Visitor legation.

Maggie shifted her position, frowning as she brushed newspaper and orange-peel fragments from the seat of her jeans. The air was baking hot—hot even for a Los Angeles afternoon in July. At least there was no humidity and little smog. Visitor restrictions on traffic had improved L.A.'s infamous smog problems, but, Maggie thought, this was definitely a case where the solution had proved far worse than the problem.

"Hand me the timer, will you?" asked Chris.

Maggie blinked in the sun as she handed over the device. "How can you stand to wear that jacket?" she asked. "It's gotta be ninety-nine degrees out here."

He shrugged heavy shoulders philosophically. "Used to it, I guess." With his jaw-length shaggy hair, wispy blond beard and mustache, he resembled a cross between a sixties demonstrator and a grizzly bear. As Maggie looked at him, she experienced a sudden memory of the moments following Brad's death, when she'd looked back at the flaming hell of the hydro plant that had become his pyre. She'd lost it for a few minutes then, and come back to find herself flailing wildly at Chris's chest and midsection. Her fists had hurt because what she'd thought was beer gut was mostly muscle. He'd stood there, letting her pound out her anguish and grief until she'd collapsed, sobbing, and then his arms had encircled her, giving her something to lean against while she cried.

He glanced up at her now, and she looked quickly down at her watch. "Let's check our time," she said. "I've got two thirty-eight."

He nodded in that offhanded way of his, pushing the bomb casually aside. "Six more minutes. You still scared?"

"Yeah, but I can handle it."

"Betcha can't tell me a Visitor joke I haven't heard," he challenged, his pale blue eyes crinkling at the corners.

"Hmm . . . what do Visitors call joggers?"

"Fast food. That's an oldie."

Maggie grinned, feeling some of her anxiety abate in spite of herself. "I'll have to update my collection."

"Time the boss showed up." Chris had barely finished the sentence when Ham Tyler stepped from a recessed doorway on the other side of the building and beckoned to them.

Maggie didn't know the ex-CIA man well, but then, no one did. The solidly built man with the thinning brown hair was an enigma, his dark eyes seldom revealing anything except calculation and contempt.

"We're all set," said Chris, tossing him one of the bombs with what seemed to Maggie appalling casualness.

Ham nodded at Maggie. "Okay, hon, it's show time."

Pulling a plastic squeeze bottle out of her bag, she squirted herself liberally with theatrical "blood," so that it dribbled down her face and chest. At the mouth of the alley, she checked to make sure the street in the old warehouse district was deserted, then gave the thumbs-up without looking behind her.

Face to the wall and crouched into a protective ball, she covered her ears and counted to ten. An instant later, a loud explosion rocked the asphalt beneath her, and debris showered from the exploded Fairlane as its gas tank caught fire with a *whoosh*. Maggie darted into the middle of the street, then fell, sprawling safely away from the heat of the burning hulk.

Minutes dragged by as she forced herself to lie still, the makeup itching maddeningly as it dripped from her scalp in the direct sunlight. Finally she heard the rumble of a heavy vehicle as it came around the corner.

For a horrible instant, Maggie wondered whether they might just run over her, but then the engine noises changed, gears clashed, and the truck rolled to a halt less than ten feet from her.

The sounds of a door slamming open and booted feet clumping up to her filled Maggie's awareness.

"You fool!" an alien-resonating voice boomed just above her. "What do you think you're doing?"

"I'm hungry," said another voice like cold metal. "This one looks freshly killed, and—"

"Surprise," Maggie murmured as she rolled over and blasted the alien in the face with the lasergun she'd been lying on. The other Visitor fell back with a startled cry which turned into a death scream the next instant as he was hit from behind.

"Ain't we got fun?" Ham asked from the rear of the Visitor vehicle, gesturing with his weapon. "Watch your backs, kids."

Maggie scrambled to her feet as the side hatch split open and five Visitor shock troopers spilled out, weapons raised.

Ham felled another of them, then dodged left as a laser bolt charred the place he'd been standing an instant before. More blasts crisscrossed the air in front of them, leaving crazy afterimages behind, and the air smelled of ozone and charred Visitor flesh—like a chicken left on the barbecue way too long.

Maggie squeezed off a couple more shots, which only scored the side of the squad vehicle as she raced toward the back.

Chris was aiming point-blank at the one wearing officers' insignia as the alien stood in the back door of the vehicle. As he squeezed the trigger, a forlorn whine came from the weapon as the beam turned pale and scattered. "Son of a bitch," he muttered, his face shocked as the alien staggered back a moment, then jumped him.

He grappled hand-to-hand with her; her small size belied her strength. Raising the butt of his weapon, he slammed it against the Visitor's head. The false human skin split and flapped down her cheek, revealing the greenish reptilian scales beneath.

Hissing, the Visitor opened her mouth wide. Maggie saw the flash of what looked like a second set of teeth, and Chris screamed as venom sprayed into his face.

Smiling hideously, the alien raised her own weapon for the kill, then fell forward against Chris, her back a mass of blackened leather from Maggie's laser blast.

Ham shot one of the two remaining Visitors, but the other had scrambled back into the vehicle and was starting it.

"Nice shooting, kid," he said, squatting beside the injured Chris, who was frantically pawing at his eyes and cursing. "Come on, we've got to get out of here before the reinforcements arrive."

"Can't see a damn thing," Chris muttered as Ham helped him stand up. Maggie glanced up at a sound overhead to see a Visitor skyfighter swooping low, strafing the ground around them with laser blasts.

"Go!" Ham yelled, shoving her in the back. Grabbing Chris's hand, she stumbled toward the shelter of the alley as the skyfighter circled back.

Ham waited until the last possible instant, standing in the road, almost daring them to strike; then he sprinted for the shelter of the alley. He fiddled with a device hooked on his belt, then covered his head. A loud *whuump!* came from underneath the moving ground vehicle as it burst into flames.

The concussion caught the belly of the alien aircraft and sent it rocking wildly out of control. The craft tried to pull up, but the tall billboard at the end of the street loomed in front of it. Crashing right through the smiling face of the Marlboro man, the vehicle plummeted into the roof of an old warehouse and exploded.

"We didn't get the goddamn energy cells, but at least now they're not gonna do the scalies any good either," Ham said as he joined them. "How's Chris?"

"We've got to get him to a doctor," Maggie said, dabbing cautiously at the big man's face with the tail of her T-shirt. Faber stiffened but made no sound as she wiped the viscous liquid off his face. "See these burns? He got it in his eyes, as well as around them." She focused suddenly on a spreading red stain on Tyler's upper arm. "You're hurt too."

"Nah, it's nothing. Let's head back and call the clinic. Doc Akers knows his stuff *and* how to keep his mouth shut."

Slowly, Chris between them, they walked toward Ham's car.

* * *

"No, I don't like it." Elias Taylor, owner of the Club Creole, frowned and shook his head at the pencil sketch.

"How about this, then?" Miranda Juarez sketched rapidly for a few moments, then pushed another drawing across the bar in front of him.

"No, that's too preppy looking. See, what I really want here is something classy, a statement. Not just another piece of tacky advertising, you understand, but a true status symbol. Something the owner can use to say, 'Hey, I have the good taste to eat and drink at the hottest spot in L.A., and the rest of you turkeys better get on the program.'"

Miranda made a rude noise. "Yesterday he was a punk street kid hustling quarters and stolen watches. Today he's Mister Big-time Fashion Designer."

"Hey, if it's bringing in the bucks . . ." Elias stopped when he saw the teasing grin on the young woman's face.

He had hired Miranda as a waitress after they'd met in the resistance, and she'd proved invaluable in both roles. A registered nurse who'd served in Vietnam, the young Hispanic woman possessed a street-savvy toughness that could give way to a surprising gentleness when someone needed comfort or stitches. Elias found her long blue-black hair and high-cheeked features very attractive, and had several times considered asking her out—but was it a good idea to mix social and business relations? Elias wasn't sure.

As their gazes clung and held, Miranda turned away suddenly, her cheeks flushed. "Hey, Willie! Can you come over here a second?" She waved at the bartender, who came forward, wiping his hands on a dishcloth.

Wearing jeans and a T-shirt, he was a shortish, compact man with curly blond hair and features that were open and pleasant rather than handsome. "Yes, Miranda?" The unmistakable voice resonance identified him as a Visitor.

William had begun his pseudo-human life as "Ahmed," learning to speak Arabic for his expected assignment in Saudi Arabia. But the Visitors, advanced as they were technologically, proved to be just as prone to bureaucratic snafus as humans. He had wound up as a technician at the Richland refinery in L.A. with little English and even less instruction in the social customs of American humans.

Decency and a sense of morality were not confined to the

human race, however. Willie had risked his own life to save
Caleb Taylor, Elias's father, from a cryogenics accident at the
plant. Since then, he had had a lot of associations with humans
and had come to respect them not only as individuals but as a
species equal in intelligence to his own.

A vegetarian himself, Willie had been shocked to discover
the real mission of the Visitors. When he was captured, he had
already decided to help the humans in any way he could, and
chose to remain with his adopted people willingly. Part of this
decision had been due to Harmony Moore, the first human
woman he had ever met. Sweet and gentle, she had learned
what he really looked like and said she loved him anyway. That
revelation had come only days before she'd died in his arms
from a Visitor laser blast.

"Which one of these do you like the best?" Miranda spread
out the series of sketches.

"Um . . . they are all most excellent, Miranda."

"Yeah," said Elias. "But which one *really* grabs you,
Willie? I need the one that knocks your socks off, makes you
want to *die* to have it, y'know?"

Willie blinked uncertainly as he struggled with the collo-
quialisms. "I cannot see how a piece of paper could restrain
me and remove my socks, and I'm sorry, Elias, I do not wish to
die to have any of these."

"He means which one is your favorite, Willie," said
Miranda. "Which one would you most like to buy?"

"Oh." Looking at the designs, the Visitor pointed to one,
then another. "Perhaps a combination of these designs—the
palm trees from here, and . . ." Taking a pencil, he drew a
small sketch beside one of Miranda's larger ones.

"I'll be damned!" Elias said, his dark brown eyes widening
with surprise—then pleasure—as he looked down. "That's it!
Willie, my man, make yourself a drink. I'll order twelve dozen
of 'em and get hold of a friend of mine who lives in—"

The door to the Club Creole opened, and Caleb Taylor
entered. "Hey, Pop!" Grinning happily, Elias hugged his father
and gestured him to a seat at the bar. "Have a beer on the
house."

"Hello, Caleb," Willie said, smiling as he brought a draft.

The elder Taylor grimaced a little as he eased himself onto a
stool. "Hey, Willie."

"How's your arthritis doing, Pop?"

"Could be better. I can't go running around at all hours of the day and night like you young folks anymore. It's . . ." Caleb's glance fell on the scattered drawings on the bar. "What the hell's this?"

"Design ideas for the new line of sport shirts I'm introducing for the club. Should make a bundle. Here's the winner—Willie's idea."

Caleb snorted. "A *lizard* under a palm tree?"

"Yeah, a little inside joke, you know? With the club's initials."

"Yeah, well . . ." Caleb shook his head, grinning, then looked around the room. "This place has shaped up real nice."

His father's expression of frank admiration at the tasteful wood decor, the rattan furniture, the profusion of plants made Elias smile. He'd worked hard on this place to create an impression of both spaciousness and intimacy.

"Who would ever have thought my son would own the hottest night spot in town?"

"Aw, Pop . . ." Elias laughed. "I'm a businessman now, and it pays the mortgage." The phone buzzed softly, and the flashing light beneath the bar told him someone had just entered the secret tunnel leading to the resistance headquarters in the subbasement. "Excuse me," Elias said, then picked up the phone. "Club Creole, may I help you?"

"You and Miranda better get down here right away. Tell her to bring her first-aid kit." Ham Tyler's voice sounded brusque as usual, but there was an odd, underlying strain to it. "Have Willie call Doc Akers. Chris took a shot of venom, and he's blind."

"Diana, I need those power packs right away!" The graying man with the no-nonsense look about him leaned forward in his plush executive's chair.

On the TV-like screen on the desk in front of him, Diana's classical features remained serene and unconcerned. "Nathan, if I said I would see to it that they are delivered to you, then I will do so. Surely you, used as you must be to dealing with bureaucracies of many sorts, realize that these things take time."

Nathan Bates, head of Science Frontiers, leaned back in his chair, thinking quickly.

He was used to walking the tightrope between dangerous

and daring ever since the day his dream of heading up an independent, high-powered research-and-development think tank had come true. People alternately feared, admired, hated, and envied those in positions of wealth and power—he'd learned that early on.

For the population of L.A., Nathan Bates was either a hero or the worst turncoat on the West Coast, depending on who you listened to. When the red dust bacteria had died out in the frost-free areas of the world, Bates had bargained with Diana, now commander of all Earth-based forces, to make the City of the Angels an "open city." In exchange for certain concessions, such as helping to stamp out the disruptive resistance efforts, he had agreed that Visitors and humans were to be free to move about the city unarmed.

It seemed reasonable to Bates that he should become the head of the provisional government that now ran Los Angeles—why make the rules unless you could also enforce them? From his point of view, his actions had saved his city from the destruction and occupation visited upon less fortunate southern cities.

He'd bought time for the human race, and Science Frontiers now provided a place where the best minds could work together to come up with a solution to the Visitor infestation once and for all. If his actions also brought him greater position and profits, well, so much the better. He was not a particularly introspective man, and his philosophy of life could be pretty well summed up as, "You do what you have to do."

"Diana," he said as he leaned forward to face the screen again, "as you know, all of my computers and security systems were modified to run on your power packs. We're down to a seven-day reserve, and, frankly, my people are getting a little nervous about it."

"Can't you return to your old supplier of electricity?" she asked reasonably.

Damn her! he thought, bending a paper clip into a twisted clump of wire. The bitch knew good and well that the generators, transformers, and linkages of Pacific Edison had been badly damaged in the Visitor strikes and counterstrikes over the past couple of years. He couldn't trust his massive data banks to the current surges and brownouts that happened much too frequently these days.

He wished Juliet Parrish were here. His number-one assistant was a scientist, not a businessperson or a diplomat. But she had a calm, matter-of-fact way of looking at problems and coming up with reasonable and practical solutions that had proved invaluable over the past months.

"Have you forgotten about that raid I tipped you off to three weeks ago, Diana?" he asked gently.

"Of course not, Nathan." The beautiful woman-face's smile had a patronizing touch to it. "But someone also warned the underground that *we* had been warned. When our strike forces arrived, the area was deserted." She gave a mock sigh. "I realize you humans have not cultivated patience as we have. I suggest you try and learn more about this particular virtue—it will stand you in good stead. In the meantime, I will see what I can do. Good-bye."

The image faded, but Bates stared at the blank screen for nearly a minute before he reached over to turn it off.

Bates is a fool, Diana thought, turning away from the communications board on the bridge of her Mother Ship. She really didn't have time to waste thinking about a foolish and insignificant human, however. The bridge communications signal had just flashed, indicating that a transmission of extreme importance had just been received and was being decoded.

It might be from one of their other Mother Ships, reporting on a special problem or victory. Possibly it was from their home world, providing updated status reports on the environmental and other crises they wcrc struggling through. Or it could be from her beloved, the Great Leader himself.

As she keyed in the codes for acknowledgment and receipt of the message, she thought about the last time they had been together in the privacy of his hunting lodge. He had rubbed her crest and back ridge in that special way of his, remarking for the thousandth time upon the beauty of her coloration, the perfection of her patterning. He had said that he would see to it that she would be fitted with a pseudo skin that was as beautiful, in human terms, as she truly was beneath it. It was a pity that the humans' lack of sensibilities and their undeveloped sense of aesthetics prevented them from appreciating her true form for what it was. It was just another example of their inherent inferiority, he supposed.

The message began flashing across her viewscreen. "My

Most Exquisitely Scaled and Beloved,'' it said in her native language, "the situation here has become most grave. Our water supplies are now at critical levels, and many are dying every day. Effective immediately, you are to direct the efforts of all personnel in your immediate area into reactivation of the desalinization plants, so that an emergency shipment of water can be made to our home world. I have already dispatched a special ship for this purpose. Our people look to me with great confidence that I will lead them through these dark and troubled times, and I, in turn, have the greatest confidence in you that you will not fail me.''

He had signed it with the private self-name that she had given him during one of their best and most leisurely dances of love in the sands of their home world. Sirius had been hot and bright on their backs, the way a sun ought to be, not like the weak, pale yellowness of this system's star. An echo of that remembered warmth touched her as she tapped in the commands to acknowledge the message's end and transfer its only record to her personal data banks.

The Supreme Commander Pamela had once snidely observed that if the Great Leader couldn't bear to be without Diana, then why had he sent her trillions of miles away? The remark was one of many reasons why Diana had taken special pleasure in killing her when she stood in the way of their plans for total domination of Earth. Now this message had come, reconfirming what Diana had always known—that she and the Leader were one, though apart. Diana smiled, and her fingers caressed the console's edge.

No one could really understand the special depth of feeling between herself and the Leader. In part, it was based on a shared vision of a galaxy united and thriving under one central government—theirs. In rare, private moments, she imagined herself returning home a great heroine, acknowledging the acclaim and adoration of her people as she stood, claw to claw, with the Great Leader.

Of course, there had been, and would be, others. One had to take what small comforts one could in a battlefield environment, and only humans held the strange, parochial notion that sexual relationships should be monogamous. She had discovered there was even a certain pleasure in making love while wrapped in these tight, strange-smelling skins. Mostly, her present life meant sacrifice, however. She missed the pink, endless sands, the shouts and games of the children during the water rituals, the excitement in the Leader's eyes as he described his plans. Diana knew she was crucial to the fulfillment of his plans, dreams, and goals.

Perhaps, she thought idly, she would accompany the water shipment back home for a hero's welcome. Surely she was due a small vacation after the privations she'd suffered during these years on Earth. The Leader would be thrilled to see her, and she was growing very tired of the taste of rodents.

"Good evening, Diana." Lydia's cool, clipped voice sounded suddenly beside her.

"Good evening, Lydia." She nodded at the blond, elegant security officer.

"I see that you have received your highest-priority message."

"Yes." Diana's smile warmed. "It was a message from our Great Leader himself, addressed to me personally. He wanted to inform me that the water shortages have turned critical, and—"

"Yes, I know." Lydia's own smile turned rueful. "You must be pleased to know the Leader continues to have so much confidence in you. He expresses such warm sentiments, even if they *are* rather misplaced."

Diana's crest flared with outrage beneath her wig, and she barely restrained herself from spraying venom as she whirled to face the other. "How *dare* you read my personal communiqués? I'll have you—"

"Control yourself, Diana, dear. It is my duty, as head of security for the fleet, to screen all incoming priority communiqués. As you are well aware."

"You should have informed me immediately," she said, but in a lower tone. Lydia was right—damn her.

"May I remind you that at the time of its arrival, *you* yourself were in communication with Nathan Bates. I was merely following standard procedures." Lydia smiled reassuringly. "That way, I could be certain you wouldn't—accidentally, of course—*overlook* something vital like this."

Diana glared at her but decided to let the matter drop. Lydia's ambitions, though not nearly so nobly motivated as her own, nonetheless ran deep. Sooner or later, she would run afoul of standard procedures and could be eliminated at that time. For now, Lydia would bear close watching.

"I will continue to do my utmost to fulfill the Leader's faith in me," Diana said, straightening her shoulders. "I trust that you will do the same."

"Of course, Diana."

"Make arrangements so that I may brief the officers and other senior personnel on our new mission as soon as possible. Also, prepare a transmission for my voice-over to the commanders of the other Mother Ships, informing them of these latest developments. Keep me informed of your progress. You're dismissed, Lydia."

"There are so many things that I don't understand," said Elizabeth Maxwell, scuffing the toe of her sneaker in the dirt.

"I wish I understood more about how this carburetor is supposed to fit together." Wiping his forehead on his sleeve, Kyle Bates frowned down at the metal pieces spread out on the blanket in front of him.

The air was hot and still this afternoon, perfect for racing his motorcycle up and down the hard-packed trails near his home on the outskirts of Los Angeles. The Yamaha waited patiently nearby—more patient than Kyle was at the moment. The engine had been idling a little roughly, indicating a dirty carburetor. Taking it apart and cleaning each piece was proving a lot simpler than getting it all back together again.

"Try this one," Elizabeth said, pointing to a small washer that had slipped off the blanket onto the lawn.

"Thanks." Kyle's hands moved expertly again for a few moments, then he glanced up at the young woman and smiled a little sheepishly. "I'm sorry—you said something, and I wasn't paying much attention."

"I have so much to learn about myself and the world." Her lovely eyes were preoccupied as she stared toward the distant mountains, shimmery in the heat. "About—being human."

"That's a very human thing to be confused about," Kyle said, smiling gently at her. He always felt that he had to be gentle with Elizabeth, as though she might shatter if you touched her too hard. With her pale hair and blue eyes, she looked like a Dresden figurine. "Believe me, everyone has problems being human."

Wiping his hands on a rag, he took her hand and squeezed it gently. "The thing is, Elizabeth, you're one up on a lot of people, 'cause at least you realize there's stuff you don't know.

Some folks can't admit it when they don't know or understand something."

"One only learns by asking questions," Elizabeth said, speaking as if the phrase were a catechism she'd learned by rote.

"Who taught you that?" Kyle asked, watching her intently.

Elizabeth turned away, and Bates had to strain to hear her reply. "Diana."

"Well, she may be a bitch, but nobody's ever said she was dumb," Kyle said, tightening the last bolt. "She's right—for both Visitors and humans."

"But there is that other part of me. . . ."

Kyle reached over awkwardly to pat her calf. "I know it's gotta be hard for you."

And I thought I had it rough, he mused, watching her averted face. His father, the rich and legendary Nathan Bates, had always been away at a lab somewhere, while his mother, a gentle, introspective woman, had been distant in another way. She had coped with her husband's long absences, which alternated with his rigid, domineering ways when he was home, by retreating into herself. When Kyle had been eight years old, she suffered a full-fledged nervous breakdown and had been hospitalized. She had remained there, alone with her thoughts where no one could reach her, ever since.

Kyle, angry and bitter, had turned to gangs and motorcycle racing as ways of getting acceptance and approval. He had been drifting around at the fringes of the law when the Visitors arrived, and he had found a new purpose in joining the resistance efforts against their common enemy.

"What was it like before the Visitors came?" Elizabeth asked.

Kyle thought back. "We never appreciated what we had," he said slowly. "You could go almost anywhere in the world with no trouble. You could buy anything so long as you had the money. No rationing. No shortages—at least not in this country. We were rich, really wealthy here."

"You mean *you* were."

"Well, yeah, my dad was always rolling in it, but even the average guy had two cars and a house. You could eat steak a coupla times a week without hocking your stereo. Everyone went on a vacation each year. There were no travel permits, no curfews. It was great."

He remembered living in this house back when he'd had nothing more on his mind than riding his bike and picking up chicks. Then the Visitors had come. He'd met Robin Maxwell on a desert road in Visitor territory and after a daring escape, the two of them had made a perilous journey to reach Los Angeles again. There, they'd settled into a platonic (although Kyle knew Robin had hopes for more) relationship while sharing his house, and he wound up joining the resistance. Kyle had learned that Robin Maxwell had a daughter—and that her daughter was the being they called the Starchild. Elizabeth had come to live with them, and Kyle's already muddled feelings had become even more mixed after he'd met her.

Elizabeth was a lovely young woman who looked about eighteen years old (her mother's age), but in reality was only about eighteen *months* old. She was the result of a cruel experiment in hybrid genetic engineering that the Visitors had performed upon the unwilling Robin. Although she looked completely human, Bates could never forget that she wasn't— nor could Elizabeth herself. Their relationship was a strange mixture of affection and awkwardness, complicated by Robin's obvious attraction to Kyle.

Some had hailed Elizabeth's birth as a possible bridge of peace to link the humans and Visitors together. Others saw her as a new and dangerous threat to humanity. Kyle just wanted to make sure nobody hurt her; she was so vulnerable in spite of some strange, inexplicable talents she'd evidenced from time to time. He'd seen her stop engines and break windows just by *thinking* about it—not that she could do it all the time, but even sometimes was unsettling.

It wasn't hard to believe that Elizabeth felt confused about life.

"It's lemonade time." Robin's voice came cheerfully out of the window. A moment later, the screen door banged open, and she appeared carrying a tray loaded with glasses and a pitcher.

"Thanks," Kyle said, hastily moving away from Elizabeth and trying not to notice the hurt look that flashed across Robin's face as she set the tray down.

Twelve cans of lemonade concentrate, Mike Donovan thought, peering irritably through his sunglasses at the shopping list again. Fumbling through his wallet, he looked to see if there were any discount coupons for lemonade.

Save twelve cents on Campbell's Tomato with Rice soup, twenty-five cents off on family-size Cheer, Aquafresh toothpaste— He replaced the coupons in disgust.

Back when he'd still been married to Marjorie, he'd discovered that near one A.M. was a good time to go grocery shopping. Few people frequented the twenty-four-hour Safeway this time of night.

Black olives for Maggie, artichoke hearts for Ham, five packs of Bazooka Joe bubble gum for Chris . . . Mike grimaced. The members of the resistance had strange and expensive eating habits. He remembered Elias's expression when he had doled out today's grocery money, and his admonition to Mike to spend it carefully.

That was a real challenge these days, with all the weird and sporadic shortages. At the moment, there were plenty of canned tomatoes, but corn was going for six dollars a can. Booze and candy were really hard to come by—the Visitors had acquired these favorite human vices for themselves. Going past the nuts-and-candy section, he searched the long and nearly empty shelves for any possibilities.

Miracle of miracles! Two Hershey's chocolate-with-almonds bars, not too badly mashed looking, still sat next to a bold-lettered sign proclaiming the special price of $5.69 each.

Donovan looked into his wallet again. Julie was a self-confessed chocaholic, and Hershey bars had been her special favorite. Mike thought about how long it had been since they'd seen each other and how her eyes would light up at the sight of the candy. She would never spend the money on herself, but if it was a gift . . . He could take it by her place tomorrow evening, and they could—

Smiling at the thought, he took out his calculator, punching in numbers with quick, eager jabs. The smile faded as he made the calculation again before slamming the calculator angrily shut. With the kind of taxes Nathan Bates and the Visitors were imposing on things nowadays, he would be $1.48 short. A quick check of his jeans revealed twenty-three cents in change. Banging the cart around, he pushed it away from the candy counter, swinging it viciously into the check-out line.

Before the Visitors arrived, Mike Donovan had been a top-notch news cameraman, highly respected in his field. He had been more daring and reckless then. If he'd put his life on the line a dozen times or more in pursuit of the best, most complete story, then he had also been very well paid for it.

He was in El Salvador with his best friend and soundman, Tony Leonetti, literally dodging bullets, when the silver spaceships floated into view overhead. Mike had scooped some exclusive footage of the Visitors' arrival, and later he'd been the one to film the aliens' true faces and discover their actual reasons for coming to Earth.

Mike liked to think he might have gotten an Emmy for that filmed discovery if the broadcasting industry had remained under human control. As it was, he'd become a wanted man, a fugitive living in the shadows while he searched for his son, Sean, who had been captured by the Visitors along with his mother, Mike's ex-wife, Marjorie. Donovan had lived for weeks on the edge, only a misstep away from capture, torture, and death at the hands of the enemy.

The only worthwhile part in that whole black period of his life had been meeting Juliet Parrish. At first he'd had trouble believing this diminutive woman in her mid-twenties was leading the whole L.A. resistance effort. Later he had come to respect how much good leadership meant, when he was put in charge for a couple of weeks and discovered how cranky people could become when you forgot to requisition toilet paper.

Still later, a deep and special caring for Julie Parrish had developed, and—

Toilet paper! The one thing on the list he couldn't do without, and he'd forgotten to pick it up. Muttering apologies to the elderly woman behind him, he backed his cart around and rolled down the aisle toward the paper products.

Checking his money once more, he saw that he had just enough for four rolls—two less than requested.

Damn, but it was demeaning, having to count pennies this way! He took a corner too sharply and had to pick up several scattered boxes of saltines. *They* were on sale, he noted automatically.

Things had gotten better again for a while following V-Day, when the red dust bacteria had driven the Visitors back into space. He had accepted a job as anchorman for the nightly news with L.A.'s NBC affiliate—as national heroes, they'd all had their pick of offers. If he'd been happier behind a camera than in front of it, Mike had nonetheless drawn a six-figure salary that eased the discomfort considerably. But the failure of the red bacteria in L.A. and the Visitors' return had relegated him to nonperson status again; his features were now always concealed by caps and sunglasses, and he was always having to badger Elias for the money to buy the stuff they needed.

"Don't I know you from someplace?" The tall, gray-haired woman behind him was tugging at his sleeve, her expression curious.

"No, I don't think so," Donovan said, hastily piling his purchases onto the conveyor.

"You been in the movies? Or on TV?"

"Oh, no." He grinned feebly as he counted out his money. "I just look like the guy, that's all."

The woman shook her head. "If you take off your sunglasses a minute—"

"I can't. I have an eye infection, makes them sensitive to light." He began bagging his supplies, pocketing his change without counting it.

Then he spotted them—two Visitor guards strolling past the produce toward the meat counter.

Grabbing his bags, Donovan bolted for the exit, crossing his fingers that he hadn't been recognized.

He took a more circuitous route than usual back to the Club Creole. It was only when he got there that he discovered that he'd left the toilet paper sitting on the counter. And he'd paid for it, too.

Chapter 2

Class Act

At precisely 0900 hours in the morning, Diana entered the crowded auditorium of her Mother Ship. Murmurs of conversation instantly ceased, and the heels of her boots made a satisfying click on the floor as she strode to the platform at the front of the room.

Smiling slightly, she glanced around at the one hundred or so Visitor officers in attendance. The specially dispatched water transport had entered Earth's orbit last evening, bringing about thirty new recruits who would be staying on to serve the Leader by helping Diana conquer this new world—or die in the attempt.

For an instant she felt a small pang of jealousy. No doubt many of them had enjoyed one last submersion in the love-pits before making the journey to Earth, or had strolled along the paths of contemplation to watch the moons rise as they cast their pale multishadows over the sands. Diana had overheard two of them say that the Leader himself had made a rare personal appearance to honor them and wish them good fortune just before their leave-taking. He'd just emerged from his most recent molt, they'd said, looking more patterned and splendid than ever.

This was a noticeably smaller group than the last one she had oriented three months ago—grim testimony to the losses from the war here, and drought and famine back home. Their records showed that they were quite young for their new responsibilities, and their human faces reflected ages in the low to mid-twenties. There was something vaguely pathetic about their youth, despite the well-fitting red uniforms and new, gleaming insignia of rank, they had no real conception of the responsibilities of command. The human-seeming masks could be molded to reflect any age, of course. But their psychologists had discovered that adjustments to a new appearance were easier if their outward selves reflected some inner truths, at least on a relative scale.

"Good morning, *ladies and gentlemen*," she said, smiling, but her eyes roved the class eagerly to see whether any of them failed to comprehend the human greeting.

"Good morning, Diana." The chorus came back, enthusiastic if still a little ragged—except for one young female. Forgetting to speak in English, she had tried to use her altered vocal apparatus to address the commander of Earth-based forces in her native language. Her hissing screech filled the hall and echoed off the walls, tearing a two-inch gap in the corner of her mouth.

Rage flared up in Diana, and she strode down from the podium. "You—must—remember—to—speak—English—at—all—times!" Each word was punctuated with a ringing slap across the young officer's face. At the last blow, the recruit's head snapped back, and a large flap of skin ripped and fell away from the ruined mouth onto her neck, revealing the glistening green scales beneath. Hissing softly in pain, she crumpled to the floor, unconscious.

"Take her out of here," Diana said to the recruits sitting ramrod straight on either side of the sprawled figure. "Tell Lydia I said that this one needs one of her special lessons in remembering to use English."

As they hastily dragged the limp body out of the room, Diana turned back to face her raptly attentive audience. "That is the first lesson I want all of you to remember. As long as you are on or above this planet, you will speak the language of the humans in the area of your assignment. Is this understood?"

It was, and Diana's smile returned. "Very well. You have come to Earth at a very crucial time in our mission. As you all know, while the food and water shortages on our own world have reached critical proportions, the resources on Earth are abundant. It is only a matter of time before we claim this entire planet in the name of Our Leader. It is our own rightful domain, since we are superior to the humans in all ways."

A red-haired young Visitor raised his hand. "Then why must we take on their forms?"

Diana pushed a button in the lectern, and a large screen slid smoothly down behind her. "Yes, we wear their skins and have been trained to mimic their sounds, movements, and behaviors. This is because they lack tolerance for appearances that are different from their own. We have even observed them fighting with members of their own species with different skin pigments or whose eye sockets were shaped differently."

A shocked murmur rose in the room.

"Yes," said Diana, "I know you were prepared for dealings with a primitive race, but such realities may be hard to accept. Now you can see the wisdom of adopting these guises. Imagine our difficulties, were we to attempt our mission in our true forms. But remember, while lacking our higher level of intelligence, the humans *do* possess a certain treacherous cunning. You must be on your guard at all times."

She crossed the stage, her boots tapping loudly again. "Lydia, our chief of security, will instruct you in specifics of self-defense at a later point. My purpose this morning is to update you on our progress to date and to impress upon you the importance of knowing as much as you can about our enemy."

The room darkened, and holographic images filled the screen—Visitor troops marching in triumph through the ruins of Mexico City, Buenos Aires, Johannesburg, New Delhi; thousands of humans herded along, hands behind their heads, into waiting shuttlecraft, transported to looming Mother Ships; the Nile and Amazon rivers diminished more each day by the newly erected Visitor plants that were pumping them dry.

"You see, we *are* winning," said Diana. "But it is a slow and often costly war." A briefer series of scenes depicted the burning shells of the two Newark plants, ambushed Visitor vehicles, scores of dead and injured, and, finally, one vast glassy plain slagged into black and gray unrecognizability, surrounded by a scorched heat-blasted desert which seemed to stretch forever.

"You are looking at what was formerly the city of Beirut. When their cursed red dust died out in this region and we attempted to reoccupy the city, fanatic terrorists indigenous to this region managed to obtain and detonate a nuclear device. Our Mother Ship in the area, commanded by Abdul, was destroyed with its entire crew. The waste of potential food and water resources is immeasurable.''

The picture behind Diana shifted and resolved itself into various shots of Los Angeles. "Here, in the city below us, we need not fear such radical events. I have crafted the appearance of a truce between us and the humans of Los Angeles—which will continue, of course, only as long as it remains useful to us. In the meantime, I want you to become familiar with these particular humans.''

The Hollywood hills gave way to the features of a handsome man in his mid-thirties, with green eyes and brown hair, laughing, frowning, looking pensive as the various poses merged into one another. "This is Michael Donovan, one of the most dangerous criminals on this planet. He has killed or injured hundreds of us. Anyone who aids in his capture in any way will be richly rewarded and receive the Leader's personal accolade.''

The screen continued to flash with the faces as Diana identified each enemy—Ham Tyler, Maggie Blodgett, Chris Faber, Sancho Gomez, and other known members of the resistance.

"We must be especially alert for any signs of them and their subversions at all times. And here are two other people I want you to be able to recognize, although I must stress that they are to be captured *unharmed*.'' A picture of two smiling young women, both in their late teens, shimmered and formed behind her. "Robin Maxwell, with the dark brown hair, and her . . . sister, Elizabeth. They are both very special to me. In the event of a capture, I want them well treated and brought directly to me.''

The room lightened and Diana stepped forward again. "This brings us to the present. You and I have been entrusted with a special mission by the Great Leader himself, and nothing must stand in our way. You will all be privileged to assist me in this effort to renew our desalinization of the oceans and prepare a shipment of water to our home world. I have spared no time beginning this project. Even as we speak, the water is being collected, and—''

She hesitated, annoyed, as a thin, brown-haired Visitor entered the back of the auditorium. He edged closer, and she recognized the insignia and short, jerky strides of her senior botanist.

"Why, Bernard!" A smile stretched across her mouth but didn't touch her eyes. Diana hated to be interrupted during one of her lectures, even by members of her personal research staff. "I am pleased that you could join us. Ladies and gentlemen, this is Bernard, who is leading our efforts to test and collect the water."

"Ah, yes. Thank you, Diana." He glanced quickly around the room, then looked back to her.

"As I was saying, we have already begun filling our holding tanks, and—"

"Diana, if I may interrupt for a moment . . ." Bernard faltered into silence.

She glared, then her features smoothed into glacial impassivity. "Perhaps *you* should continue this portion of the lecture, Bernard."

"Oh, no, I—"

"Please, Bernard."

"No, Diana, really—"

"Come up here, Bernard."

With a small, helpless shrug, he walked up the aisle, came up to the platform, and faced the crowd. "Uh, well," he said, "we, uh, we definitely have made some progress."

Diana smiled slightly. She would speak to him later about barging into her presentation. For now, she was content to watch the shy botanist squirm under the public scrutiny of the young officers.

"We . . . all feel we benefit greatly from working with Diana. She provides excellent guidance and leadership at all times, even when the occasional difficulty arrises. Uh—" He glanced at his commanding officer in desperate appeal, then down at the floor.

What in parching thirst was he talking about? Diana frowned at him. The normally terse, direct Bernard was babbling.

His eyes slid sideways to her again, pleading. "Yes, when troubles arise, Diana is always alert to them and is extremely responsive in suggesting possible solutions. She embodies the essence of, uh, true leadership in being able to recognize *immediately* when a problem exists."

"Why, thank you, Bernard." Diana summoned a confident smile as realization dawned. "I can see that it is just about time for lunch. Why don't we break for an hour and reconvene after that?"

Moving over to the lectern, she pushed another button. Along the side wall, a row of paneling slid back, revealing several rows of cages in which mice, rats, and guinea pigs squeaked and scurried.

As the students eagerly rushed over for their meals, Diana drew the scientist into the corridor. "What is it, Bernard?"

"The ocean water has been poisoned."

"What?" All sounds, all movements, everything in the universe seemed to Diana to shrink down to the tiny lights in Bernard's eyes as he gazed mournfully at her.

"The humans have developed another form of red dust that is now reproducing in the local seaweed plants. It enters the water as a by-product of the kelp's wastes. It's proliferating rapidly, and . . . we can't filter it out. Harmless to their own life forms, it's death for us."

"Damn them!" Diana barely restrained herself from using her native speech. *"Damn them all."*

Chapter 3

Wishes, Dreams, and Nightmares

Pausing a moment to wipe the sweat off her brow, Julie Parrish bent over the microscope again, adjusting the focus. From this perspective, the kelp took on a weird, spectral beauty, a symmetry all its own as cells jostled up against one another, following a blueprint known only to them.

"Well, Andy, looks good," she said, straightening. "Of course, we won't know for sure until the fifth or sixth generation of cells has been cultured, but as far as I can tell, the bacteria has settled into the cytoplasm and into a healthy and mutually productive symbiosis."

"You mean they like one another," Andrew Halpern translated, grinning. His eyes lingered on her appreciatively, and Juliet was suddenly conscious of the sweat that had collected under her breasts, plastering her cotton shirt to her rib cage. All of southern California had been languishing in the heat wave of the last couple of days, and even Catalina's breezes had turned hot and muggy under the unrelenting sun.

Tugging the fabric away from her skin, she said, "Yeah, something like that."

"Does that mean we get to go home?"

"Yeah." Amelia Anderson looked up eagerly from the slides she was staining. She was a short, intense woman of about forty, with a wonderful laugh that would burst out at unexpected moments. "I've forgotten what my husband looks like. These three clowns are starting to look good to me, so I *know* it's time to go home."

Bill Kendall chuckled. "Joe 'n' me had some rough times with women, but never anything worse than listening to this one snore all night." He jerked a thumb at Amelia, who made a face at him and flipped him the bird. Kendall was a tall, laconic Vermonter who possessed a slow grin and an endless supply of tall tales about his hound dog Old Joe. He was also an avid collector of Depression glass and loved Mozart. Julie wasn't sure whether Old Joe was, or had ever been, real, but she certainly had learned a lot about her companions during the past two days.

"I'm sure that my nocturnal warblings are more musical than your sad attempts to whistle Symphony Number Fifteen," Amelia retorted, winking at Juliet.

"I've got to get back to my own bed and some decent cooking," said Juan Perez, patting the broad expanse of his stomach. "My wife makes the best sweet-and-sour chicken known to mankind. Even fresh sea trout gets to be old hat after a while."

"Especially when it's your main dish every day," agreed Amelia, "and Halpern cooks it."

"See the ingratitude I have to put up with, Julie?" Andy spread his arms and affected a saintly, long-suffering expression. "Take me away from all of this, and I will be your grateful slave forever."

Julie's stomach lurched queasily at the mention of Halpern's specialty. She'd run out of Maalox and was now working on a roll of Di-Gel that Kendall had given her. Her abdominal distress was beginning to worry her.

Smiling a little ruefully, she said, "I wish I could. I can't okay the closing of this station until we're absolutely certain that there's been no adverse effect on any of the marine life or the kelp itself."

There was a chorus of groans, and Perez said, "Come on, Julie! There are no absolute certainties in biological science. You know that."

"We're running almost ninety-one percent sure," said Halpern, looking at her intently. "Yeah, a few of the cultures died, but that could be due to inherited DNA defects rather than anything we did to it."

"I'd still like it to be closer to one hundred percent," Julie said. The air in the tent was stifling her, and she wondered if she were going to throw up again.

"Thought you said Bates was in a hurry for this," said Kendall, shoving his hands into his pockets.

"He is. Dammit, we all are!" Shoving a hand through her hair, which felt glued to her scalp, Julie paced beside the workbench along the side of the tent. "But I'm not going to take the chance, however small, that we are creating something that could be a bigger ecological nightmare to our planet than the Visitors themselves!"

She went to the entrance of the tent, pushed the flap aside, and went outside onto the beach. The sand was hot and harsh beneath her bare feet, but she didn't care. The air was cooler here, with fresh, wild sea smells. A soft pink twilight was settling on the Pacific and the hills behind her, which pushed one another up toward the clouds. A crescent moon stretched near a palm tree, way up near the top of a cliff, and she saw a couple of dark spots beside it.

"Bison," said Andy Halpern, coming to stand beside her and pointing upward as though he guessed her thoughts. "We met a tour guide from Avalon named Carlos when we first arrived. He told us they're part of a herd that was brought over from the mainland in the twenties for filming a silent Western. When the movie crew left, the bison stayed and did what bison do. There are several hundred now."

"*They* don't eat seaweed, so we don't have to worry about them, I guess," Julie said. She was conscious of his closeness, the warm, musky smell of his sweat, and she hugged her arms. "I'm sorry I went off in there."

He nodded amiably. "It's the heat. We didn't mean to push you either. After three weeks of cold salt-water showers, sleeping bags, and the stink of seaweed, I think we were all hoping we'd get a reprieve out of you and Science Frontiers."

"It should only take another couple of weeks for you to collect the additional data. In all probability, you'll be able to march into my office, wave the results in my face, and give me a resounding 'I told you so!'"

He grinned suddenly, looking more like a college student than a widely known and respected botanist. "Did you ever think, when you were nine years old, that you'd be doing anything like this?"

She shook her head and watched the progress of a fishing boat heading toward the harbor.

"I was going to be a fireman," he said. "Rescue babies out of burning buildings, save lives, that kind of stuff."

"I always wanted to be a doctor, ever since I could remember." She shrugged a little. "I still do. I was a medical student with a side interest in research. After the Visitors came, pursuing research seemed to make more sense."

"Yeah," he said. "You know, in a couple of weeks, after I've come in to harass you about being overcautious, I'd like to take you out for a drink. I hear there's a great new spot in L.A. that is *the* place to be—the Club Creole—and—"

She shook her head, smiling. "Thanks just the same."

He looked at her, and his mouth quirked gently. "I'd like to assume it's because of somebody else and not me."

"You're quite right. As a matter of fact, you remind me a little of him."

"Lucky guy."

"*I'm* lucky." She looked at her watch. "I guess I'd better get my stuff. Mac will be here soon to pick me up."

Gallantly, Halpern proferred his arm, and they strolled back toward the tents in the gathering dusk.

Night had crept into the hills and canyons of Los Angeles like a dark, silent animal. From the old rocker on the back porch of Kyle's house, Elizabeth Maxwell watched for a long time as the stars thickened above the glow of the city. Her thoughts were vague and troubled, and neither the soft scents of the night nor the breeze that ruffled her hair could rouse her from her uneasiness. *Something was coming.* . . .

The Starchild sensed danger with that indefinable sense that she knew set her apart from both sides of her heritage. Something bad, something potentially devastating was brewing. Elizabeth hugged her arms against her small breasts, shivering. She had no tear ducts, but her eyes and throat ached dryly.

All of the lights in the house had long been out when she finally got up and went into her bedroom. She undressed and got into bed, but sleep was slow in coming as she tossed and turned. Finally, she drifted downward. . . .

. . . into a soft red mist. Elizabeth was groping through it, blinking in confusion. The featureless mist surrounded her, merging light and darkness into a uniform redness the color of dried human blood.

Her hand was barely visible as she held it in front of her face, but against the whiteness of her flesh, she could see the mist was actually millions of tiny specks of dust, rising and swirling around her.

"Mother?" she tried to call out, but no sound rose from her throat to mar the silence of the dust.

Fighting down panic, she stretched her arms in front of her and groped forward, walking at first, then running. Even the ground beneath her seemed soft and insubstantial, and she was alone, so very alone.

Then her hands slammed up against a smooth surface, cold and hard. Jerking back her stinging fingers, she reached forward more cautiously, recognizing the feel and curve of glass. She was standing in front of a large translucent cylinder.

As she circled around it, the dust within the cylinder began to clear away, and she could make out the form of a young man in Visitor's uniform. Pressing her face to the glass, she could see that his handsome features were contorted in agony, and he was yelling and pounding on the glass, pleading with someone she couldn't see.

She groped around the circumference, frantically seeking some opening or entrance. The young man began to scream— she could hear the sound as a muffled groan and feel its awful vibrations through the glass under her fingertips. Then he fell writhing to the floor, clutching his throat, tearing at his face. Terrible gashes tore his cheeks and forehead, exposing the glistening reptilian hide beneath, and he turned glazed, dying eyes to her, one still blue and human, the other orange, with an alien, slitted pupil, both full of pain and reproach as he died—

"—NO!" Elizabeth screamed, and jerked upright, her eyes huge and rolling, her hands wildly trying to push away the awful red death-dust.

"Elizabeth, honey, what is it?" Still blinking sleep from her eyes and wearing only a shortie nightgown, Robin turned on the light and rushed in to hold her daughter.

Elizabeth sat stiffly, staring at nothing, neither pushing away from nor responding to her mother's embrace. Human caresses were something she had difficulty comprehending. Finally,

Robin, sensing her discomfort, drew back. "What happened, Elizabeth?"

"A nightmare," she explained haltingly. "It was awful . . . and it seemed so real."

"Tell me about it," Robin said.

Elizabeth shook her head as Kyle Bates came in, pulling an old bathrobe around himself. "What's going on?" he asked.

"Elizabeth was having a bad dream," Robin said, looking up at him.

"Oh, Kyle." Elizabeth let her head drop onto the young man's shoulder as he sat down on the edge of the bed and put his arms around her. She stayed that way for a long time, her eyes wide and staring.

Willie stared at the blender for several moments, considering. Then he reached over for the vodka on the shelf behind it, poured a couple of shots in, and pushed the start button.

It was two-fifteen in the morning, and the Club Creole's last customers had left half an hour ago. While he tackled the nightly cleanup operations, he continued his search for the perfect mixed drink—Visitor style.

It was also something to do to delay going back to his empty room a little longer. Willie had watched his people as they talked together this evening, had seen their sidelong glances at him, and felt he needed something to help drive back the loneliness. He liked the humans, and believed in their cause, but nothing could change the fact that he wasn't one of them and never would be. Sometimes he wondered if he'd made the right decision when he'd elected to cut himself off from his own people.

"Willie, my man." Elias Taylor waved as he came in the front door carrying a large bundle. "What are you making?"

"I am creating a new commotion, Elias," the Visitor announced proudly, taking three glasses down from the shelf.

"You mean 'concoction,' Willie." Miranda Juarez paused over her broom to grin at Elias. "Although from here, it certainly has been sounding like a commotion."

"I would be honored if you would be the first to share this with me." Willie poured the blender's contents into the glasses and pushed them across the bar toward Elias and Miranda.

The Hispanic woman sniffed cautiously at the thick, grayish

liquid and frowned. "What's in this, Willie? Eye of newt and hair of toad?"

"I don't believe we stock those ingredients. This is made with several kinds of liquor, combined with milk, mustard, peanut butter, mayonnaise, and—"

"Say no more!" Miranda pushed the glass aside and looked a little queasy.

"Uh, I think I'll pass too," Elias said.

Willie shrugged philosophically and gulped his down in several jerky motions, his throat rippling as he swallowed, then smiled triumphantly. "This is most fine! We have been getting more Visitors as customers lately, and they will like this much better than the sweet drinks."

"Better them than me," Miranda muttered, going back toward the tables.

"Wait a minute. I want to show you the latest." Elias unwrapped his bundle and spread out several polo-style shirts in various pastel shades. Stitched in green over the left pocket of each was the tiny lizard logo with a monogrammed "CC."

"These look great, Elias!" Miranda held up a yellow one. "Can I have one?"

"Yes, great." Willie nodded.

"You can both have a couple," Elias said expansively. "Wear 'em on duty so the customers can see 'em. I'll be getting more. These are just samples from somebody I'm negotiating with downtown. I think I can get them faster and cheaper, though, if I can sneak a call to a friend of mine in—"

"What, did I take a wrong turn and wind up in the garment district?" Ham Tyler's flat voice was suddenly loud behind them. "Or are you collecting rags for Goodwill?"

"These are the shirts that Elias is going to sell to our customers," said Willie, his expression reproving.

"Hello, Ham," Miranda said. "How was Chris today?"

"Better. He can make out shapes, but they're still fuzzy. Doctor said he's apparently real sensitive to the venom." Ham looked at Willie with a grudging expression. "He also said if you hadn't provided him with that venom, he couldn't have made an antidote, so I guess we owe you one."

Willie shook his head. "I wanted to help—you know that."

"But he *can* see a little?" Miranda asked anxiously.

"Yeah, and Doc thinks it'll get better. It's just going to take a little time. He's still gotta keep the bandages on." The hard-faced man jerked a thumb at the entrance behind him. "And I thought I told you people to keep all three locks on when you close for the night. One good kick, and you coulda wound up as some lizard's late night snack. What is this?" He leaned on the bar, staring down at the remaining glass.

"A new drink I am making," Willie told him.

Ham sniffed it, shrugged, and chugged the contents before the amazed stares of Elias and Miranda. He stared thoughtfully at the empty glass, then shrugged. "I've had worse, in Saigon," he commented. "But not everybody's gonna go for this. You oughta save it for the lizards, Willie."

"I think that was the idea," Miranda said dryly.

"As I was saying, I think we could make these the latest status item in Visitor leisure wear." Elias collected the shirts and began folding them up. "I was showing a few around today, and a lot of our regular customers were really interested, humans as well as Visitors. I got about thirty-five orders just today. Now, I figure if we mount a full-scale advertising campaign, using the shirts—"

"Too many of the damn scalies around here as it is, and now you want to make T-shirts for them!" Ham's habitual expression of disgust turned even more pronounced. "You know, it's getting to be really dangerous around here, with them crawling in and out all the time. I think you should make the club off limits, cover or no cover."

Elias ignored him. "I'm thinking about a line of tennis shorts to match. Pretty soon it won't be Adidas you hear about anymore, but Ee-li-as! Maybe later on, we could even—"

"Hey, Taylor, I ain't talking to the goddamn wall!" Ham whirled suddenly, and Elias backed away instinctively as the ex-CIA man grabbed the shirt out of his hands and tossed it on the bar, where it landed in a little blue heap against the whiskey bottles. "Starting today, declare this place off limits to lizards."

"No way, man." Glaring at him, Elias went behind the bar to retrieve the shirt. "You don't give the orders around here."

"Your little hidey-hole downstairs is resistance headquarters for all of L.A., and it isn't safe. With our power packs almost zip, we're practically standing around here with our pants down, inviting trouble as long as they're sliming around."

"Their money's just as green as their blood," Miranda said.

"Besides, who's going to suspect this place when we invite them in freely?"

Elias nodded. "That's right. And now that I'm a businessman, my bottom line has got to be where the buck stops. In this case, it's that cash register over there."

"Is that where you keep your loyalties, too?"

"The Visitors are our best strippers, Ham," said Willie.

"*Tippers*, Willie, tippers," Elias corrected mechanically, still staring stonily at Tyler. "You know, maybe I'm not involved so much in the tough-guy big-shot fighting anymore, but I'm doing more of the *funding* than anyone else. If it hadn't been for the Club Creole, the underground would have gone *under* long ago. War is hell, right, but it's also damn expensive. The Visitors pay well, and I say they're staying."

"Taylor, you disgust me," Ham said, but before he could say more, the front door rattled open, and Juliet Parrish stepped inside.

"Hello, Julie!" Willie called, glad to see her and even more relieved that the tension had now been diverted, at least for the moment. "You are quite later this evening."

"The helicopter pilot was delayed with some mechanical troubles before he could pick me up from Catalina," she said. Dark smudges were prominent under her eyes, and the pink tinge of sunburn on her nose and cheeks couldn't hide the lines of fatigue. "I just stopped by for a Coke and to drop off some data disks. What's new?"

In terse sentences, Ham told her about the abortive attempt to obtain more power packs and described Chris's eye injuries.

"I'm glad you got Dr. Akers at the clinic," she said. "There's no one better. I'll stop by Chris's house tomorrow myself and take a look at him."

"So how is the great seaweed sweepstakes going?" Elias asked, pouring a Coke into a glass and handing it to her.

"We're making progress on red dust number two," she said, swallowing gratefully. "It looked good in the lab, and so far it seems to be successfully assimilating itself into the life chain of the sea. Our present tests indicate that it will only reproduce in the ocean. Even so, that's three-quarters of our planet, if it will adapt to colder waters. We're also trying to coax it into mutating into a form that will adapt to land-based flora of subtropical and warmer climates."

Miranda blinked. "Wow. You sound like some of my biology profs."

"Sorry." Julie ran a hand through her tangled blond hair. "That's what comes of hanging around marine specialists for a couple of days."

"How long is this latest and greatest red dust going to take before we can hit the lizards with it?" Ham asked.

"I don't know. It'll be at least another three weeks before we can be reasonably sure this strain is safe for widespread manufacture and distribution in the world's oceans. As for another variant, well, we start the process all over again in the lab, and—"

"'All over again'? This isn't some high school science-fair project we're talking about here, Doc. Can't you hurry it up a little?"

"We have to be careful about the delicate balance of the ocean's ecology."

"For some lousy seaweed?"

Julie set the glass of Coke down with exaggerated care. "That 'lousy seaweed' you're complaining about, Ham, happens to be a vital link in the food chain for the whole ocean. Break that link, and the results could be catastrophic in the sea *and* the land. I'm not interested in going down in the history books as the scientist who helped rid the world of the Visitors—only to destroy the world's oceans in the process."

"You and Gooder make a real swell pair, you know that?" said Ham, heading toward the door. "Well, kids, it's been real, but I gotta go. I got a sick friend to visit."

Julie took a sudden interest in the ice at the bottom of her glass. "Speaking of Mike, has anyone seen him today?"

"No, I have not." Willie was lining up more ingredients on the counter beside the blender. The others shook their heads no.

Julie frowned as she watched the peanut butter go in, then her expression turned queasy when Willie reached for the mayonnaise. "Willie, do you have any Pepto-Bismol?"

"Now, that is a fine idea, Julie!" Smiling, the Visitor began rummaging in some bottom cupboards, found a bottle, and began glopping the thick pink liquid into his "commotion."

"Oh, God. . . ." Julie had to turn away.

"Are you all right?" Elias asked, concern obvious in his dark, handsome features.

"Yeah, I . . . must have picked up some low-level flu bug or something." She slid off the barstool and placed a large manila envelope on the bar. "I think I'll just go home, get a long shower and some sleep. Can you lock these downstairs for me before you leave?"

"Sure thing," Elias said. "Can I get you anything? A glass of milk or more Coke, maybe?"

"No, I'll be fine." She didn't look too convinced as she headed for the door. "G'night, everybody."

Maggie Blodgett worried about Chris as she parked her old station wagon next to the curb in front of his house.

Three days after the abortive raid for the power packs, L.A. was resigning itself to another scorcher of a day. It was still midmorning, but the air was hot and windless, making the distant hills appear shimmery and insubstantial, as though they would fade into another dimension at any moment.

Hauling out the grocery bag from the back seat with one hand, she shaded her eyes with the other to peer over at the number on the house in front of her. She was surprised that he lived in such a residential area, where individualistic bungalows presided over well-tended yards in front and swimming pools in back. She had always figured him to be the apartment type, where home was wherever you slung your hat and your M-16.

She rang the doorbell and listened, hearing something bang to the floor, a muttered curse, then the gruff shout: "Who is it?"

"It's Maggie."

After a while hesitant footsteps approached the door, and she saw that his eyes were still bandaged. "C'mon in."

Inside, the house was cool and dark and smelled of freshly brewed coffee. A small, frenetic dog with masses of hair and a face like a chrysanthemum came barreling out from the kitchen, barking loudly as it danced around her legs.

"What the heck is this?" She laughed as she stooped to scratch the dog's head, and the pom-pom tail swished happily.

"That's Druid. He's a Shih Tzu."

"Druid?"

"Yeah," Chris said, deadpan. "He worships trees. Want some coffee?"

"Sure. I can get it."

"No, sit down." Determined, he groped his way back to the kitchen, fumbled out cups and spoons, and managed to pour the coffee without spilling much.

"How do you feel?" she asked, watching him from the kitchen table.

"All right. The burning feeling's mostly gone. Doc Akers said I took a pretty good hit, and I'm allergic to the venom. If it hadn't been for that antivenom he managed to conjure up, I might've died. That's why it's taking me so long to get over this."

"You'll be all right," she said, hoping it was true. He looked very vulnerable and not nearly so large, as though the bandages had somehow shrunken him. What both of them knew but neither mentioned was the doctor's concerns that recovery might not be complete.

"I've got another lizard joke," she said. "Your dog reminded me of it. What do you call the Visitor who owns a pet shop?"

"Well fed." Chris snorted. "Hon, that's older'n God."

"Oh, well. I brought the newspaper." She put it on the table. "I'll be happy to read it to you. And here are the groceries. I even managed some Wrigley's Spearmint."

"Thanks."

She looked around as she put the groceries away. There was a cheerful neglect in the way things were stacked or placed in apparently random locations, but counters and dishes were reasonably clean.

"Let's go in the living room," he said.

That was a real surprise. The paneled walls on two sides were floor-to-ceiling shelves full of books. She quickly scanned the titles. There were history books—three whole shelves were devoted to the Civil War and another two to England—biographies, and copies of *National Geographic* for the past eight years. Physics and chemistry books jammed up against science fiction and mystery paperbacks and *Carpentry for Fun and Profit*.

"You've got a real collection here," she said, taking the couch as he settled into the easy chair across the room. "I didn't know you were such an avid reader."

He shrugged, a great rolling movement of one shoulder. "I can't go around blowing up trucks and shooting at lizards all the time. Want to put on a record?"

Maggie grimaced. If Chris's tastes in reading were eclectic, his record collection consisted almost entirely of country-western music, which she hated. "Why don't I read to you instead?" she suggested, getting up again. "I could get the newspaper."

"I think I'd rather hear the biography of Stevie Wonder."

She looked at him, uncertain whether he was kidding or starting to feel sorry for himself. Then she spied one of her own favorites, a story about overcoming adversity in the face of great odds. "How about *Watership Down*?" she asked.

The small brown rabbit reared up against the wire mesh, sniffing eagerly as the lettuce was placed in its cage.

"I'm glad somebody around here likes the food, Fiver." Dr. Andrew Halpern grinned and scratched behind the rabbit's ears as it began nibbling the lettuce.

"He seems to be thriving, red dust or no," said Amelia Anderson, looking up from her report.

"Too bad the dust doesn't like lettuce as much as he does. I was hoping that a plant with a high water content might prove to be—"

Fiver stiffened suddenly under his hands and then began to race frantically around his cage. An instant later, the tent flap was ripped open, and four Visitor shock troopers stormed in, laserguns raised.

"What in Christ's—?" Anderson started to rise from her makeshift desk and immediately sat down again, a look of profound astonishment on her face as a laser bolt lanced into her chest. Her eyes glazed, and she fell over, dead.

Juan Perez threw a bottle full of a reagent at the closest Visitor, who shrieked and clutched his head as the glass shattered against it. Shoving a wooden workbench full of test tubes in racks and petri dishes toward them, Perez sprinted past as it toppled forward in front of them, blocking their pursuit. He almost made it to the door before a laser bolt caught him in the thigh. Screaming, he clutched his injured leg and fell to the floor.

"Kill him," one of the aliens ordered. "Diana said she only needs one alive." Another bolt sliced the air, and Perez's moans rose in one last crescendo and were stilled.

Andrew Halpern froze, not breathing, not thinking, as the

Visitors advanced. Bill Kendall was still outside, collecting samples of kelp. If he only stayed away long enough . . .

"Take all the papers and data disks you can find, then destroy the equipment," the officer said, then turned to the trembling scientist. "Do you have any information hidden in these tents?"

"Nuh-no," he stammered out. His voice sounded old and weak.

"You're probably lying," said the Visitor. Raising his rifle, he sighted at Andy's head.

"No, I swear to God, there's nothing that isn't right out here!" Halpern backed up against the wall, hands clutching at the tent fabric behind him as though he might tear a hole in it and get away.

Grinning, the Visitor turned his weapon around and swung the barrel into Halpern's head. As though in slow motion, the botanist sagged to the canvas floor while red-gray waves of pain started in his head and began rolling through his whole body.

He heard a muffled cry outside, the dull *fuh! fuh!* of a lasergun, and knew that Kendall was dead now, too.

Through blurring vision, he watched the Visitor pull the squealing rabbit out of its cage and hold it aloft. The alien tilted his head back, and his jaw stretched open impossibly wide as the animal was shoved into it.

The still-wiggling bulge traveling down the Visitor's throat as he swallowed was the last thing Andy Halpern remembered before he lost consciousness.

Chapter 4

Matters for Confession

Andrew Halpern came back to consciousness to find himself propped up against a hard, cold surface that vibrated slightly. His hands were tied, and his head hurt so violently he was afraid he might vomit. Those were the only things he was sure of at first.

"Good evening, Dr. Halpern."

Then Andy became coldly certain of a couple of other things. He was a prisoner aboard a Visitor craft, and his life as he'd known and enjoyed it would never again be the same.

He didn't have to open his eyes to recognize the resonant tones of Diana, commander of the Visitor fleet—he'd seen her too many times on television. Halpern let his chin sag into his chest even more deeply, not moving.

"It's no good, Dr. Halpern. I know you're awake. Look at me."

A boot tapped his thigh, moving upward with unmistakable purpose toward his groin. Andy opened his eyes, reluctantly focusing on the petite brunette who stood in front of him, arms crossed. She was so stunningly beautiful, with her blue eyes and wavy cloud of dark hair, that Halpern had to forcibly remind himself that this was the reptilian creature who had ordered the execution of his three colleagues and friends.

"I trust that you are not too uncomfortable to answer a few questions for me." Diana smiled winningly. "We know that you have been working on a new form of the red dust bacteria. I want its exact genetic composition."

46

Halpern remembered how annoyed he had been when Juliet Parrish refused to tell him what the formula was, would only provide the culture samples and instructions for growing them.

"Dammit, we're a team!" he had groused. "I'm a scientist, not some damned kelp farmer! How can I make any intelligent observations for you if I don't know what the hell I'm working with? Besides, we're pretty well camouflaged here."

"It's a remote chance that anything will happen, but I feel safer doing it this way," Julie had said.

For that reason he *couldn't* give anything away now, and that certainty gave him a sense of relief coupled with a bitter satisfaction. Andy also knew that Diana wouldn't believe him and that he was almost certainly going to die within the next few minutes. He was astonished at how calm he felt.

"I'm waiting, Dr. Halpern."

Andy looked around him, savoring every breath he drew, every color his eyes could take in. He found himself memorizing every detail of the ship's metal bulkheads, the gleaming braid of Diana's uniform, the curves of her breasts (or what her bodysuit presented as breasts) beneath the snug-fitting red uniform. He tried to visualize scales lying beneath her lovely skin, but was unable to see her that way. *Just as well*, he thought wryly.

Diana frowned impatiently at his silence. "Please, Dr. Halpern, don't be tiresome. Aboard my ship I have drugs that will ensure your telling me anything I want to know."

Andy felt a cold lump settle in his throat and realized just keeping silent wasn't going to be enough. He was going to have to engineer his own death. He couldn't allow Diana to dope him up so he could then expose Juliet as one of the leaders of the L.A. resistance. She'd told him how hard it had been to establish her cover with Nathan Bates. Halpern wondered frantically what to do, whether he was equal to this sudden, final challenge. And the worst thing was, no one would ever know his fate.

He tried to think, remembering resistance horror stories about Diana's egomania, her aggressive temper. That was it— her temper.

The Visitor leader's gaze bored into him. "Dr. Halpern, you are annoying me. I am not a patient person."

Andy moistened his lips. Strangely, he experienced little

fear, only anger that his life meant nothing to her. Slowly, he shook his head. "I don't know anything to tell you."

Diana's gaze flickered over to a large Visitor shock trooper standing on the other side of the compartment. Two quick strides, and the alien's black-gloved hand smashed across Halpern's face. Once . . . twice . . . three times. Pain lanced redly across the scientist's field of vision as his head slammed into the metal wall of the bulkhead.

"Perhaps that has helped refresh your memory?" Diana suggested helpfully.

You have no right to do this, he thought, shaking his head in an attempt to clear the ringing sound in his ears. *I'm only twenty-eight years old, I'm up for a Rhodes scholarship, my mother's a widow now since Dad died on V-Day. I deserve to live, goddamn you.*

Halpern started to speak.

"Yes, Dr. Halpern?" Diana leaned closer . . . closer . . . then jerked back as the mouthful of bloody spittle caught her full in the face. Her scalp seemed literally to crawl, and Andy vaguely realized the crest beneath her wig was erect with anger. "Thomas," she said through stiff lips.

More pain flared across his face. Halpern lost count of the blows. Darkness nibbled at the fringes of his mind, and he was tempted to yield to it . . . so tempted. He tried fuzzily to remember why he shouldn't just slip away. One final fist smashed against his mouth, sending the blackness looming toward him like a tidal wave of promised release. *Mustn't . . . black . . . out.*

Andy groaned and spat out a couple of teeth as salty-warm blood gushed over his lips from his broken nose. A fear deeper and more terrifying than any he had ever known gripped him then, and he knew with a detached sort of certainty that if he had known the formula, he would have told them.

"Nuh—nuh—" he gabbled, not even sure what he was working to say.

"Who are the people you're working for?"

Lucid speech was beyond the capacity of his ruined mouth, but he dimly hoped she could read the hate in his eyes as he faded toward unconsciousness.

A splash of icy water felt like acid against his face, and Halpern tried to scream. A thick, gobbling sound was all his throat could manage.

Diana turned to Thomas again, her rage obvious, and Andy tensed as the alien kicked him twice in the back, sending white-hot agonies up his spine and into his kidneys. "Do we have a crivit with us, Captain?" the Visitor leader asked, staring down at Halpern.

"No, Commander," Thomas answered. "They don't like the water."

"A pity. Well, I suppose the sharks will appreciate a little offering." Diana stepped over to the hatchway, released it, and Andy saw nothing but blue sky and clouds streaming by. The helpless scientist realized they were flying thousands of feet above the Pacific Ocean.

Diana stepped back over to Andy's slumped body, raising her foot, and Halpern knew his death was at the end of that polished black boot. She kicked him in the stomach, once, twice, and he could only grunt his protests, struggling feebly to free his hands and grasp something, anything to hold on to as he was rolled toward the hatchway. The floor of the craft was relentlessly smooth, and Andy could feel the chill air streaming by.

The next blow caught him full in the throat, smashing his trachea, and then he was supported by nothing. Andrew Halpern gurgled his last sounds into the ice-cold wind whipping around him as the ocean whirled below, closer and closer . . .

"You *killed* him?" Lydia's normally imperturbable features were a study in amazement.

At her science-station console, Diana deliberately keyed in two more entries to her notes before turning to face the junior officer. She had to admit to a grudging respect for Lydia's resourcefulness and contacts. Diana had returned to the Mother Ship less than an hour ago.

"Yes," she said with a shrug. "He was useless to us."

"You didn't even attempt to use your precious truth serum."

"Lydia, I have spent sufficient time with humans to know when they are lying. He knew nothing of value to us."

"Diana, I have thought of you in many ways, but never as stupid—before now." Lydia's expression of surprise rapidly gave way to something dark and crafty. "You have just tossed away our best chance to discover the nature of this new substance. I wonder what our Great Leader would think if he were to learn of your impetuous tactics."

"Dear Lydia." The security officer tensed as Diana patted her cheek. "You continue to underestimate me. That is why I continue to outrank you. At this moment, one of our finest botanists, Bernard, is analyzing the data we obtained and will doubtless come up with a solution. In the meantime, I have a contingency plan—as always."

"And what is that? So that I and my security forces can provide you with the best possible assistance, of course."

"Of course." Diana smiled gently. "But we both enjoy our little secrets, don't we? For now, let it suffice to say that I believe the L.A. resistance must be behind the development of this new form of the red dust. If we strike at the heart of their resistance, then it will die out as surely as their red dust and any other feeble efforts they might try against us."

Diana leaned suddenly across her console. "I am going to finish the resistance by finishing Michael Donovan."

Despite the raging afternoon sunlight, Mike Donovan was in a black mood as he turned the battered Chevy onto Santa Monica Boulevard.

The forgotten toilet paper had prompted the need for another supermarket trip earlier that day. His initial annoyance at that had turned to pleasure when he'd discovered he'd had almost six dollars to spare, thanks to some good coupons on laundry detergent and toothpaste, and a two-for-one special on English muffins. But when he went to the candy section to pick up the Hershey bar for Julie, the shelves were bare.

Then he had phoned Julie at work, hoping that they could at least get together for lunch afterward, but she had been "in conference" with Nathan Bates for most of the day—whatever the hell that meant.

Mike was beginning to wonder if it was ending between them. With all his being he hoped not, but after one ruined marriage and several dead-end relationships, he couldn't kid himself that such things didn't happen as long as people loved each other. Relationships ended for all kinds of reasons, even between people who still cared very much for one another.

He'd last seen her two days ago, right after Chris was injured, and she'd seemed preoccupied and distant, even during their lovemaking. And the manner of that lovemaking—Donovan frowned. The moment they'd been alone, when he'd tried to hold her, talk to her, she'd turned to him, kissing him hard, tugging at his belt buckle, almost as though she were using sex as an excuse *not* to talk. Admittedly, the couch in the resistance's subbasement headquarters wasn't the most romantic place they had ever been. But then again, it seemed to be getting harder for them to get together under *any* circumstances.

Squinting into the late afternoon sun as he hunted for a place to park, Mike felt resentment settle into his gut like heartburn. Julie had a very important job, of course, with a very important salary, working for the very important Mr. Nathan Bates. The logical part of his mind said yes, it was good that she had gotten a position of trust, working so closely with the head of Los Angeles's provisional government. Many times, she had been privy to inside information that had proved invaluable to the resistance—saving lives more than once. And yes, it was also good that at least one of them could be contributing to the profession he or she had been trained for and loved.

Julie seemed to be so busy all the time, though. He knew research took a lot of time and didn't respect regular hours, whether you were tracking news leads or microbes. But now there was always Nathan Bates, and Donovan didn't trust the financier any farther than he could throw a shuttlecraft.

Bates had made no secret of the fact that he found Julie attractive, and she had felt obliged to tread carefully around his feelings. Maybe that wasn't so hard for her to do. Bates had wealth and power, and supported the work that was almost the most important thing in her life. He also had a certain amount of charm, with his thick salt-and-pepper hair and green eyes.

Damn you, Donovan, you're jealous! he thought, scowling at a BMW as it pulled out in front of him, making him brake sharply. It was an unworthy emotion; hell, it was unworthy to consider even for an instant that Julie might be having an affair with Bates. Why couldn't things be different? he wondered. He wanted to marry Julie, settle down somewhere with her and Sean, maybe even have a kid or two of their own. But how could that ever happen as long as the Visitors dominated even part of this world? Or while Julie continued to have so many other things on her mind?

His thoughts remained gloomy while he parked and walked up to the Club Creole. It was a real effort to work up some enthusiasm for Elias's new line of shirts and Willie's latest version of his blender-madness, which had proved to be quite a hit with the lunchtime Visitor crowd. After a few minutes, Donovan escaped to the comparative quiet of the secret room in the subbasement.

"Hey, Gooder." Ham Tyler glanced up from a map of L.A. spread out before him. "Find any kitties stuck in trees while you were out?"

"Can it, Ham. I'm not in the mood." Mike stretched out wearily on the old couch jammed up against a wall.

Elias had discovered this room in the subbasement of the club the first week he'd moved in. It was securely hidden behind a secret door and also had a second entrance, a tunnel leading under the street to a nearby alley. They'd figured the place had probably been constructed as a speakeasy during Prohibition. Several coins dating from the 1920s lent credence to this theory. The tarnished pieces of silver had been unearthed when the underground members cleaned up the place, moving in old furniture and equipment, turning it into the L.A. headquarters for the resistance.

It had a certain jumbled comfort, filled as it was with racks of arms, boxes of munitions, utilitarian desks, pin-dotted strategy maps, and bulletin boards jammed with various bills and memos. Miranda, Elias, and Robin had hung up a few prints, and someone had turned one of the old "VISITORS = FRIENDS" posters into a dartboard; Diana's and John's smiling faces were riddled with holes.

All the scrubbing and painting hadn't been able to get the smell of age and dampness out of the place, though, and empty Styrofoam coffee cups and overflowing trash cans also seemed to be a permanent part of the decor. Donovan sighed at the nibbled bits of papers and droppings in one corner that said mice used it as their regular hangout, too.

"Sounds like you could use a little vacation," Ham said, interrupting Mike's thoughts.

"Couldn't we all?" Donovan shook his head. "Only thing is, the Visitors have relief crews and we don't."

"How about a busman's holiday, then? A trip to beautiful New York, where the lizards ain't around."

"That would be great. Except we're fresh out of matter transporters or ruby slippers."

"Spare me your cute metaphors, Gooder," said Ham,

looking pained. "I'll tell you what we're practically out of, and that's power packs for the laserguns and our other scaly toys. I got word to our friends in the New York contingent, and they said they could spare a few and asked if we could courier some things around in return. Since you're turning into such a regular errand boy around here anyway, I elected you for the job. Take the lizard buggy out tonight around three, fly low under radar range, and you should get there by nine A.M. Eastern Standard Time."

"Tyler, that's cold, real cold, even for you." Mike sat up abruptly, causing the couch to creak alarmingly. "You figure the power packs on the shuttlecraft will last long enough for me to ditch in Lake Michigan, or should I plan for somewhere in the middle of the Great Plains?"

"Fly easy, stay out of trouble, don't use the auxiliaries, and you should make it. I don't want to lose that aircraft."

"Your concern for me is touching."

"You're replaceable. The shuttlecraft isn't."

"Ham, if you've got a heart anywhere in that cold granite—"

"Hi, Doc." Tyler's flat-brown eyes flicked uninterestedly past Donovan to Juliet Parrish as she entered the room. "How's that seaweed surprise coming?"

"Slow," she said, smiling over at Mike, who smiled back.

"Well, I got better things to do than argue with Gooder here about the obvious, so I'll see you later." Folding his map, Ham sauntered out.

"Arrogant S.O.B.," Donovan muttered as he went over to Julie and put his arms around her.

"He just likes pulling your chain, Mike."

He leaned over to find her mouth, but her head moved, and his lips brushed her cheek instead.

"I've missed you these past couple of days," he said, pulling her down to sit on the couch, his hand stroking the blond shimmer of her hair, then moving down her neck. "Seems like you're either off working somewhere, or I'm busy making sure the resistance isn't going to run out of groceries."

For a moment her body was tense under his hand, then, as he pressed a kiss against her ear, he could feel her relax.

"There's always tomorrow night," she whispered, and there was an appeal Mike couldn't identify in her voice. "I'd like to see you. Maybe we could talk."

"Damn it." He sat back to look at her as memory struck him. "I can't, Julie. Ham just told me I've got to make a courier run to New York tonight to pick up some power packs. We're running so low that we've gotta grab whatever we can get."

"Couldn't Maggie go? She's a good pilot."

"She's looking after Chris these days, and I have a little more flying experience."

"Oh. Well, I understand. Fortunes of war and all that." Julie's smile tightened at the corners.

Mike was suddenly struck by her pallor and the tiny blue-edged lines of fatigue around her eyes and mouth, and he looked at her with concern. "Hey, are you feeling okay?"

"I don't know. I'm tired—maybe I'm getting a cold or the flu, God forbid."

"I sure hope not." He continued to hold her but shifted back a bit. "I'll see if I can bring back a couple of steaks from New York, maybe even some champagne. We'll have a special night together, just you and me."

"That . . . would be really nice, Mike," she said, but her shoulder remained tense under his hand.

Robin Maxwell stood behind the window curtains of Julie's fourth-floor apartment near Santa Monica, peering out, waiting. It was six-fifteen, over an hour past the time Julie had said she would be home, but there was still no sign of her.

Pushing a hand through her cropped hair (a recent attempt to disguise herself), Robin continued her vigil, scanning the street outside. Despite her rising panic, she was careful to remain just out of sight behind the curtain. She had learned a lot since becoming a fugitive and, later, an active member of the Los Angeles resistance, and some of the lessons were bitter ones.

All of them had suffered at the hands of the Visitors, but Robin felt she had experienced more than her share of anguish. When the Visitors had begun their hate campaign against the scientists, she had been ridiculed by the other high school seniors for being the daughter of an anthropologist. Her humiliation had soon given way to incessant fear as her whole family was forced into hiding, then smuggled to the first resistance headquarters.

Scared, lonely, and only seventeen, she had sought comfort in dreams of a relationship with Brian, the handsome Visitor

Youth leader. But when she had been captured by the Visitors, she had been subjected to some kind of internal alteration just before Brian had seduced her (actually it was more like rape). She'd soon discovered that Diana's meddling had in reality been a successful attempt at gene splicing—Robin had found herself pregnant with the first Visitor/human child.

With Mike Donovan's help, Robin had escaped from the Mother Ship, only to witness her mother's death and then suffer through her strange pregnancy which culminated in the birth of alien twins. One, reptilian and forever nameless, had almost pushed her over the edge when she saw it; mercifully, it had only lived a few hours.

The other, Elizabeth, was outwardly human, beautiful, and a source of cautious happiness. Her daughter, however, had undergone several molts, growing and maturing at such a rapid rate that she now appeared to be eighteen, the same age as her mother—and they were both in love with Kyle Bates.

Robin's father, the brave and gentle Robert Maxwell, had died not long ago, sacrificing his life to save many others. After so much loss and upheaval in her life, Robin now peeked out of windows and watched clocks with a special intensity, living always on the bare edge of fear and anguish. She tended to worry easily if people she cared about were late. . . .

She was picking up the phone to call Julie's office for the third time when she spotted the white VW Rabbit pulling up to the curb across the street.

"I'm sorry I'm late, Robin," Juliet Parrish said minutes later, panting a little from running up the stairs. She had a shopping bag in her hands, which she put on the kitchen counter.

"I was worried about you, Julie." Robin put a hand over her mouth to hide the sudden trembling of her lower lip.

"I wound up working later than I'd planned, and then I had to stop at the Club Creole. Then Mike happened to be there, and I ended up talking to him for a few minutes."

"You could have called."

"You're right." Julie came over to give her a hug. "I should have called. I'm sorry."

"We've having beef burgundy." Robin smiled, beginning to relax. "I finally got around to trying out that crock-pot recipe you gave me."

"It, uh, smells wonderful."

V

"And for dessert, I made . . ." Robin frowned and looked at her friend more closely. "Julie, are you okay?"

"Oh, sure, fine." The blond scientist didn't look at her as she pulled off her lab coat on her way into the bedroom, returning a moment later with a silky red caftan on a hanger. "Look what I bought yesterday."

"Oh, Julie. It's totally awesome. I mean, it's really beautiful, and the color is perfect for you."

Smiling a little too brightly, her friend smoothed down the translucent fabric. "It cost a chunk of my last paycheck, and it is a bit extravagant, but Mike and I are planning this special dinner together when he gets back from New York. He says he's going to scare up steaks and a bottle of champagne, and it will be a really special occasion, for just the two of us, and—"

"Julie, what's wrong?" Robin asked suddenly.

Julie looked as though she had been caught trying to rob a bank. "Why, nothing! Everything's fine."

"You've always treated me as an adult, whether I deserved it or not, and you've always been honest with me, whether I wanted it or not." Robin shook her head slowly. "I've kind of gotten used to that kind of treatment from you, and I hope things aren't starting to change between us."

Juliet bit her lip, and Robin saw tears welling up behind her eyelashes. "I'm late, Robin, and I've been sick to my stomach all the time for the past week. I'm afraid I might be pregnant."

"Oh, Julie." Robin came over and hugged her, hard. Suddenly she felt strong and very adult. This was something she had been through, and now she could help Julie for once. "Are you sure? Have you gotten any test results?"

"It's still too early for a conclusive test."

"I thought you were on the Pill."

"I am." She moved restlessly into the living room, her face drawn and shadowed. "There's been a rumor out of the Seattle underground that the Visitors have been secretly tampering with shipments of contraceptives so that they're rendered ineffective."

"Why would they do that?" asked Robin, confused.

"To make more fat, bouncing little humans for their food chambers, I suppose," Julie said bitterly. "Oh, Robin, I *can't* have a baby, not now! Not until we've got our own world back! What am I going to do?"

"Have you told Mike yet?"

Julie shook her head wearily. "No, and I'm not going to. It's my problem at this point. He's got enough worries about Sean without losing more sleep over the possibility of another child. At any rate, it wouldn't be fair to mention it until I'm sure. This *might* be a reaction to the stress I've been under. Or it could be due to some bizarre side effect of that new kind of red dust I've been working with."

"I think Mike would want to know." Robin patted her shoulder gently. "He really loves you, Julie. He'd want to do whatever is best for you."

"I know. But I'm so unsure of everything right now."

"If it's true, would you have an abortion?"

"I don't know, Robin." Julie's voice was soft and haunted. "I just don't know."

Chapter 5

Connecting Flight

"I don't know," said Mike Donovan darkly, looking up from his scan of the controls in the console of the shuttlecraft. "In some ways trying to read these things is always guesswork, but I've never seen the power indicators look this low."

"You'll make it." Ham Tyler, leaning against the doorway of the vehicle, examined a hangnail. Behind him, the night sky up here in the Los Angeles hills was starry and bright under the gaze of the quarter moon.

"Easy for you to say," Mike muttered, going back toward the storage bay, "since it's not your butt that may be in a sling this time. Flying at six thousand feet may not be much as aircraft go, but it's more than enough to kill me if I crash."

"C'mon, Gooder. Where's your usual flag-waving, rah-rah, for-the-good-of-God-and-country optimism?"

"Maybe cynicism is more contagious these days." He stooped to check one more time on the items he was carrying. Crates of fresh oranges and grapefruits dominated the small cargo hold, along with lettuce, avocados, and other produce. There were several courier packs containing papers and computer disks for the New York–based resistance group, code-named White Christmas, as well as various other parcels and packages. Some of these latter were small gifts from Julie and the other scientists to friends in the Brook Cove research group.

Former hotshot recon pilot in 'Nam, award-winning news cameraman and evening anchorman—now he was the local greengrocer and Purolator courier. *Hell of a comedown,* Donovan thought, tightening one last strap.

Satisfied that everything was secured, Mike swung himself into the pilot seat and strapped in. "Zero-four-niner to control tower, requesting permission to take off, over," he said, looking at Ham.

"Hit the skies, Gooder." Ham stepped off the ramp. His rock-still expression never altered, but he lifted a hand. "Give my regards to Broadway."

Mike smiled a little as he touched the controls to raise and seal the ramp door of the hatchway. "Want me to bring you back an issue of *Variety*, Tyler?"

Ham's thumbs-up gesture was the last thing that Mike saw from the ground, then the shuttlecraft was nosing toward the star-sprinkled night.

The alien engines were eerie in their almost total silence. The faint, low-pitched hum and the rush of wind along the craft's streamlined sides told him that everything was working as it should. Only the night-dark blurs of houses and highways and the occasional headlights of a passing car flashing by underneath gave him any real sense of movement.

As the San Gabriel Mountains began to stretch below him, Mike made adjustments for the thermal currents and reflected once again how much easier it was to fly the Visitor ships than any human-made machines. Certainly, his flight training in various aircraft, coupled with fast reflexes and good instincts, had helped save his skin the first time he had stolen a skyfighter, but the little craft were basically designed to be flown by a moron of any humanoid species with a minimum of training. Donovan wished that the resistance had one to spare, that he and a couple of flight engineering types could tear down and examine without having to worry about putting it all back together again.

Once he had crossed into the frost zone, safely out of Visitor airspace, there wasn't much to do. He put the craft on autopilot, then set the radio transmitter to broadcast the special signal the New York resistance had provided which advertised the pilot of this alien craft as a friend. Then he settled back in his seat to gaze down at the moonlit clouds and snowcapped peaks of the Rockies gliding by.

The cabin was cold and dark. Although the interior was equipped with lights and a heater, Mike felt he had to conserve every erg of energy he could from the shuttle's weakening power packs.

Shivering, he drew his suede jacket more tightly around himself, then frowned down at the scrapes on the sleeves, the frayed ends of his shirt cuffs underneath, and his faded jeans. These were his best clothes these days, he thought, and he tried to remember the last time he had bought a new suit or jacket. Life as a resistance fighter and fugitive tended to be tough on clothes, and even tougher for making any kind of money to replace them.

He ran a hand through his hair, grimacing at the feel of the ragged patch behind his left ear. The results of Robin's earnest attempt at a haircut before he'd left had fallen short of the forty-five-dollar stylings he had regularly gotten during his days on national television. So he wasn't there for his looks— still, it was demeaning to accept handouts and walk around with two bucks in his pocket most of the time.

"Freedom and dignity, Michael." He could picture his mother, Eleanor, the way she used to walk back and forth in front of the fireplace of her elegant home, hands clasped primly in front of her. "That's what money means more than anything else. More than diamonds or furs or anything material, money buys your freedom from drudgery, the small and meaningless things in life, and dignity through self-respect and respect from others."

Now that a year had passed since she had died, Mike thought he could understand a little better why someone like Eleanor Dupres might have thrown in her lot with the Visitors. His mother had grown up in "a little hick town in Louisiana," as she had often told him. Donovan knew she had married his father partly for money; when Patrick Donovan had died several years ago, she had promptly remarried a rich industrialist, Arthur Dupres.

When the Visitors had landed with their bogus plea for assistance in manufacturing a chemical that would save their dying world, Eleanor had pressured Arthur into bidding for the contract. His Richland plant had been among the first to begin operations, and they were well rewarded for their efforts. While the rest of the world was being slowly crushed under the weight of the Visitors' growing domination, Eleanor had ridden high on the wave of freedom and dignity in the company of the Visitor officer Steven. Diamonds, position, power—she had it all.

Maybe she had gotten in too deep, and her old values, such as caring for other people, honesty, and all the other ones she had instilled in her only son, had been lost along the way. The last time Donovan had seen her alive, his mother had pulled a gun on him, threatened to kill him, and had almost gotten him captured by the Visitors.

She had died on V-Day while Donovan was on the Mother Ship trying to prevent the nuclear destruction of the world. Robert Maxwell had broken the news to him later, saying she had come screaming out of the Los Angeles Visitor headquarters when the resistance had stormed it. Telling them to hold their fire, she had claimed that she had been held prisoner by Steven and forced to do his bidding. Moments later, Steven had stepped out from behind her, his laser flaming at her back. It didn't help that a few minutes later Ham Tyler had poured red dust into Steven's face and watched him die.

Mike knew Eleanor had always been an opportunist, ready to grab the best of every chance that came along. Hell, there was something of that in himself. He liked to think, though, that his mother had meant what she'd said at the very end, that she really had been trapped and had only realized it too late.

There were a lot of things he had wanted to ask her, arguments to settle, and some small things that had never been said between them but should have been. There would never be a chance now. . . .

In the coolness and silence of the cabin, Mike Donovan thought about his mother as he flew over the moon-washed wheat fields of Nebraska and Iowa, and for the first time since her death, allowed himself to grieve.

Eventually, his thoughts turned to his son, Sean, who was the source of another kind of heartache.

Sean and his mother, Marjorie Donovan, Mike's ex-wife, had been captured early in the initial days of the struggles with the Visitors, along with thousands of other residents of San Pedro. Sean had been put through Diana's "conversion" process and used as bait to try to get to the resistance through Donovan.

Mike had turned himself in to the Visitors in exchange for his boy's safe return, subjecting himself to Diana's torture and her truth serum. He had betrayed his friend Martin, a Visitor

member of their own fifth-column resistance, before the two of
them had managed to escape.

Mike remembered how good it had been at first to have his
son back following the initial defeat of the Visitors. Sean had
had problems readjusting to a normal life, though, and after
some troubles at school, Mike took him to a psychiatrist. The
doctor confirmed his suspicions that the boy was suffering from
the lingering aftereffects of Diana's conversion process and had
recommended a special school for boys where some of Sean's
inner conflicts might be smoothed out.

Donovan had reluctantly agreed, a decision which turned to
anguish when he had learned his son had been recaptured by
the Visitors and brought under the tutelage of the deadly Klaus.
Mike remembered the last-ditch effort to rescue his son, the
easy familiarity with which Sean had released the safety of a
.357 Magnum and aimed it at him. Sean hadn't fired it, but
Diana had summoned the boy at that moment, and his son had
turned from his own voice to follow hers.

"He's ours or no one's, Mr. Donovan," Diana had gloated
just before she had spirited the boy off. The last Donovan had
heard was a scrap of intelligence gleaned from the San
Francisco resistance network that Sean was in some sort of
Visitor-run camp for boys in northern California. Mike had
spent more than one wakeful night trying to think of ways he
might learn the camp's location and free his son. Right now, the
situation looked pretty hopeless.

Mike knew he would continue looking for his son as long as
he lived—but not with the same blind singlemindedness of
purpose he had felt once before. He was still haunted in his
deepest nightmares by the fact that Sean had *chosen* to go with
Diana. And if there had been a glimpse of something in Sean's
eyes that gave Mike hope that his son might be his again, there
were also other people to think about.

Now there was no one to take fishing or camping, throw a
baseball to, or talk with about the Important Things on the
minds of all twelve-year-old boys. God only knew what kinds
of things ran through his son's mind these days. Maybe he was
teaching eight-year-olds how to fire Uzis or laserguns at human
targets.

Wincing, Mike shut his eyes, then after a while he ate the
two ham-and-cheese sandwiches and the apple that Miranda

had packed for him, all the time frowning into the predawn darkness of Illinois below.

Then he must have dozed. The next thing he knew, he was bounced hard against his safety harness as the shuttlecraft hit a pocket of air turbulence.

A quick look at his flight plan and instruments told him he was in Ohio, about seventy-five miles from the Pennsylvania border. Near eight A.M. local time it was strangely dark. Then he saw the greenish-black clouds roiling toward him from the south.

Thunderheads! He pulled hard on the controls and banked sharply, intending to fly out and above the turbulence, when a sudden downdraft pummeled the craft like a fist. The boxy shuttlecraft had never been designed for flight in bad weather. Alien metal creaked and groaned throughout the ship, and something broke loose in the cargo hold and began rattling around the storage bay area with a hollow, spectral thump as Donovan fought to regain control of his ship. Sleet and rain cracked against the windshield and fuselage while lightning tore the sky into hellish jigsaw fragments.

Another downdraft sent him plunging sickeningly for several hundred feet before Mike could bring the nose up again. A sharp, peppery smell filled the air, and he realized that one of Miranda's bottles of homemade salsa had broken. Hail the size of Ping-Pong balls battered into the left side of the craft, and he heard an odd coughing sound in one of the jet engines used for maneuvering. Then the engine began to whine alarmingly, signaling an overload. He had to shut it down.

The steering control in his sweating hands went stiff and sluggish, and Mike cursed. The tightly controlled turns that would allow an escape from these weather conditions were out of the question now. Somehow he would have to ride the storm out.

Far to his left, near the horizon, an inky cloud began to turn and twist into itself, and lightning sent blue-white streaks across his line of vision. The roaring of wind and the pummeling of the rain and sleet were almost deafening. *Oh, God,* he thought, fighting the urge to shut his eyes, *am I going to wind up in Oz?*

Fascinated in spite of himself, he watched the tornado form, a huge black snake that turned downward and began sniffing the ground as though for mice. The newsman that still lurked within him wished for a minicam with a zoom lens as a barn lifted itself whole from the ground, did a sluggish pirouette, then imploded into splintered lumber. Trees nearby bowed down almost to the ground, as though in worship of an ancient and terrible god; one broke off and turned into a spinning missile that drilled itself into the side of an old farmhouse.

A tractor lifted itself into the air and attempted a missionary mating with the four-by-four parked across the yard. The truck didn't fancy being on the bottom, and rolled over onto the John Deere, instead. Debris pelted the side of the shuttlecraft even from this distance, and Mike yelped in pain as the ship lurched sideways, slamming his wrist down hard against the control console.

Trying to ignore the agony which flared up his right arm, he wrestled with the steering control. The ship had turned into a living creature, a bronco determined to buck him off. At one moment, he was plummeting toward the ground, which stretched like a wrinkled old Army blanket in front of him. The next, he was facing the clouds, where a few were turning white again around a growing patch of blue sky.

Mike locked the craft into a course aiming for that small bright spot. The ship shuddered violently, as though the invisible giant behind him had made one last grab for it. Then he was flying smoothly again, and the sun was shining through the settling dust as the winds died down.

Donovan rolled up his sleeve and moved his arm experimentally, wincing as pain defined lateral and circular movements. He hoped it wasn't broken. Jury-rigging a splint out of a newspaper and some tape, he swallowed a couple of aspirin and checked the indicators for any additional signs of damage.

The power reading was nudging into the dangerously low zone—he'd used up a lot of power battling the storm. Long Island and the Brook Cove lab were still almost five hundred miles away.

He climbed slowly, nursing the controls, taking every advantage he could of air currents and wind direction. Shutting power down on all systems except those related to flight, even the radio beacon, he divided his attention between his eastern heading and the readings on his console. He didn't want to attempt a gliding, powerless landing—the fuselage and short, stubby wings weren't built for it.

Over New Jersey, the greenish-brown blur of Long Island

was just coming into view at the horizon when the engines began to hiss shrilly. Sucking air through his teeth, Donovan banked the ship and began his descent.

Once again he was grateful for the simplicity of the controls. As it was, it took all of his skill, learned from fighting the nasty, hot winds in Southeast Asia, to bring the craft down more or less in one piece. It was a bumpy landing in a pasture several miles short of the Brook Cove facility, and he saw several horses bolt in fright in front of him as the belly of the shuttlecraft churned turf into mud in a broad swath. Finally the shuttlecraft shuddered to a halt.

Mike's legs felt a little weak as he fumbled for the catch of his safety harness and stood, the floor comfortingly solid and unmoving under him. Leaning over the console, he switched on the small battery-powered CB radio they had installed for emergency use. "Breaker one-nine, this is Hollywood Joe, do you copy?"

The speakers answered only wth the weak crackle of static.

Donovan frowned and tried several times more to no avail. He was wondering whether he'd have to walk it—and in what direction, for that matter—when he heard a muffled thumping on the shuttlecraft's cargo doors and a shouted, "Hey, fly-boy!"

Unsealing the hatch, he stepped out into the gray, mist-damp air to see a tiny white-haired woman in enormous galoshes cheerfully waving an umbrella. A young woman wearing a down vest, her strawberry-blond hair in a ponytail, stood beside her, while a plump man in jeans and a plaid hunting shirt came up the slight rise from the road, puffing a little.

"Hard landing, wasn't it?" the older woman asked.

She pronounced it "haahd," and Mike found himself grinning. "A Bostonian, born and bred. You must be Dr. Hannah Donnenfeld."

"And you're Mike Donovan." She smiled and stuck out her hand. "I remember your stories on the hungry kids, the victims of war in Laos and El Salvador, in *Life* a few years back."

"I remember when you won the Nobel Prize. Glad to meet you." Mike started to extend his hand, but pain twinged up his arm and he withdrew it, grimacing. "Rough flight. I just about ran out of gas."

"You've got some swelling there," the young woman

observed, the freckles on her forehead bunching into a frown. "I'll take an X-ray when we get back."

"This is Sari James and Mitchell Loomis," Hannah said, indicating each in turn. "My favorite chaperons, rabble-rousers, and—"

"—and personal cheering section." Sari's engaging grin revealed a slight gap between her front teeth.

"Enough nonsense!" Hannah made shooing motions at them, her expression mock-stern. "Mr. Donovan has had a long trip, and he's much more interested in a hot toddy than your hot air."

Her brisk stride belied her diminutive, fragile-looking appearance as she led the way to a jeep waiting by the roadside. "Mitchell, be a dear and grab Mr. Donovan's bag, will you?" she called over her shoulder.

"I love it when you talk sweet to me, Hannah." He vanished into the cargo hold. A moment later, they could hear his excited shout all the way to the road as he reappeared, holding Mike's battered suitcase and a bag of oranges. "Hey, look! Fresh vitamin C! Thanks, Mr. Donovan."

"Call me Mike." He smiled. "There are a lot of neat things in there. Julie sent me along with a bunch of stuff—computer disks, reports, pictures. It's all in the blue vinyl carrying cases."

"Mitchell, grab them as well," Hannah shouted, then got into the driver's seat. Turning to Mike, she said, "We'll bring over a power pack and Sari'll fly the whole thing back to Brook Cove later."

"Sounds good to me." Donovan leaned back in the seat. His arm ached dully, and it was good to let someone else take charge for a while.

"I wanted to be a scientist, and I wound up as a pack mule," Mitchell groused good-naturedly as he swung the bags behind the rear seat and clambered inside.

"It's good exercise, and you need it," said Sari, poking playfully at his broad abdomen.

"What I really need is a woman who loves me for my mind."

"Julie also sends her love, by the way," Mike said as Hannah started up the jeep. Donnenfeld gave him a quick glance.

"She's such a lovely girl. How is she?"

As they bounced along the winding, tree-lined road, Mike filled her in on Julie's activities and her progress on the new kelp-based bacteria as best he could. Hannah asked him a couple of questions, but when he floundered to a halt, she shrugged. "Sorry, Mike. I get carried away when somebody talks technical to me. I wish Julie had been able to come along, too."

"So do I," he said, looking out at the lush greenery of the fields, so different from California's palm trees and scrub.

Hannah nodded sympathetically. Sari touched his shoulder and pointed. "Welcome to Brook Cove Laboratories."

Dark and boarded-up as it was, the old mansion on top of the hillside still had an imposing aura about it, and it didn't look as much deserted as merely asleep. Donovan looked around, a little confused, expecting to see more signs of activity.

Driving the jeep into a garage heavily camouflaged by bushes, Hannah jumped out and led the way to a small storage shed nearby. Inside were crates piled on top of one another and shelves of books. "Here's our heart and soul, Mike," she said, reaching behind one of the bookcases. A section of it swung outward, and stairs descended to a highly sophisticated research complex behind a metal door eighteen inches thick.

A number of people, their ages ranging from early twenties to late sixties, were working at various tasks. Casually dressed in T-shirts, jeans or cut-offs, and sneakers, they looked cheerfully incongruous in this gleaming, high-tech environment. Computer terminals, microscopes, and pieces of ultramodern equipment Donovan couldn't even begin to name were arrayed throughout the labs.

As Donnenfeld led him through the compact, well-designed warren of living and working quarters, introducing him to the members of her team, her pride in this dedicated group was obvious, and they just as plainly held her in the highest esteem.

"This is one hell of a setup," Donovan said an hour later, leaning back in the leather easy chair in the library. After X-raying his wrist, Sari had pronounced it sprained and had wrapped it up, saying he should use it as little as possible for the next several days. Then she and Mitchell had taken a power pack out to the shuttlecraft so that they could fly it back to the grounds to a spot protected by rocks and pine trees. Sari, it seemed, was a fair pilot herself.

"Julie is a gifted researcher." Hannah peered up at Mike

over the reports in her hand. "I know she's got more resources to work with now, but half the time it's like magic, the insights she gets."

Donovan grinned. "The first time I ever met her, she was wearing a beat-up sweatshirt and jeans, with her hair all stringy. She looked about as much like a scientist as I look like Einstein. How was I to know she could think almost as well?"

Hannah laughed. "You should hear her talk about you. I was expecting a cross between Indiana Jones and Bob Woodward."

Cupping a snifter of good brandy in his hands, Mike chuckled at the image. "I bet you have things down here even Science Frontiers hasn't heard of. And the location—it would even fool the scalies, as Ham Tyler would say."

"It did once." The fine lines around Hannah's mouth tightened for a moment at an old memory, then she sighed and settled back into an overstuffed chair in the small library. "I miss the fireplace back at the house, though. Ah, well. We all make our sacrifices. Tell me, how is the ever-charming Mr. Tyler?"

"Like fingernails on a blackboard, as always. If he weren't the fastest lasergun in the West, we'd send him over to the Visitors for Thanksgiving. But he's probably too tough a mouthful even for Diana."

She laughed, inquired after Maggie, then stood with Julie's folders. "We'll get this stuff into our data banks right away. We're one of the most protected research facilities in the country, so we've been collecting data and acting as a sort of clearinghouse for the results of all scientific research aimed at sending the Visitors packing back to Sirius."

"Hi." Sari, her face dirty and her expression cheerful, came bouncing in, followed by the slower-moving Mitchell. "We've checked your shuttlecraft inside and out. One of your jets took a load of debris from that storm you went through and needs to be flushed."

"Also your landing gear needs realignment, and one of the struts is cracked," Mitchell added, reaching for a cookie from the plate beside Hannah. "We've got a couple of good engineering types hanging around down here, and it's about time they earned an honest day's wage. Even so, it'll take about four days to put it all back together."

"Wash your hands, Mitchell," said Hannah, affecting a severe expression.

"Can you get a message back to L.A., let them know I'm okay, just delayed?" Mike asked.

Her forehead wrinkled a moment. "It's hard to get messages in and out, especially any distance, but we'll see what we can do."

"Yeah, communication is our biggest problem around here, as a matter of fact," Mitchell said, reaching for another cookie.

"Don't talk with your mouth full, Mitchell." Hannah swatted him on his plump backside with Julie's folder. "Our various scientific communities risk duplication in some areas of inquiry while ignoring others just because we don't always know what the hell's going on. We sneak off occasional phone calls or bounce through somebody's satellite dish antenna, but it's hard keeping track of everybody's progress."

"We do have some nifty stuff happening here on the East Coast, though," Sari said proudly.

"Like what?" Mike asked.

"Let's see . . ." Donnenfeld ticked off people on her fingers as she spoke. "In Maryland, the Mariahs are looking at the Visitors' genetic makeup from the samples they've collected, seeing if there's a weakness to exploit. Keller's people in Connecticut are trying to find a drug that will render the Visitors catatonic but is harmless to humans. Kate Weaver in Toronto is researching weaponry, and Dr. Hathaway . . ."

She waved her hand. "I'll get this all written down so you can bring it to Julie along with an update on our own pursuit of the perfect frost-free red toxin. In the meantime, I guess you're stuck with our humble East Coast entertainments for the next few days, but we'll try to do our best."

They did their best, and then some. Mike had never passed four days more quickly or pleasantly.

A lot of items were rationed, so the oranges and other fresh fruits and vegetables he'd brought from California were very much appreciated by the members of the resistance.

The "engineering types" that Mitchell had jokingly referred to turned out to include an aircraft technician, and repairs on the shuttlecraft progressed smoothly. When Mike wasn't helping with that, he had plenty of opportunities to stroll along the beach, watch the waves break over the rocky Long Island shores, and unwind—especially after the high-speed printer at

Brook Cove tapped out the message from L.A. that they had received his message and understood that he would be delayed.

On Saturday night, two days after he had arrived, they took him to see a revival of *Cats* on Broadway. Times Square was a little quieter than he remembered it. Some of the gigantic neon signs, damaged in Visitor attacks, hadn't been repaired, and people didn't seem to hurry as much. Perhaps the Visitors had taught New Yorkers a lesson in the value of taking time to enjoy the present moment.

Most of all, it felt good to Mike to walk freely and openly down the street—more or less. Here in New York, he was still a national hero, not a wanted criminal. People recognized him, shook his hand, or asked for his autograph. The sudden attention and hero worship, after the last year of living behind sunglasses and upturned collars, was a little unnerving.

The best time of all came on Sunday night when they went back into New York and a little Italian restaurant in lower Manhattan named the Bella Capri. The proprietor, a cheerful little Italian by the name of Guido, bustled the group to tables with candles dripping over Chianti bottles and covered with red-and-white checkered oilcloth.

There was plenty of exquisite lasagna, antipasto, and wine. Mike got to meet other members of the New York–based resistance. It was a special pleasure to meet Peter Forsythe, former star third baseman for the New York Yankees. Mike immediately liked the stocky, droll man with the thinning, curly blond hair. Pete, a fourth-year medical student, was now completing his studies at Cornell Medical Center.

"I used to take my son, Sean, to the L.A. Dodgers games all the time," he said, grinning as he shook Pete's hand. "I remember that game in seventy-nine. You got two homers and helped whomp the hell out of us."

"Yeah, those were the good old days."

"Anno pre-Lizardarius." The attractive dark-skinned woman sitting beside Forsythe made a face, and Donovan grinned appreciatively at Lauren Stewart. He remembered her from their first brief meeting almost two years ago on the roof of the UN Building in New York. As special assistant to the Secretary General, Olav Lindstrom, she had accompanied Lindstrom on his historical first contact with the Visitors' supreme commander, John.

"Are you and Olav still working at the UN?"

"Yes," she said. "We manage to stay surprisingly busy too, despite the fact we've lost virtually all of our members in the equatorial and subtropical zones."

They talked about politics and the various states of the world for a while, then Pete stretched his legs, grimacing a little as he rubbed his knees.

"So how are you and the most famous knees in baseball doing?" Mike asked.

"We're hanging in there." Pete rattled the ice in his glass of Diet 7-Up. "They're treating me a lot better than I did them. I can't sit still for too long in one place, is all."

"I guess you don't get much of a chance to play since the leagues were dissolved."

Pete nodded. "School and my . . . extracurricular activities keep me pretty busy these days. We take time for a pickup game once in a while, though. Some of the refugees from the southwest belonged to the Oakland As and the L.A. Dodgers, as a matter of fact, and—"

"Mike! Hey, Mike Donovan!"

A beautiful, slender woman with black hair ran over from the entrance across the room and almost landed in Donovan's lap from the force of her enthusiastic hug.

It was Denise Daltrey, an anchorwoman for the CBS morning news in New York. Mike had dated her a few times after the breakup of his marriage. It had stayed casual between them, and both of them had dated others before he had met Juliet Parrish . . . but he had always liked Denise.

"I heard a rumor that you were in this part of the world again," she said, pulling up a chair after she had exchanged greetings with the other members of the group. "Damn, you're looking good! Better than anyone suffering the deprivations of the West Coast has any right to. How the heck are you?"

For quite awhile they talked, and she brought him up to date on what was happening in the New York television news scene. Mike was sorry to learn that some of his colleagues had died, and pleased that others had done well.

"You know, Mike, you're a real hero," said Denise, leaning back.

He shrugged and made a self-deprecating gesture. "I've kept busy, although not necessarily out of trouble."

"You miss it? Lights, camera, action . . ." They'd drunk a

fair amount of Chablis, and pink colored her wonderful cheekbones as she grinned at him.

"Yeah, sure."

"You ever think of coming back this way?"

He looked at her, then scraped a bit of candle wax off the wine-bottle holder with his thumb. "Once in a while."

"Snow's never looked better than it has the last couple of years, Mike. You could get a really good job here. I'd talk to my producer. You could be my co-anchor, I bet."

A blur of conflicting emotions rose in him, even through the gentle haze of the wine he'd drunk. Here was his chance to be a respected professional again, with the salary and prestige to go with the work he loved. There would be shows, nice restaurants, decent clothes, and money in his wallet again.

And Julie, along with a whole bunch of people who had come to depend on him, would be three thousand miles away.

"God, Denise, I'm flattered, but . . . I don't know." It was the most honest thing he could say.

Her hand casually moved onto his and squeezed it. "Think about it."

Chapter 6

Conflicts of Interest

Lydia walked briskly down the corridors of the Mother Ship, her boots beating out a sharp, angry staccato along the polished deck. Officers of lower rank stepped aside with murmured apologies as she brushed past; the enlisted personnel flattened against the walls and pretended to be invisible.

She hated Diana's imperious summonses. The arrogant bitch had nothing better to do, it seemed, than haul Lydia out of her vital work as chief of security so that she could gloat over some trifling scientific success.

Of course, there had been that delicious little upset the other day, when Diana had learned that her precious water-collection scheme had gone awry. Lydia smiled slightly, remembering the rage Diana had flown into when she had learned from Bernard that the seawater had been poisoned by a new form of the bacteria deadly to their species. Lydia was beginning to suspect her commander was becoming unstable from the strains of dealing with the humans. Then again, Diana had never seemed particularly well suited to the rigors of command.

Certainly not nearly so well suited as Lydia herself . . .

Composing her face into her habitually neutral expression, Lydia announced her presence outside the door to Diana's laboratory.

"Come in, Lydia."

Diana sounded more than usually pleased with herself, and Lydia sighed inwardly. Doubtless today's lecture would be especially long and tedious, and she wished she'd scheduled the briefing on personal security for the new recruits this afternoon instead of tomorrow morning.

"Yes, Diana?" she said, steeling herself for the inevitable as she walked in. A young blond woman was sitting quietly in a chair behind Diana, and Lydia looked at her in surprise, then at the commander.

"I know how interested you are in being kept informed of all scientific matters," Diana said, smiling. "I have two things to share with you. One, Bernard is making excellent progress on the bacteria-infested kelp. He has already begun identifying the specific plants so affected and is planning appropriate means to deal with them. And two, I want you to meet someone special."

Diana crossed the room to lay her arm across the slight shoulders of the blond woman, who raised her head and smiled. "She looks splendid, wouldn't you say, Lydia? A perfect subject for my improved conversion process."

"She certainly does not look used up, the way some of your conversion subjects have appeared," Lydia admitted, raising her eyebrows. The woman did indeed look healthy, with good coloring.

"With those communiqués we intercepted from the Denver courier last week, she'll be accepted into the L.A. underground without question."

"Diana, I think that you put entirely too much stock in your conversions. Among other things, the humans usually spot them as soon as they use their hands."

"You weren't listening to me." Diana's smile made Lydia's venom rise in her mouth. "This is my *improved* process. In her case, I've been able to solve the problem of the brain hemisphere switchover *without* bringing about the left-hand dominance that was such a giveaway."

"You sound so sure of yourself, Diana."

"Confidence is the hallmark of the true leader, Lydia. This is an area that you could improve in yourself."

"What is so special about *this* particular person?" Lydia eyed her commanding officer suspiciously. "Why would the underground accept her readily, even with planted documents?"

Diana turned to the younger woman and smoothed back a lock of her soft gold hair. "Tell Lydia your name, my dear."

"Marjorie," the woman obediently replied, smiling up at Diana with the trusting expression of a child.

Diana patted the woman's shoulder and glanced sideways at Lydia. Her expression was a study in triumph, and Lydia felt her lunch move heavily in her stomach, knowing that her commander had gotten incredibly lucky once again. "I meant your married name, Marjorie," the commander amended.

The blond woman smiled. "I am Mrs. Michael Donovan."

Mike Donovan had forgotten what stores full of merchandise looked like. As he wandered the departments and aisles of Macy's, eyeing the counters full of clothes, jewelry, and toiletries, he calculated furiously.

Just before he'd left L.A., Elias had pressed one hundred dollars into his hand, saying, "Here, my man, have a good time." It had turned out that L.A. dollars weren't the same as New York dollars anymore, although there was some reciprocity.

With almost half of the United States effectively under Visitor control, the aliens had managed to do what the Civil War had not—divide the country in half. In his darker moments, Mike wondered whether they would ever get the greatest nation in the world back together again.

In the meantime, it was a real challenge figuring out the current rate of exchange. No one in Brook Cove had allowed him to spend a dime up to this point, anyway. So when Hannah asked him what he'd like to do today, his last in New York, he'd promptly replied, "Go shopping."

Candy was expensive in New York City too, but $3.50 was still a hell of a lot better than almost $6 for a Hershey bar, and he got two for Julie.

He caught Peter Forsythe grinning at him after the third time he'd run his hand over the racks of men's jackets, and smiled back a little self-consciously. "I feel like a hick, or the world's biggest tourist," he said. "Shopping malls used to be as common as palm trees in California, yet here I am, gaping around like a kid at Christmastime. There are so many shortages back home . . ."

"Don't forget to pick out something for yourself," Forsythe said. "I'm Santa Claus, and Christmas is early this year."

"No, I couldn't—" Mike began, but Pete raised his hand.

"Look at all the stuff you brought back for us. Hell, the fresh oranges alone were worth it."

"Yeah, but—"

"Come on, Mike. Don't forget who you're talking to. The man who for fourteen years got paid obscene amounts of money for playing a kid's game—and had a great time investing it well. I've got more than I know what to do with. You're someone I admire a lot, and I'd really appreciate it if you'd take something back from me. Anything you'd like."

"Okay. One thing," Donovan said. "Thanks, Pete."

"Think of it as a loan." Forsythe grinned. "You can remember me kindly when you're a famous newsman again and I've faded into obscurity as a kindly old M.D."

"Right." Mike grinned back. Walking resolutely past the menswear section, he led the way to ladies' lingerie. He was fingering a shimmering sapphire-colored silk negligee and nodding approvingly when Forsythe caught up to him.

Pete blinked. "Definitely your color, but I'm a little dubious about the fit."

"Real funny, Pete. This is for Julie. You said I could have anything I wanted, and I want something special for her."

"You know, I used to head over this way after my ex-wife and I had a fight and my conscience was bothering me," Forsythe said, his expression rueful as he pulled out his wallet. "The bigger the fight, the smaller and frillier the item of intimate apparel. It didn't do any good in the end, but it was fun while it lasted."

Mike looked at him and frowned slightly, wondering about his own motives for choosing Julie's gift. Denise's offer had remained in the back of his mind throughout his time here in New York. No matter how he tried, he couldn't forget it. And that was beginning to scare him.

"Have you thought about my offer?" Denise Daltrey asked.

"Day and night," Mike admitted, toying with his Risotto alla Milanese.

They had met for lunch and more of Guido's wonderful minestrone soup, antipasto, and homemade bread at the Bella Capri.

"I've already talked to my producer, and he thinks it's a fabulous idea." Denise leaned back, regarding him measuringly, and raised her wineglass. "You and I would make a terrific team, Donovan."

"What about the power packs and the shuttlecraft? They still have to get back to L.A. tonight. Everything's ready to go, and I know how crucial our supplies are."

"Sari mentioned she'd love to fly the shuttlecraft back and hang around for a while with Julie to help with your West Coast ocean bacteria studies—kind of an exchange student."

"You have to be as good with a rifle or a lasergun as you are with test tubes in L.A.," he said sourly, breaking off another piece of bread. "You want some more?"

"It's fattening." She shook her head. "You sound really tired of it, Mike."

"Hell, yes. Everybody's tired of it."

"Then give it a rest. You've done more than your fair share. Nobody could ever accuse Mike Donovan of shirking his civic duties."

"I don't know, Denise. Let me think about it. I would have to go back to L.A. anyway to straighten out some things. I'll let you know in a week, okay?"

"Fair enough," she said, and reached for the check, shaking her head at his protests. "Oh, no, that's all right. You can pick up the next one—when you're back."

"I hate good-byes." Hannah Donnenfeld hugged her arms in the cool night air and peered up at Donovan. Her wispy white hair, sticking out from under a beat-up Red Sox baseball cap, seemed to glow in the moonlight.

He came back down the ramp from the shuttlecraft's hatchway and tugged her visor playfully. "The next time I come, I'll try to bring you a *real* team's cap from L.A."

"You're just lucky I didn't know you were a Dodgers fan *before* you landed without the proper radio code!"

"Hey, ease up there, Donovan!" Peter Forsythe said, scowling. "When we get the leagues going again, the Yankees will whup your asses every time!"

"I'll bet you ten bucks on the next game." Mike shook his hand warmly. "Thanks for everything. And listen, Pete—can I have your autograph?"

Pete took out a pen. "I'll give you mine if you give me yours."

"Make it 'To Sean.' I know he'll be thrilled when I . . . get a chance to give it to him."

Mike made one last round of hugs and handshakes as the small group waited on the hillside next to the shuttlecraft. The air was clear and still, the salty-clean smells of the Atlantic below fresh in his nostrils, and he knew he would miss this place and these wonderful people.

"Take care of yourself." Denise's kiss lingered just a bit longer than sisterly on his mouth, and he was surprised at how good it felt. "Call me soon with the good news."

He waved from the cockpit, they stepped back, and the shuttlecraft raised and pointed itself toward the darkness in the west.

Later, after he got up to use the facilities (thank God the Visitors' forms also followed function, and their plumbing wasn't vastly different from humans'), Donovan noticed the several large brown-wrapped packages with his name on them in the back storage compartments, which now held several other items and courier packs for the L.A. resistance.

Puzzled, he fumbled open the wrappers and pulled out a sports jacket, two pairs of slacks, three pairs of Levi's, and a new brown suede jacket. They were all perfect in style, color, and fit, and Donovan grinned all the way back to L.A.

"Diana is such a bitch!" The beautiful blond in Visitors' uniform leaned her elbows on the bar and peered owlishly at Willie over her drink.

Nodding sympathetically, he topped off her glass with the contents of his blender.

"It's bad enough that I was reassigned to southern California when my bodysuit was thermally designed for the climate of Great Britain, now I have to work for *her*."

Willie could personally appreciate the strange and often baffling results of bureaucracy. "I have heard Diana can be difficult to work for," he ventured.

"Oh, you don't know the half of it! She thinks she's so damned clever and wastes no opportunity to tell us all how wonderful she is. She makes me ill."

Willie nodded again, watching the slight rise of her hair as her crest bristled in indignation beneath it. He tried to picture what she really looked like under her artificial skin. She must be finely patterned indeed if her human analogue was any indication of the true beauty of her appearance.

It had been a long time since Willie had been with a female. The results of his last mating had proved disappointing from a genetic standpoint, so he had been authorized only short-term, recreational types of couplings. The trouble was, he had never found anyone who had really interested him—until he came to Earth and met the human woman Harmony Moore. He and Harmony had shared something special. Even though she had learned what he really looked like, she had said she loved him.

But Harmony had died in his arms well over a year ago, and meanwhile, this exquisite creature sat in front of him, seeking a sympathetic listener.

"Well, I do not think Diana is so clever," he said. "She was captured and imprisoned by the humans for an entire year, and she has still not been able to stop the Earth resistance groups."

Taking a swallow of her drink, the blond Visitor tossed her head back, her throat rippling as she gulped. She nodded at him. "Yes, it would be quite a coup if I could locate and destroy the Los Angeles resistance right under Diana's nose!"

Willie didn't like the cold, deadly look that came into her blue eyes and immediately regretted that he had brought up the subject of the resistance. Laying a hand on top of hers, he stared earnestly at her. "You must be very beautiful."

"You're not the best-looking one of us I've ever met, but I rather like your smile." She looked at him through half-closed eyelids and smiled slightly. "What's your name?"

"Willie. What is yours?"

"Lydia."

"That is a lovely name, Lydia." Willie had been a bartender long enough to overhear some of the more common premating ritual words used on Earth; now they might be useful to him.

"Did you know that I am head of security for the entire Visitor fleet?" She drew herself up proudly, if a little unsteadily.

"I am not surprised." Willie poured himself a glass of his special drink and leaned forward. "That is a most important position and must be very interesting. Tell me more about it."

"Christ on a pony, Taylor, when are you going to listen to me?" Ham Tyler's normally impassive features were coldly angry as he paced in the secret downstairs room of the Club Creole.

"When you suggest something that makes sense." Folding his arms, Elias Taylor made an effort to keep his voice level. "Kicking out a bunch of my best-paying customers who also happen to be Visitors isn't in that category."

"Do you *know* who's up there right now, making time with your bartender?"

"A whole lot of eaters and drinkers are up there tonight," Elias said, glancing over some figures in a ledger. "Hard to believe it's a Monday night with a crowd like that. Word must be getting around—"

"Yeah. Word's out all right. We got Lydia, Second Queen of the scalies, slithering around maybe fifteen feet above your goddamn thick head. I'm telling you, Taylor, get rid of the lizards! Put 'em out until we can at least defend ourselves, for chrissakes."

Elias felt his mouth tighten. "Maybe it's time for another one of our talks on who owns and operates this place."

"And maybe it's time you looked past the dollar signs in your eyes and wised up to what's going on. We are low, L-O-W on power packs. We get down to our own ammo and guns, and they'll mow us down like wheat."

"I thought Mike's bringing back some from New York tomorrow."

"A *few*, Taylor. Very few. And when they're finished, this resistance is finished too, because Uzis and Teflon-coated bullets aren't going to stop any large assault force of lizards and their new improved body armor. The more of them crawling around this place, the more likely somebody's going to tumble onto something they shouldn't, and we're all dead."

Elias slammed his book shut. "Let me remind you of the way things are. You run things down here, and I run them upstairs. Accordingly, the Visitors stay."

"Stalemate." Ham pulled a toothpick out of his pocket and began chewing on it thoughtfully. "Suppose we get another opinion from a senior member of our little clubhouse down here. Let's ask Caleb Taylor what he thinks about his son's decision to put money before the safety—"

"Tyler, you wouldn't—"

"Elias." Miranda slipped in through the door, her large dark eyes troubled. "There's an argument starting upstairs over who will get your last shirt. You'd better come up and straighten things out."

"Right with you," Elias said, getting up without a backward glance.

They were both males, one a Visitor in uniform and the other a twenty-one-year-old with spiky blond hair who sported the latest in punk fashion. Their aggressive and somewhat unsteady stances as they faced one another said they were both pretty drunk. Other patrons at the bar stepped back, their expressions half fearful, half expectant.

". . . saw it first, Lizard-breath," the young man was saying as Elias came up. "So slither off."

"Perhaps we should step outside to settle this dispute." The Visitor spoke softly, but there was something unsettling under the resonance of his voice and in the look he gave the other.

"Gentlemen, may I help you?" Elias asked, smoothly interposing himself between the two of them. "I'm Elias Taylor, owner and manager of the Club Creole."

"Yeah," the kid said. "Tell Dinosaur-brain here that first-come, first-served is the way we do things around here on Earth."

"I had money down on the counter before you opened your mouth, you little—"

"Why don't we toss a coin?" Elias suggested, digging into his pocket.

"Why don't we toss this alien creep out on his leathery ass?" the youth asked, advancing. His hand moved toward his belt, and Elias recognized the gesture of someone carrying a blade. But before he could react, there was a noise from the other end of the bar.

"How about an auction?" The deep, rumbling voice came from behind the crowd, and then a huge black man, at least six-foot-five and weighing over 250 pounds, elbowed his way to the front. His gold chains, rings, and well-cut suit fairly shouted money, and Elias's mouth dropped open as he recognized an old crony from his street-hustling days, "Honeybee Al."

"An' who's the clown with the big mou . . ." The young man turned around as he spoke, and the words died in his throat as he looked up into Honeybee Al's face. "Uh, yeah. An, uh, auction."

"The dude what wants it worst pays the best." Smiling gently, Al held up the controversial green shirt, then laid it down on the bar like a gauntlet between them, and neither seemed inclined to argue with the man-mountain. Three minutes and sixty-eight dollars later, the Visitor walked away with a smirk on his face and the shirt under his arm, while the young man stomped out, muttering not so quietly about "the stinkin' lizards."

"I'll have more in a couple of days," Elias called after him, then grinned as he pocketed the cash and turned to the large man. "Well, what do you know? Could have figured you'd come sliding back into my life sooner or later."

"Can't keep eye-den-tee-cal twins apart too long, Elias." He wrapped his arms around Elias in a bear hug that left the much thinner man gasping for air.

"Al, my man, dinner and drinks are on the house tonight." Elias grinned as he freed himself from Al's grip and led the way to a front table. Miranda, looking sharp in a pink Club Creole sport shirt, came up to take orders.

"Miranda, I want you to meet Alfred Lewison, alias 'Honeybee Al.' He's an old pal of mine from . . . way back."

"A mover, shaker, and ladies' heartbreaker." Al grinned, revealing a gold-capped front tooth. "How are you, sweet thing?"

"Pleased to meet you," Miranda said, and her smile suddenly seemed quick-frozen to her face. "What would you like to drink?"

"Double margarita," he said, his eyes lingering on her breasts.

"Rum and Coke, Miranda," Elias said, frowning a little. "Thanks."

As she disappeared into the kitchen, Al grinned and rubbed his expansive stomach. "I like your little hot tamale there, Elias. You developed a taste for Mexican food these days?"

Elias's jaw muscles tightened. "Al, I don't want to hear that kind of talk about Miranda. She's a classy lady, and—"

"Hey, the ol' Honeybee never stings when he can be sweet, you know that. Be cool, brother." He looked around at the Club Creole's interior, the well-dressed people and Visitors enjoying themselves, and the expression across his broad, scarred face grew speculative. "This is one fine establishment you got here, Elias. Yessir, mighty fine. Must bring in big bucks."

Suddenly wary, Elias shrugged. "It's all right. Most of it goes to the bank to pay the mortgage and the loans."

"Hard to believe that little Elias Taylor is a serious businessman!" Al looked up at Miranda in exaggerated astonishment as she placed his drink in front of him. "Why, I knew him when he was a skinny teenage dude, ripping off little Sony TVs from the rich white folks and selling dime bags of reefer."

"Some people grow up," she said, dodging his hand as he reached for her behind.

Al laughed, a large, booming sound that had little mirth about it. "I like your little taco, Elias—and she's right. Some people do grow up. How 'bout you? You ready to play with the grown-ups?"

"What do you mean?"

"Two-for-one specials, happy hour, T-shirts—nickel and dime stuff, Elias, real small time. I watched you and I saw your potential way back, and you can do better than this, man. How 'bout doin' a little work for me?"

"What do you have in mind?"

"Not so much." Al took a large swallow of his drink. "You got a nice place in here. Good location, quiet, discreet—a good place to do business."

Elias thought about Al and his "business." Numbers running, stolen goods, prostitution, gambling, drug dealing . . . Honeybee Al had had a finger in just about every illegal pie there was in and around Los Angeles before the Visitors came. While regular society had done a topsy-turvy under the aliens' domination, the underworld had flourished, with new interests in extortion of scientists, spying, the black market—and Al had obviously done very well.

"I bring in some people, we eat and drink, do a little talkin', pass a few packages under the table, and you keep your mouth shut. Naturally, there'll be a little something in it for you—say, a percentage of my gross business?"

Elias stared into his drink. The club needed a new roof, and he wanted desperately to buy the parking lot next door for eventual expansion. Maybe if he just let Al use the place for a month or two . . .

Or would he be getting himself—and the resistance—in so deep that there wouldn't be any escape, ever?

"Excuse me, Elias." Willie approached the table with two menus. "Miranda said she had received a headache and asked that I take your orders."

"Willie, I'd like you to meet my old—"

"A goddamn lizard!" Al recoiled so fast that he almost fell

over in his chair, and his face twisted into the ugliest expression Elias had ever seen. "You gone soft in the head, letting a lizard work for you?"

Willie looked chagrined. "I . . . am sorry. I will request one of the others to—"

"Stay right here." Elias's voice was very soft, but each word carried distinctly so that both Willie and Al froze in their places. "Willie is my friend, and you'll remember that while you're here, or anywhere near me."

"Hey, it's all very fine and good takin' their money, but I ain't doing business with any lizard lover." Al stood, deliberately tipping over his glass. A dark stain spread into the tablecloth, then began dripping onto the floor. "I figured you for a smart dude, Taylor, but it seems I was wrong. Too bad."

Elias looked at him and saw an older, fatter version of himself as he once was and might have been today—willing to sell out anyone or anything for money. "I'm smart enough to tell you to get the hell out of my club," he said, and walked away from the table.

Elizabeth stared blearily at the clock on her bedside table and wished for the sunrise. But the red digits proclaimed the time in bold, relentless numbers: 11:17.

She was becoming afraid to sleep. Sleep brought the dreams of red dust and destruction more and more frequently.

She tried reading for a while, something light and gentle that Kyle had recommended to her. "*Alice in Wonderland*," he had said earlier that day, handing the book to her. "It was one of my favorites as a kid. And you remind me of Alice in some ways, with your blond hair and blue eyes, and the way you're always looking at the world with a kind of wide-eyed astonishment, as though you'll see six impossible things before breakfast."

For a while it helped, and Elizabeth lost herself in Alice's extraordinary adventures down the rabbit hole. Then fatigue tugged at her eyelids and obliged her to close them just for a moment . . .

. . . and she was falling down a dark and red-tinged hole herself, and the blood-colored dust was swirling around her. She screamed soundlessly into the void as she tumbled helplessly, down and down into the place facing the glass-walled chamber of death.

This time it was larger, and she saw the shadow-shapes of a number of people. The dust cleared, and she recognized other faces besides the Visitor's. Mike Donovan, Julie Parrish, her mother, Elias, her grandfather, Robert Maxwell, and Willie— all the people she had known and loved were wandering uncertainly around in the chamber, their expressions apprehensive.

She pounded on the glass until her hands were bruised and aching, shouting a warning for them all to leave, get out, but no one could hear her. And then the dust rose again, blurring everything except the people within. Before her horrified eyes, she clearly saw them grabbing their throats, their faces twisting in agony. They tore at their faces, ripping them off, and blood gushed from long, hideous rents, revealing bone-white death's-heads as they died, one by one . . .

Elizabeth clutched at her own face, her heart racing in her chest as she jerked upright. Stifling her dry sobs in a pillow— she would not wake up her mother and Kyle again, tonight— she turned out the light and lay in the dark for a long time, shuddering quietly, alone. . . .

Smoothing the folds of her new red caftan, Juliet Parrish smiled at Mike Donovan's back as he headed toward the kitchen in search of a corkscrew. He was wearing one of the terrific new outfits the Brook Cove group had given him, and Julie thought she hadn't seen him look so good since his days as a news anchorman.

She shifted a little on the couch, her thoughts warm and languorous as she imagined the well-tailored jacket and slacks coming off later that night and being draped across a chair next to her caftan.

"Give me a hint," he called from the kitchen.

"Try the second drawer down, Mike." A moment later, she heard the triumphant pop of the champagne cork, and he reappeared carrying a tray with the bottle and two glasses.

"Here's to us," he said, linking arms as he raised his glass. "I missed you."

They sipped. "Ohhhh, that's fine," she murmured, feeling her nose tickle deliciously. "I haven't tasted imported champagne since V-Day." He nodded, leaning over to kiss her ear.

"Did you miss me?" he whispered.

"You know I did," she said, looking at him seriously, then,

realizing if they kept on in this vein she would end up putting the steaks back in the fridge, she sat back. "Tell me all about New York."

"Okay. But first, I brought something back for you."

Touched and a little surprised, she looked at him. He had brought back an armload of presents for all of them when he had arrived earlier that afternoon, but here he was producing another tissue-wrapped box with frothy ribbons spilling off it. Her fingers fumbled with the lid for a second, then Juliet pulled out an exquisite sapphire-colored negligee. Two Hershey's chocolate-with-almonds bars nestled beside it.

"Oh, Mike," she said, holding it up to the light to admire the shimmer of the expensive silk. "It's gorgeous."

"You can model it for me later on," he said, kissing her. "And I'll thank Pete Forsythe next time I see him. He's the one who helped me pick it out."

"How is Pete and everyone? Tell me especially about Hannah Donnenfeld. How is she?"

"Everyone's fine and she's especially fine—one great lady, even if she is a Boston Red Sox fan."

He went on to fill her in on all the East Coast people and events, the important things that hadn't been dryly explained in the reports that he'd brought back.

"Hannah, Sari, and Mitchell said they're issuing a challenge to you and Science Frontiers," he said, pouring them both more champagne. "First team with the successful warm-climate red dust is the winner and gets a case of imported champagne from the loser. The last challenge worked really well, according to Hannah, even if you did win."

"We were all lucky," Julie murmured, settling into the crook of his arm. "She's about the best there is, and she has a great team. Sometimes with Nathan Bates, I feel I'm working more for the cause of politics than science."

"She really thinks the world of you too, Julie. She'd like you to come work for her."

"Oh, God, I wish . . ." she said, feeling a brief, sharp stab of regret.

Donovan looked down at the bubbles rising in his glass. "I got a job offer, too. A possible anchor spot on the CBS morning news."

"Oh, wow," she said. Her stomach, feeling fine until now, twinged suddenly. "Are you interested?"

"You know it," he said. "Maybe we could both go to New York. We could help the resistance there too, you know."

And in New York, it's so much safer—safe enough to have a baby. Julie looked at Mike, feeling a rush of closeness with him, and she thought about confiding her fears that she might be pregnant. At that moment, she felt that he would understand, and it would be all right.

Or was she trying to hold on to him?

"I'd . . . love to be somewhere where I don't have to look at red uniforms all the time. But for now, I'd also love to see those steaks get started."

"You got it."

She was putting the napkins on the table when the phone rang, sharp and staccato over the mellow Neil Diamond record Mike had put on earlier.

"Hello?" she said, trying to keep the annoyance out of her voice.

"Dr. Parrish? I'm trying to get in touch with Michael Donovan, and I hoped you might be able to help me. It's very important that I speak to him. I'm from the Denver group, code ID 'Rocky Mountain Oysters.'" The woman's voice was soft and tentative.

"Well, I—" Frowning, Julie looked at Mike as he came back into the living room. "May I have your name, please?"

"This is Marjorie Donovan. It's very important. Please tell me how to get in touch with him."

"It's for you, Mike," Julie said leadenly, holding out the receiver to him. "A woman."

He stared at her, his expression puzzled, then took the phone. "Hello? . . . *Margie?*"

Watching his expression transform into a pleased sort of amazement, Julie's stomach twisted with a sinking feeling that their romantic evening together was over before it had even begun.

Chapter 7

New Friends, Old Friends

"My God, I thought you must have been killed during the attack on San Pedro! Where are you? . . . Wait a second." Without looking at Julie, Mike Donovan fumbled for a pencil and paper from the desk and scribbled for a few seconds. "Right away, sure. Be there in ten minutes. It's wonderful to know you're all right. 'Bye." He hung up, still smiling.

"I . . . guess you have to go," Julie said, staring down at the negligee in the box beside her.

"I'm sorry, honey. I know you understand. It's Margie. She's here in town, wants to meet me tonight at one of our . . . at a restaurant not too far from here."

"Sure. Be careful."

He kissed her hastily, grabbed his jacket, and ran out. The echo as the door slammed shut reverberated for a moment, then the apartment settled into an awful, final silence.

Julie looked at the bottle of champagne—still half full, at least—and thought it would be a pity to waste it.

She was still staring at the condensation collecting around the glass bottle when an electronic screech blared from the hallway. Startled, she looked up and noticed the faint bluish haze of smoke drifting down the hall, then the charcoal smell of burning made her nose wrinkle.

Julie raced into the kitchen to yank the steaks out of the broiler, singeing a finger in the process as she poked a hole through the worn pot holder and connected with the broiler pan.

The steaks were ruined, and Juliet didn't know whether to swear or sob as she held her smarting hand under the cold water faucet. Eventually, she did a little of both while she drank the last of the champagne.

Willie tilted the last few drops from his blender into his glass and sighed. It was well past the Club Creole's closing time of two A.M., he still had a lot of cleanup chores to do—and he would be going home alone again tonight.

He had gotten Lydia fairly drunk and through carefully casual questions, had learned a few aspects of Visitor security procedures that might be useful to the resistance. His triumph felt a little hollow, however. Lydia had gotten bored with his conversation and had wandered over to another part of the club, and he had seen her leave half an hour ago in the company of a handsome male officer.

Emptying out the bills and coins from the tip glass to count them, Miranda Juarez smiled teasingly at him. "Wil-lie's in lo-ove," she sang.

"Please, Miranda, I do not wish to make a joke at this time." He swallowed the rest of his drink without tasting it.

"Willie, you've been putting away a lot of that stuff lately," Elias said, his expression concerned as he came in from the kitchen.

"It . . . is part of my job to put the bottles and clean glasses back in their places."

"I mean you've been drinking more lately."

Willie looked at him blearily. "You said that we could have as much as we wished of the food and drink here. If you feel I am taking too much, then you may take it from my pay."

"Dammit, that's not what I meant! It's not the booze I care about but *you*. What you're doing to your liver or whatever you have inside yourself that you're pickling."

"I am all right." Picking up a dishcloth, Willie began polishing the silverware on the counter.

"Willie, you did those already twenty minutes ago," Miranda pointed out gently.

"I am tired, that is all," he said, and reached for the blender to wash it.

Miranda laid a hand on his arm. "Here, let me. You just sit down for a minute and take it easy."

He sat reluctantly, watching her as she filled the blender with warm water, added two drops of dishwashing liquid, then turned it on. "That is a good idea," he admitted. "It is getting cleaned without needing to be scrubbed."

"As my old parish priest, Father Ramirez, used to say, 'Blessed are the lazy in nature, for they shall invent shortcuts.'"

"Shortcuts?" Willie looked puzzled. "Aren't they sections of meat taken from cows?"

Elias shook his head, holding back a grin. "You explain it, Miranda," he said, heading for the kitchen. "I've gotta make sure Henri's got enough scallops for tomorrow's special."

After Miranda had explained the colloquialism, Willie subsided once more into gloomy silence as his thoughts turned, as they often did late at night, to memories of Harmony. There had never been anything approaching actual lovemaking between them, but somehow Willie hadn't missed the physical release. Finding out that someone really *cared* about what happened to him had been the most important discovery of his life. Now, although he knew that Elias, Miranda, Elizabeth, Mike, and Julie were all his friends, he still ached with loneliness. The thought of walking alone to his silent room was unbearable; the thought of lying awake in it was enough to make him want another drink. Anything to blunt the emptiness.

Miranda looked over at him. "You know, Willie, when I was an Army lieutenant serving in Vietnam, I met a wonderful person. His name was Captain Eduardo Perez, and he was tall and handsome, and he wrote songs. He would sing them to me late at night. He had a beautiful voice. They were about love and our beautiful Mexican heritage, and when he sang, it would make the heat and the jungle rot and the blood all go away for a while. Then one day he was killed doing a very brave thing which saved a lot of his men."

She paused, swallowing as a sudden brightness came into her eyes. "I missed him very, very much. We were going to be married when we both got back to California. For a long time I was . . . empty inside, and I tried to fill it with work. In Nam there was plenty of that for an Army nurse with surgical training. But even the captain's bars I received couldn't take the memories away late at night—or the tears. I tried alcohol for a while, marijuana, other things. Then I met Paul. Our relationship was short and sweet, as the expression goes, but it taught me that I was beginning to feel again, and I was ready to go on with my life."

Smiling, Miranda reached over to squeeze Willie's hand. "I know you still miss Harmony a lot. But Lydia will be back, or there will be someone else for you, even better."

Visitors couldn't cry—they lacked tear ducts. But Willie felt the tightness around his eyes, under the concealing artificial skin, which was his response to strong emotions, and he squeezed her hand in turn. "Thank you, Miranda."

"Now go home and get some rest," she said, making shooing motions. "I can take care of what's left."

Willie left the club, tasting the warm night air, seeing far above him the stars faded from the glow of the street lamps. He didn't bother looking for Sirius; it wasn't visible during the summer at this latitude. Besides, he realized with some surprise, "home" in his mind now meant his small apartment here on Earth.

Mike Donovan's hands shook slightly as he tipped the last of the second carafe of rosé into Margie's glass. He didn't know whether it was because he'd had too much to drink or whether he was still getting over the shock of finding out that she was still alive.

She looked wonderful—even more beautiful than he remembered. The hard, pinched look around her eyes and mouth that had reflected her bitterness during their separation and divorce was gone. Her blue-gray eyes were now frank and clear, and her rich laugh came often and easily as their voices tumbled over one another, each trying to bring the other up to date on the past two years of their lives.

Only one other couple lingered over coffee and drinks in the tiny, out-of-the-way Italian restaurant near Glendale that had been one of their favorite eating places in Los Angeles. (*Although the food's not quite as good as Guido's in New York,* Mike thought.) By now, their table candle was sputtering its last flickers deep within its red-plastic-coated glass, and the waitress was vacuuming in the other room.

Donovan was surprised how easily he and his ex-wife had gotten past the awkward chitchat stage. The wine had helped, on top of the champagne he'd already had with Julie, but it was Margie who was making the difference, making him forget the angry words, the bitterly charged silences. The two years since the Visitors had arrived seemed to have changed her a lot. She was vibrant, committed, and assured. Gone, apparently, was the resentment and frustration which had characterized their former relationship, especially toward the end of their marriage.

Apparently she had found confidence and self-respect in joining the Denver resistance. She showed him a communiqué detailing the group's operations, present and planned, to prove it. ("You're a newsman, Mike. I know you don't accept assertions without something to back them up," she'd said with a smile.)

Following her post V-Day release from hibernation in the captured Los Angeles Mother Ship, she had gone to Colorado to live with one of her sisters, she said. She'd deliberately avoided any contact with her ex-husband, deciding, as she put it, "that this was my chance to make a clean break and get my head on straight about who *I* really was."

Margie told Mike that she'd landed a job in Denver, working for a local newspaper as an editorial assistant, using an assumed name so people wouldn't associate her with Michael Donovan, one of the national heroes of V-Day.

"One of the main reasons we broke up was your jealousy of my work and the attention I got," he said. "Didn't you know how little all that meant to me—and how much *you* did? Did you realize that when I couldn't find you after V-Day, that I'd naturally assume you were dead?" He looked at her steadily across the red-checked tablecloth. "Did you realize that I'd grieve?"

"Yes," she said, poking her spoon into the remnants of her tortellini. "I . . . loved you too. But I couldn't face you right then. Especially then, after you became the most sought-after hero in the entire country—hell, the entire damn world!" She pushed the dish away from her with something verging on violence. "I felt empty inside, hollow, like I could never, never live up to your example. Never do anything heroic, never save all those lives. I wanted you to respect me as well as love me . . . but eventually I figured out that was something I couldn't have until I respected myself."

"Oh, Marge . . ." He looked at her, and regret was sudden

and sharp within him. *Why couldn't we have talked like this years ago?*

She shrugged. "But I did the right thing, I think, getting away awhile, thinking hard about things. I saw your face every night on television, though, when you were doing the anchor spot on that national news broadcast. Every time I saw you I missed you more—and Sean, too. So when the Visitors came back, and I had a chance to help the Denver resistance by serving as a courier, I took it."

"So what brings you to L.A.?"

"A couple of things." Smiling, she pushed an envelope across the table to him.

Donovan opened it, and his eyes widened in amazement. An official employee identification card for the L.A. Visitors' legation fell out.

"I've just gotten a secretarial job there," she said. "I suspect it will prove very helpful to your cause—*our* cause, I mean."

They talked for a while longer. Mike updated her on what little he knew about Sean and his whereabouts.

She hadn't any information to add, but the determination he read in her eyes matched his own. "Mike, wherever he is, we have to get him back."

He looked at her, again struck by how much more she was like the woman he'd fallen in love with thirteen years ago than the one he'd later divorced. Impulsively, he reached across the table to squeeze her hand. "You bet," he said.

"I know that's going to take time. Meanwhile, I'd . . . like to stay on here for a while and help the Los Angeles resistance in any way that I can."

"I . . . uh, we really appreciate that." Mike eyed the waitress as she walked by pointedly for the third time in fifteen minutes, carrying a broom.

"I guess it's time to go." Pushing back her chair, she stood. "I can't believe how fast the evening went by."

"Where are you staying?" he asked, glancing at the bill as he reached for his jacket.

"My sister Patty's." Her smile turned soft and a little wistful. "Mike, it's been really great to see you again. Better than I might have expected. I'll look forward to the next time—soon."

"Yeah, same here. Stay in touch, Marge, okay?" She

nodded, and he scribbled his home phone number on a scrap of paper. Their glances and fingertips met for a moment as he handed it to her. Hastily, he fumbled bills out of his wallet and turned away with the check. After a few steps he turned back apologetically. "Uh . . . would you mind leaving the tip?"

Michael and Marjorie Donovan met several times during the next week. At Ham's insistence, Mike had not introduced her to the other members of the resistance nor taken her to the Club Creole—Ham wanted a chance to verify the Denver documents she'd brought first. After making a few wisecracks about old lovers reunited, he had advised Donovan to meet Margie in public but not too crowded places like Redondo Pier or Santa Monica Park. Mike grumbled but, knowing Tyler was right, obeyed.

Some of their rendezvous points were old hangouts from their first dates, which couldn't fail to wake sleeping memories, but Mike salved his conscience with the recognition that their meetings felt more like the discussions between old business partners than anything more romantic.

Most of the time, that is . . .

He spent a lot of time with Margie, partly because everyone else in the resistance had his or her own projects under way. Ham was busy checking out Margie's initial information from Denver, while Elias, Miranda, and Willie were promoting shirts and making plans for expanding the Club Creole wearing-apparel line. Maggie hadn't put in an appearance at resistance HQ for days, although her daily telephone calls reassured them that Chris's vision continued to improve. Julie was cooped up in her lab, running tests on the red dust variations developed by the Brook Cove group. Nathan Bates was pushing her for greater progress, no doubt motivated by the potential for profit far more than by any overwhelming concern for humanity.

As far as Mike was concerned, Julie seemed increasingly withdrawn. The few times he'd been able to talk with her on the phone, she had sounded increasingly tense and uncommunicative. He knew she hated it when Bates put the pressure on, worrying that the quality of her scientific research might be compromised. He told himself her aloofness was due to overwork and that she needed some extra breathing room. But the coolness in her voice made him uneasy.

As much as Donovan missed talking with Julie, for the first time in his life, he found he was able to open up with Margie and talk frankly about his own frustrations with his current life-style.

"It's so damn crazy," he said, sitting on a towel on the beach at Santa Monica, resting his elbows on his knees to stare out across the searing whiteness of the sand at the relentless blue of the Pacific. Above them the sky arched, pale blue, as though the afternoon sun had leached away some of its color. "I can't imagine life anywhere but here, but I can't forget that in some parts of the world people can still live somewhat normal lives, have jobs, earn money, raise kids."

He shook his head ruefully. "No target practice, no M-16s, no crawling around in the underbrush spying on Visitor contingents, no nearly pissing yourself with fear when you feel the heat from one of those laser bolts go by your head. No having to live off handouts 'cause your face is too well-known to hold down a job. I've thought about just running away from it all, but how could I leave my friends to keep on facing it? I'd feel like a coward."

Margie rested her head on her knees, gazing at him sideways. The wind whipped her blond hair, now doubly light because of her tan. "After all you've done, nobody could ever call you a coward, Mike. Your friends would understand that people can endure only so much before they need a break."

He smiled gratefully at her but shook his head. "That may have been so three years ago, but not anymore. That's part of the thing we've all got to face: that life will never be worthwhile again on this planet unless we all give one hundred percent even when we feel like there isn't anything left."

"But sacrificing yourself—"

"Hey, Marge," he chuckled. "Don't go nailing me to any crosses. You know what it's like by now. You do whatever's necessary, moment to moment, for the greater good, but it doesn't feel noble or anything when you do it. It just feels like your job—sort of inevitable, I guess."

She looked away from him, and her words came so softly he could barely hear them. "I guess. . . ."

"Hey, here you were cheering me up, and I've infected you! Don't make me feel guilty about *that*, too!" He laughed and pulled her up beside him. For a second their bare thighs brushed, then they moved apart as though stung. "Let's get wet. Last one in is a rotten lizard egg!"

The next day, six days after her initial phone call to him at Julie's, they met along the bike path at Redondo Beach. Margie's eyes sparked with excitement as she grabbed his arm. "Guess what, Mike? I found out there's going to be a shipment of power packs from the Visitor legation in the next day or so, and I'd like to help you get them." She paused alongside a park bench, grinning. "You've mentioned how low you're running, and whatever Diana's plans, *I* can't think of a better or more deserving group of recipients than the L.A. resistance."

Grinning, Donovan shaded his eyes from the red-orange glare of the setting sun to look at her. "That's great! We sure the hell need 'em. Where are they being sent to?"

"I don't know yet. I also need to find out the delivery date and time."

"Well, even that much information is worth a dinner at Taco Bell. Come on."

That night she wound up following him in her rented car to his apartment, and they talked for several hours more. At one point, Donovan got up from his living room couch to refill their coffee cups for the third time. As he passed the cream and sugar, their fingers touched. Her skin felt incredibly smooth and cool.

She glanced up at him, then down again with a small smile.

Their conversation lulled and then slid into a companionable silence. Mike looked at his watch and was amazed to see that it was past three. "My God, I don't know how it got so late."

Margie looked rueful. "With the strange hours I've been keeping, it seems like Patty's been putting up with me, rather than putting me up, since I got into town."

Her sister still lived in Ventura, as far as he knew, and he frowned. "She lives over an hour's drive from here, and it's so late."

"All the more reason for me to hit the road." She stood up, looking around for her purse.

"Uh, look. Why don't you stay here tonight? I'll, uh, take the couch."

"I . . . don't want to impose on you," she said, hesitating.

"No trouble, really. I'd rather sleep out here than toss and turn worrying about whether you got home all right."

She looked at him, then a soft, genuine sensuality stole along the curve of her mouth. "You don't have to do that, Mike. Sleep out here, I mean."

A confusion of feelings welled up in him, and temptation was one of them as he stood looking at her, admiring the gentle push of her breasts under her blouse, her lean, tanned legs beneath the short skirt. He remembered vividly how good it had been, the times those legs had been tangled with his, the feel of those breasts against his bare chest when they'd made love. Their problems had never been in the bedroom until the very end. . . .

"Hey," he said, coming over to slip an arm around her shoulders. "I can't tell you how good it is to see you, to get to know you all over again. But let's not rush anything, okay?"

"Okay," she said, and he escorted her to the door of his bedroom.

"There's a spare toothbrush in the medicine cabinet, on the—"

"I know, the bottom shelf on the far right." She grinned. "Some things never change. Do you still keep your T-shirts in the second drawer down on the right?"

"Uh, yeah."

"Good. I'll borrow one for tonight." She paused and the smile played briefly around her mouth again. "And I won't lock the door."

Standing on tiptoe, she gave him a brief, tender kiss on the line of his jaw. Her lips rasped against the stubble, feeling infinitely smooth and warm.

He watched her close the door, leaving it ajar, then he moved like an automaton to rummage sheets, pillowcases, and a blanket out of the hall linen closet. Making up a bed for himself on the couch, he stripped to his shorts, then padded to the bathroom to brush his teeth.

He passed the bedroom door on his way back to the couch, and hesitated. He knew she was lying awake, and late, late at night had always been some of their very best times—

An image of Julie suddenly flashed into his mind—her smile, the way she had looked when he'd left her that evening almost a week ago—the last time they had seen one another. With a little shake of his head, he went back to the living room and lay down on the couch. He lay awake for a long time, listening to the night sounds outside.

"He sure makes a lot of noise." Maggie Blodgett stared down at the barking, wriggling Shih Tzu and made a mock-fierce face. "Shhh, Druid!"

"Yeah, but you know he calms down once he's outside," Chris Faber said, handing her the leash.

She smiled up at him. Only small, fading pink blotches remained on his face now, and his eyes were clear and direct as he grinned back. Dr. Akers had been very pleased with his progress, and said after the exam yesterday that he felt Chris would be spotting fleas on sparrows flying overhead again within a week. "Just keep staying out of bright light," he'd advised.

"It's just my luck to always be around when it's doggy-walking time." Laughing, she scooped Druid up in her arms and pushed open the door. "Come on, you fur ball."

The afternoon air was warm and still in Chris's sprawling suburban neighborhood, and the streets were quiet except for the occasional rumble of a passing car. Maggie pushed her sunglasses up on the bridge of her nose, admiring the hazy outlines of the hills in the distance, while Druid made a more prosaic inspection of the palm tree on the corner of Chris's lot.

In the days since Chris's injury, Maggie had found herself looking forward with more and more anticipation to her daily visits to the large man with the tiny dog. Lean, compact men were traditionally more her style, but even so, she was finding Chris increasingly attractive.

An interesting, complex mind lurked under the shaggy, dirty-blond hair, and she had been repeatedly surprised at his depth of knowledge on a wide variety of subjects. His eclectic library had only given a hint of his insatiable curiosity. If he was a consummate professional when it came to understanding weapons of all sort, he was also interested in Maggie's explanations of why certain wing shapes were more aerodynamically efficient than others.

When she had mentioned that she had a certified flight instructor's license for small-engine planes and could teach him to fly when he was better, his blue eyes had lighted up like a kid's at Christmas. Maggie was beginning to think that seeing him on a regular basis would be just fine.

Druid barked suddenly, and the sound was more a high-pitched shriek of fear than his usual playful yippings. Startled out of her reverie by the jerk of the leash in her hand, Maggie looked down to see what was wrong with the little animal. Facing the street, his whole body rigid, the little dog crouched, growling deep in his throat as though facing a mortal enemy.

A moment later, Maggie herself heard the low-pitched, alien whine of a Visitor land-patrol vehicle just before it rounded the corner barely fifty feet up the street. Grabbing Druid, she made a diving leap behind one of the low palm bushes before a cream-colored Spanish-style house, and froze, her heart racing in her chest.

From this vantage point, she could see most of the street but was reasonably well concealed (*Why did I have to wear this damned bright red T-shirt?* she wondered savagely). The patrol vehicle sighed to a halt almost directly in front of her, and four shock troopers wearing body armor sauntered out. Their casual formation and alert, purposeful glances up and down the street told Maggie that they were looking for something—and they weren't in any hurry.

Druid whimpered, and Maggie grabbed his muzzle. "Shhh, Druid!" A Visitor glanced in their direction, then away again.

Maggie knew that both she and Chris Faber were easily recognizable and wanted members of the Los Angeles resistance. While an uneasy truce existed between the Visitors and most of the human residents of Los Angeles, Nathan Bates had made it clear that he didn't sanction the resistance. Its members were fair game for human and Visitor authorities alike, and that end justified a whole lot of means, while Bates conveniently looked the other way.

She had to get back to warn Chris. Pulling off the betraying scarlet T-shirt, thanking God that her bra and running shorts were tan-colored, Maggie grasped the trembling Shih Tzu under one arm, then a foot or so at a time began slithering backward in the sandy grass. She stayed as close to the nearby high wooden fence as she could get, trying to keep the screen of brush between her and the vehicle. Druid started to protest, and she clamped her fingers around his muzzle with a hissed, "Shut up!" His puppy face blinked at her accusingly, but he obeyed.

By the time she got to Chris's back door, she was bruised, scratched, and filthy from clambering over neighbors' fences

and rose bushes. She'd also managed to lose her T-shirt. Chris
didn't answer her knock—maybe he'd seen the Visitors, too.
Druid began to whimper, and Maggie had to fight back tears of
frustration as she glanced nervously around to see if she'd been
followed. She was wondering how she could get inside without
being taken for an invading alien when inspiration hit her.
Cautiously, she began tapping out her name in Morse Code.

He was there by the second G, looking apologetic. "I saw
'em twenty minutes after you'd left. I thought they must've
gotten you for sure."

She leaned over to release Druid, who promptly ran around
in circles, barking hysterically, then paused to relieve himself
on the hall carpeting. "You were supposed to do that outside,
you creep," she said, not knowing whether to laugh or cry.
Chris glanced at her, suddenly took in her dishabille, then
wordlessly pulled off his ancient western snap-button shirt and
handed it to her. Maggie fastened the front and rolled up the
sleeves on her way over to the sink and the Formula 409, shivering as her adrenaline rush faded, then grinning a little as she
pictured what a sight she'd made shinnying over the fence.
And there went her "UFOs Are Real—They Wiped Out the Air
Force" T-shirt.

When she was done with the cleanup and had set down fresh
food and water for Druid, she went back into the living room to
find Chris standing sideways beside the bay window, peering
out from behind the drawn curtains. The Visitor squad vehicle
remained motionless two houses up.

"Here," he said, handing her a .357 Magnum in a shoulder
holster. He had already put his own on, then donned his
perpetual camouflage jacket.

Maggie had originally planned to stop for a brief visit with
Chris this afternoon and then meet up with Julie for dinner.
Now, she thought, adjusting the fit on the shoulder holster, it
looked like she would definitely be here for a while.

"I'd better call Julie," she said, but Chris placed a hand on
her arm.

"I wouldn't," he said. "They might have tapped the phone
lines, and if worse came to worst, they'd get her, too."

Maggie nodded mechanically and tried to remember a time
in her life when she hadn't been constantly on the run, hadn't
had to be so paranoid all the time—when the biggest problem
in her life had been the young flight instructor she and her

husband had hired who thought he was a real hot dog, both on and off the ground.

Chris nudged her and smiled. "Hey. Tell me another Visitor joke."

She didn't see anything at all that was humorous about the aliens at the moment, but she appreciated his attempt to lighten the tension. "Uh, let's see . . . what do Visitors call two boys and a girl?"

"A sandwich." Chris rolled his eyes. "Hon, where do you get these truly ancient jokes?"

"Mike Donovan just brought that one back from New York," she protested defensively.

"Well, God knows, things in California are bound to be old and tired by the time the East discovers 'em." He grinned.

"So since you're so smart, you tell me one *I* haven't—"

She froze just as he gestured for silence. A group of Visitors—six or seven, at least—had suddenly jumped out of the back of the vehicle and were fanning out purposefully.

"Oh, shit," she murmured as she joined him at the window. "Do you suppose it's a house-to-house search?"

"Hard tellin'."

Tensing, they waited. Their conversation was sporadic and terse while the minutes dragged by, becoming an hour, then ninety minutes. Maggie, who had quit smoking almost five years ago, found herself desperately wanting a cigarette.

Glancing up at Chris beside her, she noticed him squinting behind his sunglasses and realized he'd been rubbing his eyes more and more frequently as he scanned the sun-bright street for signs of Visitor activity. "Hey," she said. "Didn't Doc Akers tell you not to look at bright light?"

"A Visitor invasion in the neighborhood wasn't part of his prescription either," he muttered.

"Go sit down and rest your eyes," she said. When he began to protest, she snapped, "*Now*, Chris." Shrugging, he retreated.

More impossibly long minutes passed, and Chris tried to entertain her as she watched with his impersonations from old movies. Amused despite her fear, she applauded his impressions of James Cagney, Jimmy Stewart, and Cary Grant. He was beginning Henry Fonda as Mr. Roberts when the doorbell rang.

The sound seemed incredibly loud, echoing off the walls and shattering the quiet.

"Stay in here," he said, drawing his weapon and thumbing its safety.

"Bullshit!" she said. "I'll cover you."

Bracing himself before the front door, he drew a deep breath and said, "Who is it?"

"Peggy," a child's thin, piping voice cheerfully responded. "Your papergirl. I'm collecting."

"Could be a trick," Maggie muttered as Chris lowered his weapon.

He looked at her and shrugged. "Then it's been real nice knowing you, honey."

He eased open the door, and a girl around ten years old, with blond hair, freckles, and braces grinned expectantly. "Hi, Mr. Faber. It's four-fifty."

Maggie let breath out in a small sigh as Chris pulled out five dollars from his wallet and handed it to her.

"Thanks!" She headed back to her bicycle, which was lying on the sidewalk in front of his house, just as the Visitor vehicle began to whine again. As Maggie and Chris watched, the vehicle glided down the street. Peggy stuck her tongue out at the retreating Visitors, then offered a more adult form of disapproval with a grubby finger.

"Oh, God . . ." Maggie's legs turned suddenly wobbly, and she sagged against the hall closet door.

"I'll hold you up if you hold me up," said Chris, and then his big-bear arms slid around her, steadying her. "Hey, kid, it's okay."

"*Kid*." She sniffed, then grinned in spite of herself. "You have your nerve. I'm almost four years older than you are."

"And ten times better lookin'."

She put her arms around him, leaning against him, feeling his embrace tighten, change into something more purposeful—

—and then they both yelped in pain and jerked back as the butts of their holstered guns ground into shoulder or stomach.

"A fine pair of dangerous characters, aren't we?" Maggie grinned up at him.

"We better get rid of these damn things," Chris muttered, "before somebody's toes get blown off." They both fumbled at straps and buckles as they pulled off the weapons, snickering a little. Then Chris, with exaggerated care, ceremoniously hung up the gunbelts, and they both collapsed with hysteria-edged laughter.

Sides heaving, they clutched one another while the tears rolled down their cheeks. Wiping her eyes, Maggie hiccupped, chuckled, and looked up at him again. "So, you were saying?"

A gentle expression came into his eyes, and he bent to kiss her, softly, hesitantly. Maggie wound her arms around his neck and returned the kiss, feeling the scraggly brush of his beard and mustache. His mouth was soft, questing, but as her lips parted beneath his and her fingers traced the line of his ear, he responded to her demand. She felt the sudden jump of his pulse beneath her fingertips, and his hand moved to cup her breast beneath the raggedy oversized shirt.

They were both breathing hard by the time they parted. Maggie could feel the heat in her face, and she saw Chris's fair skin was flushed and his eyes were bright.

"Hey," he murmured. There was a touching sort of wonder in his expression as he looked at her. "The lizards could be back, you know. Probably not safe for you to leave yet."

"I know," Maggie said. She also knew that she wouldn't be going home that night, Visitors or not.

"I bet the scalies would like to get hold of this, eh, Tyler?" Early the following morning, Mike Donovan gestured happily at the papers spread out on one of the desks in the resistance's secret headquarters.

"How do you know they haven't, Gooder?"

"Well—hell, Margie couriered them straight from the Denver group a week ago, she said."

Ham nodded and leaned back in the creaking metal chair, hands clasped behind his head. "The info's legit. I verified it through a . . . couple of independent sources, shall we say? Now, they hadn't heard of Marjorie Donovan, but then again, you said she was using an assumed name, and they run their operations more spread out up there, especially in the courier operations."

"I guess they can afford to." Draining the last of his chicory-laced coffee, Donovan grimaced and threw the cup into the wastebasket. "Their snowfall's great, and the red dust bacteria is flourishing. Which means they don't have to put up with as many shortages, or coffee that tastes like it's been cut with mud."

"Yup, Denver is a good place to be these days, since it's run by humans." Ham's perpetually stony expression remained, but something shifted in his eyes that might have betokened humor. "Shit, Gooder, don't tell me we actually agree on something."

"An historical first," Mike said, then tapped the papers with a pencil. "Let's go for two. You agree we should try for the power pack shipment that's coming from the Visitor legation sometime soon?"

"Oh, absolutely. There's just a small concern or two I have—that we don't know the route the shipment's gonna take, where it's going, or when—but don't let me rain on your parade."

"Margie thinks she can find out the details before—"

"Hey, Mike." Elias stuck his head around the door to the secret headquarters. "Pick up on one-eight. There's a call for you."

"Hello, Mike?" It was Margie's voice, and he found himself grinning into the receiver.

"Hi, Margie. How are you?"

"Listen, I can't talk long. I'm at a pay phone. I just found out that the power packs are scheduled to be delivered to Science Frontiers at two tomorrow afternoon."

"What's the route they're going to take?" he asked, reaching for a pencil and paper.

"I don't know, but I think I can find out before tomorrow. Get a car and somebody you trust, and meet me at one o'clock in that alley about eight blocks from the legation, near Vallejo Street, all right?"

"Margie, wait—"

"Gotta go, Mike. See you tomorrow. 'Bye."

The phone clicked in his ear.

"She said bring someone I can trust," Mike said, after he had filled Ham in on the brief conversation. "I guess I'll settle for you instead."

"*Trust.*" Ham gazed up at him levelly. "Now, that's an interesting word, Gooder, and it's one you sure seem eager to apply to this woman who just waltzed back into your life after letting you think she was dead for more than a year."

"We need those power packs, Tyler." Donovan felt a sudden anger rising in him, and he worked to keep his voice even.

"She's been working hard for the resistance. She's on the level, I can tell."

"She's your ex-wife. The mother of your son. How objective can you be about her?"

"I don't care if Gabriel came down on a cloud to tell us where to get more power packs, I'd listen, and listen hard."

"I dunno. This doesn't smell right, Donovan. Seems much too easy somehow."

"Maybe it's about time our luck changed, then."

Ham shrugged. "By tomorrow afternoon, you'll either be right . . . or we'll be dead."

Chapter 8

Bad Relations

Chris Faber woke up instantly—an ingrained habit from years of living next to danger most of his adult life—and glanced over to the left side of his bed.

He still couldn't quite believe the incredible pleasure of finding Maggie Blodgett lying beside him. In the days since their vigil by the window, when the Visitor patrol had come into his neighborhood, she had stayed with him every night. Little traces of her presence were beginning to accumulate in his house—a couple of her shirts hung in his closet, an extra toothbrush now resided beside his bathroom cup, and a few articles of feminine toiletries jostled next to the rust-edged razor in his medicine chest.

Chris smiled a little, enjoying the faint odor of her perfume, which still lingered on his pillow. Asleep, she looked young and vulnerable, almost like a child. He didn't want to wake her, so he lay quietly, just enjoying her, the gentle rise and fall of her breasts beneath the shortie nightgown, the curve of her arm thrown over the pillow toward him. Her honey-gold hair tumbled across her pillow, half obscuring her face, but in his mind's eye he sketched in the details—her green eyes, finely shaped features, all encased in creamy, flawless skin.

Chris had had few women in his life, even fewer whom he hadn't paid for, and never one as beautiful as Maggie. Her presence stirred up something strange and strong within him, deep in a place where he'd never let anyone in before, not even himself, and he had to admit that the way he was beginning to feel about her frankly scared him. He wondered what Ham Tyler would say if he knew—probably eyeball him with that half-lidded look of his and tease him about being in love.

Druid, curled up at the foot of his bed, raised his head and then bounded up to lick Chris's face.

Maggie turned over, exhaling with something perilously close to a snore, then woke abruptly when Druid, wriggling ecstatically, licked her nose. "Jesus! Have a heart!" She dived beneath the sheet, and Chris, laughing, put the Shih Tzu back on the floor.

"Take a hike, pal," he advised the dog. "The only person gets to lick Ms. Blodgett first thing in the morning is me."

One green eye emerged cautiously from beneath the sheet. "I slept like a baby. You been awake long?"

"Just a few minutes. I said no, Druid." As the dog jumped back off the bed, he gently pushed her sleep-tousled hair out of her eyes and leaned over to kiss her.

"What were you thinking about?" she asked. "You looked so serious."

He grinned down at her. "About how good you look in the morning—especially right there."

"You mean you like me better in a sexy nightie than in camouflage fatigues, bristling with weapons?" she said, smiling languorously at him.

"You better believe it, sister," he said, "and as soon as I shut Druid out of the bedroom, I'm gonna show you how much."

Later, she stirred in his arms as he gently brushed the hair away from her closed eyes. "That was good," she murmured. "God, it just gets better and better between us."

"Yeah," he mumbled, turning his head to nuzzle gently at her breast. "I've never felt like this about anyone, Maggie. I—"

She turned her head away, not meeting his eyes, and he faltered to a halt. "What is it?"

"Forgot to take my pill last night," she said, sliding out from under him. "And if I don't take a bathroom break, I'm in serious trouble."

Frowning thoughtfully, he watched her stride into the bathroom, then sighing, turned over and stared at the patterns of sunlight left by the venetian blinds.

When she came back, she was dressed in shorts and T-shirt. "Okay, Faber, rise and shine. Time's awastin', son!"

He groaned. "You're a worse dictator than Tyler."

She smiled. "But I'm infinitely prettier and have other qualities that he lacks. Your turn to walk the dog, and mine to make the coffee."

A few minutes later, she faced him over a steaming mug. "So what do you think of the café Vienna? Did I add enough cinnamon?"

He took a sip, swished it around in his mouth with exaggerated care, then swallowed and smiled slyly. "You're getting better, but it's still not as good as mine."

"Faber, you're such a damned snob!" Mock-scowling, she threw a packet of Equal at him.

"I do a few things well, and I'm proud of them. Making coffee happens to be one of the few socially acceptable skills I have. Somehow people don't react nearly as positively to well-constructed firebombs."

She grinned. "If you're really looking for praise for your coffee, you should share it with some of our friends at the club."

"Uh-uh." He shook his head. "I lie in ditches and get mosquito bit for the resistance, blow up buildings for 'em, bribe black market informers, even lay my life on the line now and then for 'em. I even share *you*. But if I admitted to that mob that I could make kick-ass coffee and had a pantry full of real beans just waitin' to grind up, you know how fast they'd—"

He broke off, his grin fading at the stony expression that had settled over her face. "Maggie? What is it?"

"Nothing," she said, getting up so abruptly that her coffee slopped onto the kitchen table.

He followed her into the living room. Her back to him, she was staring out the window where they had stood together several days and countless layers of feelings ago. His nearly healed eyes made out the barely perceptible shaking of her shoulders.

She was crying.

"Mag, hon, what is it?" He tried to put his arm around her shoulders, but she shrugged it off and stepped away from him.

"You had to remind me, didn't you?" she said. Her voice was low and flat. "About what you do for the resistance.

Double-oh-seven reincarnated as a good ol' boy with a southern accent and a beer gut—the guy who gives the Grim Reaper the finger as he cheerfully wires bombs together or chases after Visitors, guns blazing.'' Her eyes brimmed over, then hot, angry tears spilled and ran down her face. "Damn you! Damn those stupid aliens! You had to remind me that it's probably only a matter of time till I have to watch you die, too!"

"Hey, wait!" he said. "What am I supposed to do? Sit around on my ass waiting for the lizards to march in and turn us all into Hamburger Surprise?"

"You always have to make a joke about it, don't you? Ha ha. Only I don't think it's funny, Chris. I didn't think it was funny when they brought you in with your eyes all bandaged up, wondering if you'd ever see again, and I don't think I'm going to be laughing a whole lot the next time they carry you in on your back."

"Hey," he said gently, putting his arms around her. "Nobody's carrying me anywhere. Maggie, you can't think you're gonna die every time you walk out the door with a gun to fight the scalies, 'cause then you wouldn't fight anymore. And then you might as well be dead."

"Yeah," she said, although she sounded unconvinced, and her shoulders remained stiff under his hands.

He forced a smile. "So tell me a Visitor joke I haven't heard before."

She shook her head, her mouth a thin, sad line. "I'm not in the mood right now, okay?"

"Okay." Quietly, he held her for a long time, stroking her hair.

Those were the only answers they had for one another at the moment.

Mike Donovan looked at Julie Parrish, seated across from him, and his mouth turned down slightly. "Aren't you hungry?" he asked. "That tuna salad looks great."

"Not very, I'm afraid," she said. "Want some?" She pushed her plate over toward him and took a sip of her Coke as he took a few mouthfuls.

They had met for lunch at a small restaurant near Science Frontiers. This was the first time in eight days they had been able to see one another, but the atmosphere between them was tense and awkward. Julie obviously had something on her mind, and she looked pale and tired, but his anxious inquiries had only met with head shakes and monosyllables. Unasked, the thought of Nathan Bates and his slimy insinuations of his "special working relationship" with Julie crossed Donovan's mind.

For a moment, her troubled blue eyes met his, and he wondered if she was trying to work up to telling him something he didn't want to hear.

Forcing a smile, he said the first thing that came into his head. "You know, even Ham Tyler admitted the information Margie brought back from Denver will be a lot of help." He glanced around and lowered his voice even further. "Of course, the best thing of all is finding out about that shipment of power packs to Science Frontiers tomorrow afternoon."

"I wish *I* could find out more about it," she said. "I tried to ask a few roundabout questions, but Nathan immediately got suspicious, and I had to drop it."

"It'll be okay."

"I don't know, Mike. It all seems so . . . convenient, Margie turning up like this."

"What do you mean?"

"It could be a setup," she said bluntly.

"Are you starting to take lessons from the Ham Tyler School for Paranoia and Misgivings?" Donovan crumbled a cracker to powder, frowning. "Her info is legit. Ham double-checked."

"What about Margie? Is *she* legit?"

"Oh, come on, Julie, you don't—"

"Mike, wake up to the possible reality. That information may be valid, but it could have been planted, and she could be a spy."

Donovan felt his jaw muscles tense. "Would you be saying this about Margie if she weren't my ex-wife, Julie?"

Her face flushed, but she looked at him steadily. "Would you be defending her so much if she weren't?"

"What's going on here? You're not trying to tell me you're jealous of Margie, are you?" His mouth twisted. "There's something else, isn't there? What is it? Bates?"

"You know my only concern in this matter is one of security, Mike," she said, glancing down at the purse in her lap. "Listen, I have to get going. Nathan has been like a grizzly bear lately, and I've got a lot to do."

Putting his share of the bill on the table, Mike again felt the sad, aching sense that their relationship might be ending as he watched her leave. Julie seemed to be slipping out of his emotional reach, and all his attempts at discussion, at bringing problems out into the open were ending in arguments that left him feeling confused and defensive. He was finding it more and more difficult to fight off a growing sense of pessimism about their future together.

And now Margie was back in the picture, a different person, stirring up feelings he didn't want to look at too closely. Maybe he needed to give some more thought to Denise Daltrey's offer about that co-anchor spot in New York City. . . .

Damn you, Donovan, why couldn't you just shut up and listen for once? In the ladies' room near her lab at Science Frontiers, Julie cupped water to rinse her mouth and splash onto her face. Her after-lunch bout of vomiting had left her shaking and dizzy, and she leaned against the sink for support.

Glancing at herself in the mirror, she catalogued the red-rimmed puffiness of her eyes, the darkness beneath them, and sighed. She pulled the ever-present Maalox and her makeup kit out of her purse and set to work repairing what she could of the damage to her appearance.

Her period was now two and a half weeks late, and it was getting harder for her to keep down any solid food. If this was so-called morning sickness, it certainly didn't seem to respect any particular time of day with her, but she knew from her medical training that some women spent their entire pregnancies fighting nausea. She should have had a pregnancy test last week, but she'd been too sick and too tired—and too scared—to learn the truth.

I'll call Joe Akers first thing in the morning, she thought. *Have him schedule me for a test the following morning.*

Juliet dabbed once more at the shadows under her eyes with cover-up stick, then carefully fixed her mascara. Popping a breath mint into her mouth, she went back to her lab feeling a bit better for having made the decision.

The enormous gleaming-white room was part of a complex filled with the most modern equipment and computers money could buy. Here the smells of kelp in seawater mingled with the more civilized scents of plastic and alcohol. Julie wistfully remembered the fresh sea-smells from the breezes of Catalina

Island and frowned a little. Science Frontiers had not heard from their research team out there in several days, and she was growing worried. Mac, Mr. Bates's helicopter pilot, had promised to go out there for a look today.

Forcing her attention back to her surroundings, she spoke to a couple of technicians and set about preparing slides from the latest kelp cultures. Here, Julie knew, she had the resources and some of the best scientific minds in southern California to help her tackle the problems of the red dust bacteria mutation that might live without frost. Even so, she often felt isolated in her work at Science Frontiers.

As her employer, Bates admired her work and gave her a lot of freedom to pursue her research as she judged best, but there was more of the profit-seeker than scientist in him as he inquired about her progress. She also missed the sense of community among scientists that she had grown up with in the pre-Visitor days, before all national and international communications had been so disrupted. Nowadays, research groups mostly had to work alone to find their answers.

As she sliced tiny bits of kelp and prepared slides for the microscope, Julie thought longingly of Hannah Donnenfeld and her Brook Cove group. The information they had swapped was proving very useful in eliminating certain types of DNA cross-strains. But how much faster it would be if they could work together.

"Where were you?" Bates's normally terse voice was even sharper than usual, and Julie jumped and dropped the slide in her hand.

"I . . . went out for lunch. I do every once in a while."

"Next time check with me first."

Anger heated up her face, and she bent to pick up the glass shards of the broken slide so that he wouldn't see her expression. "Yessir, boss. And would you like me to get permission when I step out for coffee or go to the rest room?"

"I'm sorry, Julie." His apologetic smile didn't quite make it to his eyes. "I'm a little jumpy these days. I don't like our power pack situation being this low. You know our computers, security systems, everything depends on those little alien black boxes."

"You should have kept up your payments to Pacific Edison," she said dryly.

"In any case, the situation will be remedied tomorrow

afternoon. I'd like you to adjust your work schedule so that you can assist with the computer shut-down tomorrow morning, prior to installation of the new power packs. I'd also like you to accompany me to the legation tomorrow afternoon.''

Julie frowned and bit her lip. She had been planning on remaining here so that she could help with the raid. "Nathan, I'm at a very critical point in our research. I'll be glad to assist with the information transfer to our backup computer system, but I'd hate to lose a whole day's work right now, just when we're—"

"Julie, Diana is already suspicious enough of us and our work here. She suspects we're involved in the production of the new red dust that's settling into the ocean, and she's been giving me a lot of heat about it. It may even be why she's delayed giving us the power packs this long. Come into my office. I want to show you something."

Reaching into his desk drawer, he pulled out a manila envelope and tossed it across the desk to her. "Mac took these with a telephoto lens over Catalina this morning."

Numbly, Julie stared at the pictures of destruction—the ruined, laser-blasted tents, scattered equipment, the charred torsos of Bill Kendall, Juan Perez, and Amelia Anderson, their expressions frozen into horrified disbelief as they'd looked into death.

Julie remembered the stories of Bill's Old Joe, the maybe-mythical hound dog, Perez's comical reviews of L.A. restaurants, Amelia's good-natured grousing, all the learning and laughter they'd shared less than two weeks ago, and tears blurred her vision. And there was Andy.

"What . . . about Andrew Halpern?" she asked, her voice low. "What happened to him?"

"Who knows?" Bates shrugged, his eyes flat and expressionless. "They probably got him too. At least he didn't talk, or things would be really hot around here. Anyway, that's why I want you around to help me tomorrow. No point in getting Diana any more excited than she already is."

You heartless bastard, Julie thought, going slowly back to her lab. *Sometimes I don't know what's worse—the Visitors runnings things or you.*

Diana strode down the corridors of her Mother Ship feeling more than usually pleased with herself. She had just finished talking with Nathan Bates again, and she smiled as she thought about the edge that had come into his voice when she had told him the shipment might be delayed once more. She had enjoyed seeing him squirm, the tension deepening around his usually imperturbable features. She had dragged it out for quite awhile, and then she made a show of conferring with Lydia and assuring him the delivery would be made as scheduled after all.

Except that Bates would never get it. Diana had plans for these particular power packs, and Science Frontiers didn't figure in them.

A second set of high-heeled footsteps joined hers, and Diana glanced over as Lydia came up from a side corridor. "You wished to see me, Diana?" she said. There was a note of resignation in Lydia's voice almost all the time now, and Diana smiled, knowing she was largely responsible for that, too.

"Dear Lydia, don't look so glum. I have some splendid news to share with you." She led the way to her lab complex in the science department.

During her year of confinement on Earth, when Lydia had assumed her duties and command of the Mother Ship, their efforts in scientific research had almost ended. In Diana's opinion, Lydia was at heart a narrow-minded security officer who had not been able to see the usefulness of the sciences in combating the humans. Now it was a special delight to inform her of every new development in her lab.

"Good evening, Bernard," Diana said, approaching a work area.

The slender botanist, hunched over some scientific apparatus, jumped at the sound of her voice and whirled around. His eyes widened and flicked nervously from one to the other as he faced the two most senior-ranking officers on the ship. "Uh . . . yes. Good evening, Diana and Lydia. How, uh, may I help you?"

"You are already doing much to help me," Diana said warmly, laying an arm around his shoulders. "I want you to show Lydia what you are working on."

Bernard reached over to his worktable and held up a vial containing a reddish-brown powder.

Peering at it, Lydia recoiled and grimaced. "It looks very much like the humans' red dust bacteria. Diana, surely you have not brought any of *that* aboard this ship."

"Don't be absurd!" Diana snapped. "Bernard, please explain to our . . . hasty security officer here what this is."

"While it somewhat resembles the humans' bacteria, it is darker in color, and its, uh, purpose, is completely different. This is a powdered chemical substance, not a bacterial toxin." Bernard carefully placed the vial back on the counter. "Our own red dust is a possible solution to the contamination of the Pacific Ocean waters around Los Angeles—"

"Get to the point," Lydia said.

Bernard blinked and glanced at Diana, then at the dust again. "This chemical is a defoliant designed to wipe out the kelp beds. As I told Diana, the humans' new red dust is concentrating in the bladder kelp and certain other common kinds of seaweed. If we destroy all the ocean-based vegetation along the southern California coast, we can then filter the diluted remains of the bacteria out of the water."

"And this way, the desalinization can continue as planned." Diana smiled. "Our Leader will have the water he needs to save our people and strengthen our cause. Bernard, I will see to it that you are personally commended for your efforts."

"Uh, Diana . . ." The thin botanist glanced at her, then down again, and Diana was uncomfortably reminded of the first time he had told her about the original contamination problem.

"What is it, Bernard?"

"There is, uh, one problem I must mention. This compound is extremely unstable until it actually enters seawater."

"What do you mean 'unstable'?" Lydia asked impatiently.

Bernard slowly rolled up the sleeve of his uniform to show medi-flesh swathing the inner side of his left arm. He eased the medi-flesh away, revealing a livid wound. From wrist to elbow, the artificial pink skin had been torn away, and the normally smooth scales of his own flesh were buckled and oozing. "A single spark or concussion, and it explodes violently," he said, carefully replacing the dressing. "This was caused by less than twenty milligrams. Geraldine, the technician assisting me, may be permanently blinded."

"Don't the humans have a saying about a rose always having thorns, Diana?" Lydia smiled. "A pity. This particular scheme of yours actually appeared to have some promise."

Rage crawling up her spine to her crest, Diana whirled to

face Bernard. "I want you to make manufacture of this defoliant, *our* own red dust, your number-one priority."

"My calculations indicate we'll need a large quantity of it to accomplish our purpose. The Pacific is a large ocean," Bernard said, his habitually gloomy expression turning even longer.

"Then I suggest you begin working on it right away," she said, turning to go.

"Not on this ship." Lydia stepped forward to block her path.

"What do you mean, 'not on this ship'? *I* am in command here, and you would be most wise never to—"

"As security officer, I feel obliged to point out that the instability of this substance precludes its manufacture in large quantities anywhere aboard this vessel. Not to mention the problems inherent in transporting it safely via our shuttlecrafts to the ocean."

Diana glared at her, but recognized her junior officer was right—for once. "Very well. Bernard, you can set up the manufacturing plant in one of our warehouses near the Long Beach docks. I'll see to it that you have all the authorizations and personnel you require. How long do you think it will take to complete the manufacture of the defoliant in the quantities we need?"

"Including the time to transfer and set up all the equipment and train personnel in the basic manufacturing process, it will be at least five days, Diana, before—"

"You have two. I know that you won't fail me, Bernard."

The botanist swallowed, but his features clearly said he knew better than to argue with Diana. "No," he said faintly.

"Well, there goes a busy fellow," Lydia said, watching Bernard jog away to begin shouting a jumble of orders. "It appears that you have found another project to replace the scheme you began with the little blonde you planted in Los Angeles."

"By no means, Lydia."

"But surely the only real reason you converted and released Marjorie Donovan was to learn the formula for the humans' ocean-adapted red dust. Now that Bernard has come up with the defoliant, you can dispose of her. Otherwise, she is an unnecessary risk. After all, you *did* say that her conversion was a new, unverified process."

Diana sighed and gave an exaggerated look of concern for

the junior officer as they walked out into the corridor. "Lydia, you lack a sense of imagination, which I fear is another failing that will work against your ambitions for command. I have other, even more important plans for Marjorie now. I have arranged for, shall we say, a little gift for our friends in the resistance tomorrow afternoon. After that, they'll trust her implicitly."

"For what purpose?" Lydia could barely disguise her frustration, and Diana smiled.

"Why, Lydia, it should be obvious to you. When she is fully accepted into their little group, then she can lead us to their secret headquarters—so that we can capture all of them and not just Michael Donovan." Diana raised her head, and her smile widened. "And then I'll eliminate him and those other troublemakers once and for all."

Kyle Bates whistled cheerfully as he revved up the motor of his Yamaha, listening to its smooth sound. The carburetor was clean and running well again, and he felt the satisfaction of a job well done.

Mostly, though, he was glad to be involved in some action again. Mike Donovan had asked him to help with this latest plan to obtain more power packs, and he had readily agreed, especially when he had learned that the packs were to be intercepted on their way to Science Frontiers. For Kyle, there would be a special pleasure in sabotaging one of his father's operations.

He checked the brakes once more, made a couple of adjustments with his wrench, then turned off the ignition. The engine sputtered and died, and the gentler sounds of nature returned to the hills surrounding his home. The air was clear and a little cooler than it had been, and Kyle hoped it would hold up for their raid tomorrow. Waiting around in a heavy leather jacket and motorcycle helmet under the hot sun was not his idea of a great time.

"Hi." Robin Maxwell sat down on the blanket beside him. "I made some sun tea this morning, and it looks ready."

Kyle took the tall, ice-filled glass she offered and gulped its contents gratefully. "Thanks, Robin. This is terrific."

"My mother used to make this for my sisters and me when we were kids." Robin's smile grew a little wistful as she gazed out over the distant heat-shimmery desert. "I miss my folks."

Kyle nodded and put a sympathetic arm around her shoulders. He thought he understood. His parents were still alive, but he'd lost them in other ways long before the Visitors came.

Robin brushed impatiently at the sudden wetness around her eyes. "I even miss my little sisters. I used to think they were such brats. Aunt Rebecca says they've adjusted just fine to Chicago—they even love the snow. And Polly is almost as tall as I am now, can you believe it?"

"You'll get to see them again soon. Julie'll get this new red dust all figured out, and we'll send the lizards packing into space for good."

"I hope." Robin paused as Elizabeth came out of the back door, carrying a couple of books in her arms. "Uh-oh, here comes the academic taskmistress."

"How's she doing?"

"Better than I ever did in school," Robin admitted, her expression a comical mixture of pride and envy. "She's almost up to me already. Thank God Daddy kept all of his old textbooks from way back, and we were able to get them from the old house."

"Yeah, my father had a pretty good collection himself, I'll give him that." Kyle idly tossed a pebble at a small lizard as it scuttled under his bike. "You know, I'm proud of you two, hitting the books hard every day."

Robin shrugged and grinned self-consciously. "I know Daddy would have wanted us to. He always said that education was the key that opened a lot of doors in life. Julie's going to arrange for me to test for my GED—the high school equivalency test—next week. And then . . . well, who knows? The community college just down the road has started offering some classes again."

"Mother, I have a question about the sum of angles in triangles and rectangles." Elizabeth opened a book as she sat down, and the blond and brunette heads of mother and daughter bent low in discussion. Kyle went to the garage and brought out his old bike, a Kawasaki. He hadn't given it a good going over in a while, and it was always a good idea to have a spare bike around.

After a few minutes, Robin stood. "Well, I'm going inside and take another look at my geometry notes. I can see I need some brushing up."

"I'll be in shortly," Elizabeth called after her, then looked up at Kyle and smiled shyly. "This conversation must have been rather boring to you, I'm afraid."

"Not a bit." He leaned across the saddle of the smaller motorcycle, grinning at her. "I learned something, too."

"What was that?"

"That I like the sound of your voice, no matter what you're talking about."

She blushed and smiled down at the ground, then her face grew pensive. "You're going somewhere important tomorrow, aren't you?"

"What makes you say that?" he asked, keeping his voice casual as he reached for the tire pressure gauge.

"There is a greater sense of purpose about your actions than I have noticed recently," she said. "And you . . . seem to be filled with anticipation."

"I can't hide anything from you, can I?" Sighing, he put the wrench down and went over to sit beside her. "I don't want you to tell your mother this, but I'm going to help Mike and Ham with the raid tomorrow afternoon."

She looked at him, her blue eyes level. "I would like to come, too."

"Oh, no way!"

"I can ride your other motorcycle. You taught me on it."

He shook his head emphatically. "It's much too dangerous."

"Is this what my mother calls your 'male chauvinist crap'?"

"Hell, being a woman doesn't make any difference!" Kyle said, blushing. "Margie Donovan is coming with us. But an operation like this, the fewer people involved, the better. Only reason I'm invited this time is that Chris isn't ready for any daytime action yet."

"Maybe I could help."

"And more likely you would just be in the way, and maybe get hurt."

Her lovely features hardened, became colder and more alien-looking than Kyle had ever seen her. "The circumstances of my birth make it hard enough to be human. Most of the time I feel like someone on the outside looking in. I'm doing everything I can to belong fully to this world, the one I have chosen. But all of you conspire to keep me on the outside."

"That's . . . not true," he said, finding his voice. "We love you and want to protect you, that's all."

"I feel like that princess in the fairy tale that you lent me—the one who was kept locked up in the highest tower so that no harm could come to her. She wasn't allowed to really live either." Snatching up her books, Elizabeth got up and ran into the house.

Feeling helpless, Kyle watched her go.

Mike Donovan shifted in the front seat of Ham's old Buick and opened another button of his dark-colored shirt. The car felt like an oven in the ninety-eight-degree heat, with only an occasional puff of breeze coming through the open windows to ease his discomfort. Parked on this lightly traveled side street off Wilshire Boulevard, about four miles from Science Frontiers, they had little to look at besides a couple of parked cars and well-kept suburban homes. The minutes passed leadenly—especially with Ham Tyler for company.

"Gooder, quit fidgeting, will ya? You're making me nervous." But the ex-CIA man was Mr. Cool himself, not even sweating as he leafed through the pages of the issue of *Variety* Mike had brought back from New York.

Feeling vaguely resentful, Donovan glanced at the older man. "C'mon, Tyler. I didn't think anything ever got to you."

"Only partners who can't sit still for two minutes at a time." Folding his paper, Ham leaned back and locked his hands behind his head. "You're acting like someone who's got a lot on his mind. Women troubles? You been talking to Julie lately?"

Mike felt guilt burn his face, then his typical annoyance with Tyler surfaced a moment later. "None of your business!" he snapped, hunching farther down in his seat.

"I guess that means no," Ham said blandly, checking the extra ammo clips in his pocket. "Maybe you ought to. Everybody knows you've been spending a lot of time with your ex lately, all in the line of duty, of course, but—"

"The day I need *your* advice on relationships is the day *I'm* moving to Sirius! So it's been pretty crazy lately. Julie understands." He tried to force conviction into his voice, ignoring the nagging prickle of guilt. He *had* been spending a lot of time with Margie, but—

"I'll tell you what's crazy," Ham said, frowning as he glanced at his watch, "is us waiting here like sitting ducks.

When the hell is this broad going to show? Assuming that she gave us the right route in the first—"

"Watch your mouth, Tyler. That 'broad' was my wife."

"My, my, we're getting a little touchy, aren't we?" Something changed in his flat brown eyes as he looked over at Donovan. "You're still carrying a little torch for her, aren't you? Why did you two break up in the first place?"

"You're pushing it, Tyler," he said, but it seemed too hot to argue about anything. "In case it's any of your business, which I doubt, people change, that's all. They go in different directions. They . . ."

He stopped, suddenly thinking of the last time he and Julie had been together, and how the same thoughts had crossed his mind there at the restaurant.

"You thinking of getting back together with her?"

The thought *had* crossed his mind, more than once in the last few days, but he was damned if he was going to tell Ham that. "Listen, suppose we talk about *your* love life for a while? Or would that make the shortest conversation in—?"

He stopped as he saw the old black Ford Galaxie pull to a stop in the middle of the street behind them. Marjorie Donovan, wearing jeans and a jacket, got out and lifted the hood, miming the actions of someone with car trouble.

A minute later, a white van with red Visitor logos prominently displayed pulled to a stop behind her. Margie had effectively blocked the narrow street.

"You sure got a thing for blondes, doncha, Gooder?" Ham muttered, opening his door. "Let's go."

Chapter 9

Power Plays

Mike Donovan crouched low, scuttling along the right side of Ham's car, then paused by the rear wheelbase until Ham Tyler caught up with him. Out of sight and with guns raised, they waited.

Two shock troopers got out of the Visitor vehicle and approached Marjorie Donovan from either side of her car. It was all Mike could do to hold himself perfectly still while they marched up to her, weapons held casually but ready.

"Move your vehicle," one of the Visitors said, gesturing threateningly with his lasergun. "We have an important shipment to deliver here, and we can't be delayed."

"I'm so sorry, but I can't seem to get it started again." Standing in front of her car, Margie smiled apologetically, gesturing at the engine. "I think it might be the battery. It's not a new model. Do you know anything about cars?"

The Visitor leaned over to glance indifferently under the hood while the other one came up beside her on her left. "Move the car, or we'll blast it out of the way," the second one said.

"Please, couldn't you just help me push it to the side a little, over there?"

Grinning evilly, the second Visitor raised his weapon. "Yes, Harry, let us help her move it—"

Ham and Mike leaped up from behind them, yelling in unison. At the same moment Marjorie slammed the hood down on the first Visitor, who was still peering at the motor. As the hood bounced up, Mike clubbed him down with a lasergun butt to the back of his head before he'd drawn breath to yell. The Visitor's partner reacted more quickly, grabbing Margie and dragging her in front of him for a shield, his weapon pointing at Donovan.

"Duck!" Ham yelled, and the blond woman did—just as Ham clobbered the alien from behind. The Visitor's expression of amazement went slack, and he crumpled unconscious to the pavement.

"Piece of cake," Tyler muttered, flashing one of his rare and almost humorless grins as he stooped to pull the lasergun and extra power pack off the first Visitor. "That was no way to talk to a lady, was it, Gooder?"

"My line was, 'Hey, she said *please*,' " Mike said, looking at Margie. "You okay?"

"Yeah," she said, pausing to jerk the lasergun off the shoulder of the Visitor at her feet.

"You know how to use that thing, honey?" Ham asked.

"You bet I do. Just call me 'honey' again, and I'll demonstrate my aim on your ass."

"Whoa!" Ham rolled his eyes and winked exaggeratedly at Mike. "I love tough-talkin' women, don't you, Gooder?"

"Shut up, Tyler."

Close against the left side of the still-idling van, they moved cautiously toward its rear doors.

It was one of the Visitors' regular land-transport vehicles rather than one of their armored carriers, which seemed unusual. Donovan frowned. It also appeared to be deserted, which was even stranger. There was usually at least one guard riding shotgun behind a transport on a motorcycle or in a car. On the other hand, the Visitors may not have wanted to call any special attention to this shipment by using a lot of armed troopers or an escort.

Slowly they edged around the rear, Ham leading. "Just for laughs," Tyler said, triggering the Uzi he still held. The little machine gun chattered loudly in the still, hot air. "That *should* have smoked any lizards out." Ham gestured with his lasergun. "Come on."

Weapons ready, they positioned themselves facing the back of the van. Ham blasted the handles into twisted and smoking metal, and the doors fell open.

It had gone flawlessly. Mike allowed himself a small smile

as he put one foot on the rear bumper—and stared up into the raised barrel of a lasergun.

Three Visitors in heavy body armor pushed up their helmets as they stepped forward from the front of the van. The center one grinned and aimed his weapon at Donovan's head.

Moments seemed to blur and elongate as Mike stared into the tiny round face of his own death. He felt like a cameraman again, dispassionately noting every detail, the afternoon sun glinting off the shiny alien metal of the lasergun, the way the Visitor's finger squeezed down on the trigger—

"Mike!" Margie shouted, blue-white streaked past his shoulder, and the Visitor in front of him caught the blast from her lasergun full in the face. His hideous, ululating death cry tore the air as he pawed at the smoking, charred remnants of his eyes and pitched forward past Mike onto the street, dead.

Ham used the distraction to blast one of the other two Visitors in the stomach while Mike hit the ground and rolled, coming up with weapon blasting, and the third Visitor was hit high in the shoulder.

The female officer that Ham had injured tried to spit venom at the stocky ex-CIA man, but he covered his face and grabbed her arm, pulling her onto the ground and kicking her in the face. Her false skin split across her nose and cheekbone as she snarled up at him, some imprecation in her native tongue. Donovan thought he heard Ham mutter, "This one's for Chris, you scaly bitch," as he slammed the Uzi viciously across her throat, then stood impassively watching as she convulsed into agonized death spasms. Finally she lay still.

Snarling, Mike's victim clutched his green-stained shoulder as Donovan relieved him of his lasergun. "Move it—here comes the Visitor cavalry," Ham yelled, taking aim, and the injured Visitor fell out of the van, his midriff charred into a smoking ruin of alien entrails and burned meat.

Mike's stomach lurched sickly at the barbecued-chicken smell, and even more in the face of Tyler's execution-style treatment of the prisoners, but there was no time to remonstrate with the ex-CIA agent. Another, more streamlined ground vehicle was roaring at full speed up the street behind them.

"Shoulda known somebody would be riding shotgun after all. Let's go, kids."

The three of them jammed into the cab, which had clearly been designed for just two passengers. Ham slid behind the wheel, Donovan beside him, and Margie squeezed next to Mike on the right side. "For once I'm glad Chris sat this one out," Ham muttered, glancing down at the strangely smooth floorboard. "We'd never have fit. Christ on a pony, where's the damned gas pedal?"

"Try the left hand control." Donovan glanced nervously in the side-view mirror at the rapidly approaching Visitor vehicle. "Any day you're ready, Ham."

"This thing got a gearshift?" Tyler pushed experimentally at one lever.

Sun-bright streaks of laser light suddenly slogged the road beside them, peppering the side of their van with tiny concrete missiles.

"For God's sake, Tyler!" Mike yelled, reaching over for the steering wheel just as their van suddenly leaped ahead, skidding a little. He was slammed back into his seat and Margie fell against his shoulder as Ham took the first turn wide, narrowly missing a car parked close to the corner.

The van lurched drunkenly, almost as though it resented being brought under human control. They bounced over the curb and down again at the next corner while lasers whined in the air next to them, leaving an ozone smell behind.

"Can't you drive?" Margie snapped, and Mike put his arm around her to prevent her from being thrown against the door again. The doors were featureless slabs of metal, with no locks—at least none he could identify. Glancing at Ham's tight-jawed face and then at the dashboard, he realized the problem was even worse than he'd thought. A lot of the standard controls weren't where they were supposed to be—and all of them were labeled in Visitorese.

"Don't look at it, Ham, just drive!" he yelled above the protesting whines of the engine as they accelerated sharply again, then abruptly slowed.

Another blast made an angry noise like tearing metal somewhere in the back of the van, and Ham cursed. "If they hit those power packs, we're all history," he said, twisting and throttling the wheel side to side as more bolts tore up the street around them.

"They're gaining, Mike!" Margie said, taking a cautious look out the window. Rounding a curve, she got off two quick blasts, then ducked as the laser scored the side of her door.

"Where the hell is our backup?" Ham said, opening the alien throttle wide. "Hang tight, kids, we're going for broke."

Bored and too hot in his leather jacket, Kyle Bates pulled his helmet off his head for the second time in three minutes to wipe the sweat pooling at the back of his neck. He was leaning against a fence, his Yamaha idling low and smooth underneath him. He listened to the sound and brought the throttle up a little, then down . . . up, down. . . .

It felt like he'd been waiting in this alley off New Hampshire Avenue, half a block from Wilshire Boulevard, for hours, but it had only been maybe twenty minutes. Mike and the others were due anytime . . . or maybe a little overdue.

Frowning, Kyle checked his watch again and glanced up the street. The original plan was for them to intercept and capture the Visitor truck on Mariposa, cut east down Third, then south on New Hampshire. Kyle was to escort them from there, or draw off pursuit, if necessary.

But suppose something had gone wrong? Kyle was used to thinking of anything that had Mike Donovan and Ham Tyler behind it as a practically guaranteed success. Still, there was Marjorie Donovan. In his book, she was an unknown quantity.

He was a little sorry Elizabeth hadn't been around to "psych" her out—Elizabeth was sometimes good at picking up impressions from people—but she and her mother were holed up studying, and she had avoided him ever since their conversation yesterday afternoon.

Kyle bounced restlessly on the saddle of his bike. Dammit, he was only twenty-four. The care and feeding of cars and motorcycles were far more in his league than answering thorny questions about Life with a capital L. Why did she have to look to him to provide all the answers? Why did *he* have to be the source of the wisdom of the ages for the eighteen-month-old Starchild?

He knew she loved him, and he loved her, in a cautious, protective sort of way, but he couldn't imagine treating her like a human woman, making love to her. She was still so much a child emotionally; could any love withstand for long the kinds of pressure their different heritages put them under? And yet, love was love, wasn't it? Or was it a case of—

Tires screeched a protest up the street behind him, and Kyle jerked out of his thoughts to see the Visitor van skid sideways as it came around the corner too fast. He tensed, feeling the adrenaline rush of excitement rise in him as he revved up.

Then he saw the other vehicle, smaller, meaner looking somehow, zipping in close behind the first. Laser fire blossomed like a deadly flower in the sidewalk beside the larger van, and two children playing on a nearby lawn screamed and cowered on the grass as the vehicles streaked past.

Kyle fumbled his Police Special out of its holster and waited until the pursuit vehicle was almost on top of him, then he squeezed off some shots, aiming at the windshield. The glasslike surface starred, and the gleaming white shape swerved dangerously. Pulling up to the driver's side of the front vehicle, he gave a quick thumbs-up to Ham. Then he dropped back to blast at the second vehicle again, like a Chihuahua worrying a Great Dane.

At Wilshire, Ham peeled right, Kyle left—but the van followed Ham. Cursing under his breath, Kyle did a skidding, foot-braced U-turn, cars braking and honking to either side of him. He had hoped to draw them off, that they would think him and his hand weapon an easy target—not knowing he had a lasergun hidden under his jacket. But they were still in screaming pursuit of the Visitor transport van. Kyle leaned on the throttle, and the Yamaha roared ahead.

"I see the kid behind us again," Margie reported, glancing in the side mirror again. "He's maybe fifty feet behind the second car. Obviously, they didn't fall for it."

"Hell," Ham said tonelessly. He swung the wheel hard to avoid a collision with a city bus, and then their vehicle groaned and squealed around the corner onto Wilshire Boulevard, heading toward Santa Monica. "Well, Gooder, got any of your famous great ideas?"

Mike looked at him. "Not a one. I hope Kyle has his lasergun."

As if in mocking answer, bright light sheared the air beside them, and the side mirror disappeared in a puff of smoke.

"Somebody'd better think of something in a hurry," Margie said, pressing herself even harder into Donovan's lap. "If they hit those power packs with one like that, it's all over."

They continued dodging and twisting around cars. Their

Visitor pursuers weren't so careful, sideswiping a Toyota as they roared closer.

Mike glimpsed the green expanse of Hancock Park ahead on the right through the concealing trees. The La Brea tar pits and museum located there had been one of Sean's favorite haunts years ago, when his son had been going through his dinosaur phase. Sean had enjoyed the skeletons of the woolly mammoths and giant saber-tooth tigers. Mike wondered if he was going to live long enough to ever see his son again.

Kyle was gaining, being able to slip in and out of traffic. As he wrestled the lasergun free from his jacket, he thought they all made a pretty strange-looking caravan—only now the parade was over. Balancing himself on his bike as traffic cleared in front of him, he aimed the weapon carefully at the red Visitor logo on the pursuit vehicle in front of him.

The blue-white blast caught the right rear wheel full just as the vehicle was rounding a curve. The pursuit car careened wildly out of control, crashed through a chain-link fence beside it, and sailed over the slight rise. Tar, pitch, and water cascaded up in a giant, slow-motion geyser as it plunged into the tar pit and mired like some ancient sloth who had strayed too far in search of water.

The pit already had its own denizen, a giant gray statue of a mastodon, its trunk and massive tusks lifted pleadingly toward its wild-eyed mate and calf on the land beside it. The concussion sent the life-sized statue rocking, then its base broke, and it crashed on top of the vehicle.

Tourists were gathering on the top of the observation platform as Ham slowed to a halt near the broken fence. A few cheered as one Visitor scrabbled out of the sinking vehicle and fell into the tar pit, thrashing in the black ooze; nobody seemed inclined to rescue him.

Pulling up alongside Ham and the others, Kyle pulled off his helmet, ran a hand through his thick dark hair, and grinned. "That put the lizards back in the slime, where they belong."

"Now all we need are the feathers," Donovan said, grinning back, and Margie smiled up at him.

"Nice shooting, kid," said Ham.

"Nice driving, old man. I bet—"

Sirens began whooping in the air, and Ham fumbled the van back in gear. "Let's go," he said. "Catch you later, hotshot."

Replacing his helmet, Kyle waved and moved on ahead of them. They eased back onto Wilshire Boulevard—and a laser bolt angled from above blasted down, catching Kyle's rear wheel.

"Jesus Christ!" Ham swerved hard to avoid the bike as it went down, pitching Kyle to the right, and more bolts tore up the pavement in front of them as the Visitor skyfighter swooped low past them and began circling back.

Twisting over Margie, Mike strained to catch a glimpse of Kyle, but they were moving too fast and erratically. "Tyler, we've gotta go back for him!"

"No way, Gooder." Ham braked and swung left, barely moving out of the way of oncoming traffic. "He knew the risks, and these lizard batteries are too important."

"Listen, you icy-hearted son of a bitch—"

"Maybe Kyle's okay, Mike," Margie said softly, squeezing his arm. "It didn't look like he took a direct hit. Anyway, Ham's right. We can't risk the whole shipment of power packs for one person."

Mike settled into grim silence as they raced along, running a red light at the next intersection in front of a police car. The siren began behind them—then abruptly ceased, and the squad car made a quick right turn. Evidently the officer had seen the Visitor logo on closer inspection of the speeding van and had decided there was more pressing police business elsewhere.

The skyfighter swooped low again, and a couple of people near a hotel screamed and fell to the sidewalk as more laser blasts strafed alongside the speeding van. A hapless Volkswagen truck on their right caught one in the rear, sending its two passengers scrabbling for cover as smoke and flame licked up its exhaust pipe.

"Turn and head back downtown," Margie said, checking her lasergun. "Our only hope is losing them under a bridge or among taller buildings." Leaning out of her window, she tried to get a few shots at the skyfighter, but it was moving too fast.

They were less than ten minutes away from the downtown section, but to Donovan, it was one of the longest stretches of his life. At times, as they weaved around the traffic on Pico Boulevard, it seemed as though the skyfighter was playing with them, and he wondered why they hadn't been blasted into smithereens a dozen times over.

Then he remembered their cargo. Any laser fire hitting this

many power packs would set off a chain reaction which would level ten square blocks of downtown Los Angeles. Apparently the Visitors were trying to herd them to a less populated area and then kill them without destroying the truck.

Ham drove around the monolithic glass slab of the Hyatt-Regency, and for an elated moment, they thought they'd lost their pursuers. Then the Visitor craft was banking high overhead again, and Donovan thought he glimpsed another white van with red Visitor logo pulling out from an alley on their right—

"Over there!" Margie shouted suddenly, pointing to a low, open garage. A sign over its entrance proclaimed "BILL'S CARWASH" in bright blue letters. "A perfect hiding place!"

"Or a tomb," Tyler muttered.

"There's no place else," Mike said. "Go for it!"

Ham braked, and the van screeched and skidded into the opening, then jolted to a halt. The sudden darkness after the bright California sunshine seemed total and final.

Something metallic scraped against the wheels, took hold, and the van was pulled along on the track.

"Hey!" A fat middle-aged man came running out of the office just inside the entrance, his expression furious. Waving a cigar at them, he shouted, "Hey, you can't just come in here without paying!"

"Shut up," said Ham, tapping the door of the truck. "This is official business."

"I don't care what kind of . . ." The man stopped, suddenly taking in the Visitor logo. Then a weak smile settled onto his well-fed features, and the cigar was raised in a conciliatory gesture as he backed off. "Hey, anything you say. Always glad to help out. Wash 'n' wax on the house, no problem."

"Chalk up another victory to the Ham Tyler School of Charm and Persuasion," Mike said.

"Yeah, well, I'd hate to die in a dirty car," Ham said.

"Who said we're going to die?" Margie glared at him. "If it hadn't been for me seeing this place—"

"Honey, in case you hadn't noticed, we're caught here tighter'n bugs in a Roach Motel, if the lizards happen to be waiting for us on the other side."

"And maybe we lost them," Donovan said. "Anyway, it didn't seem like we had a lot of choices, particularly with the way you were driving."

"And you think you would do a hell of a lot better, Gooder, the way those lizards were riding up our asses? Listen, you—"

Water and soapsuds suddenly sprayed into the open windows, literally drowning his words. Long-fringed brushes swiped the windshield, then thrust into the crowded cab like begging hands.

"For God's sake, roll up the damn windows, will you?" Margie sputtered as Donovan and Ham, cursing, searched vainly for the window controls on the incomprehensible dashboard. Margie buried her face in Mike's chest as foam poured into the cab.

For tense moments they waited, dripping and silent, as the van majestically rolled through more suds, water, spray wax, and giant blowers. Finally they were facing the square of sunshine that was the carwash's exit, and the van jerked to a halt at the end of the automatic track.

Slowly, his clothes squooshing with every motion, Ham inched forward and turned back toward Pico Boulevard.

People strolled down the sidewalks, cars moved and honked on the street, the sun shone down—and there wasn't a Visitor vehicle in sight.

"I don't believe your luck, Gooder," Ham said.

Donovan was more exultant. "It worked!" He hugged Margie hard, one battle comrade to another, but then her arms were around his neck, and she was kissing him passionately on the mouth.

He might have responded if soapsuds hadn't chosen that moment to drip into one eye. Jerking his head back, he rubbed furiously for an instant, then he looked at Ham, then at her. They were all soaked, soap clinging comically to their hair and clothing. Ham had developed one massive white-foamed sideburn on his left cheek, and Margie had a splotch of suds right on the tip of her nose.

He began to laugh, and Margie joined him. "We . . . we look like an Ivory Soap commercial gone crazy," she said between gasps.

"I don't know what you're talking about." With great, absurd dignity, Ham settled the collar of his black leather jacket in place, only to have more foam well out, and even he began to laugh.

Chapter 10

Room for Discussion

A man's raucous laughter rang out over the hubbub in the Club Creole late that night, and Bernard the botanist raised his head, feeling vaguely resentful. "I'm glad *someone* is having a good time this evening," he remarked to the bartender.

"Yes." The bartender nodded and poured more of his special drink into Bernard's glass. "This is a good place to come for a good time."

Lifting the glass, the botanist gulped gratefully. The drink was suitably viscous for his swallowing apparatus, and had none of the annoying sweetness of most human alcoholic beverages. Bernard knew he shouldn't be here; Diana would be furious if she found out he'd slipped out for a quick drink and a chance to rest his eyes from the harsh glare of the warehouse lights, rather than continuing to oversee their own Operation Red Dust. But he'd been so sick of being cooped up inside with the noxious smell of his defoliant that he'd risked going out— just for a little while, he told himself. Just a few minutes . . .

The manufacturing plant had been set up in record time very early this morning, and his assistants were working feverishly to produce the quantities of defoliant Diana had demanded for tomorrow night. They were far more afraid of Diana's wrath than his own; he wasn't needed to keep discipline this late at night—at least for an hour or so.

"Do you lick your drink?" The blond-haired bartender looked anxious as he wiped his hands on his apron.

Puzzled, Bernard looked at him. "Usually, I swallow them."

The other gestured. "My English is not good. I learned Arabic to come here, and then central personnel screwed my transfer orders. What I wish to know is if you love my drink."

"Yes, I . . . like it very much." Bernard smiled slightly. He knew how bad problems with the military hierarchy could get.

"My name is William, but my friends call me Willie." The bartender extended his hand. "I am pleased to meet you."

"I'm Bernard," he said, ironically acknowledging the human custom. This fellow was one of his own kind and seemed a decent sort, someone Bernard felt he could talk to, someone who had experienced his own troubles with high command—someone who could understand and sympathize with how horrible his lot in life was at the moment. "Indeed, your drink has been the best thing in my entire miserable day. I'm working on a special project for Diana, and she is a horrible person to have breathing over your crest."

"So I have heard." Willie nodded sagely and reached for his blender again. "That she has no respect for opinions other than her own, and she drives others very, very hard."

"Exactly right!" Bernard's own nod was vigorous, making his head feel a little dizzy, but pleasantly so. Somewhere deep down, he knew he was getting drunk, but somehow couldn't summon the wherewithal to care. "She's given me less than two days to complete this vital project, when four was my estimated minimum." He stumbled over the word "minimum" and grinned at Willie.

The bartender leaned over the bar with his own glass. "It must be a very important project."

"Oh, yes, it is." Feeling suddenly very important himself, Bernard winked slyly at Willie and swallowed more of his drink. "I shouldn't be talking about it at all. It's top secret, you see, but—"

"Excuse me, everyone." A tall, slender dark-skinned human was striding up to the small stage at the opposite end of the room and clapping his hands for attention. "Excuse me. The Club Creole is closing an hour early tonight in order to accommodate a special party. Five minutes, everybody."

"Oh, no, Elias," Willie muttered, as though to himself. Amid a chorus of groans and boos, the man on the stage smiled apologetically and raised his hands. "I'm sorry for any inconvenience, and I appreciate your understanding and support. See you all tomorrow, okay? In fact, if you come in tomorrow evening, first drink is on the house."

"Just my luck." With a philosophical shrug, Bernard gulped the rest of his drink and started to rise. "I will be much too busy tomorrow evening to take a drink, free or otherwise."

"Then have it now," Willie said, and the blender was being upended over Bernard's glass once more. "On the home—I mean, house. There is time before the others leave."

"Well, thank you, my friend." This one tasted especially warm and good as it eased down his gullet, and he smiled gratefully at Willie."

"I have a good position here." Willie put his elbows on the bar, his expression wistful. "And I was grateful to get it. After V-Day, there was no longer need for my services as a cryogenics technician, and I feared I might be shipped home. And I do not need to tell *you* about the conditions there. But I . . . miss knowing about the goings-on among my own people."

Bernard smiled gently at him. Poor little fellow, it would no doubt be a real thrill for him to hear about Operation Red Dust. Just a few hints would probably light up his bleak existence among these dim-witted humans, and give him hope.

He drew himself up a little crookedly. "I am personally heading *the* most important project our people have begun since we lost control of this backward waterhole. I am authorized by Diana to generate files using my own name-based access code to our computer network. For the duration of this project, I have even been declared exempt from security checks, in order that my mind not be distracted with worrisome details."

Willie looked suitably impressed. "I never heard of that being allowed before. What did you say this project was?"

"It's a plan to use our own—"

"Five minutes, ladies and gentlemen, please." The black man was shouting and waving his arms again. "And don't forget to check out our brand-new line of Club Creole sportswear with the famous little logo. The shirts come in a variety of sizes and are only fifteen ninety-five, a real bargain."

Willie looked as if he would like to kill the man for a minute, then his face smoothed into a smile again. "My boss. He gets so exited sometimes. Please, go off with your story."

"'Operation Red Dust.'" Bernard nodded proudly and placed his empty glass onto the bar with exaggerated care. "That is my own ironic title for an operation using a defoliant that I have developed, which *does* resemble—"

"Dee-foal-lee-ant?" Willie's mouth moved uncertainly over the syllables.

"It's a substance to destroy all water-based vegetation in the southern California ocean waters. The humans have been working on more of their own red dust to drive us off Earth, but now we have outsmarted them. I will no doubt receive a personal commendation from the Great Leader himself once this is completed, within the next—"

"Excuse me, sir." Bernard broke off to find the black man tapping him on the shoulder, his expression polite but firm. "Time to go. We're closing now."

Waving a hand at Willie, Bernard grinned blearily, fumbled a wad of money onto the bar, and lurched out into the cool night air.

"Why didn't you *tell* me, Willie?" Elias Taylor asked, pacing unhappily in front of the bar.

Behind him, laughter and voices were punctuated by a chorus of pops from champagne corks. After the last customer had walked or staggered out of the Club Creole, the members of the L.A. resistance had emerged from their basement headquarters to celebrate their victory in obtaining hundreds of new power packs.

The party was already in full swing, and Willie had to shout to be heard over the noise. His English slipped even further in his agitation. "I *tried* to capture your vision, Elias, but you were not watching at me!"

Elias stared at him blankly, then his mouth quirked. "You mean, 'catch my eye.' Yeah, if I'd known you were pumping that dude for the secrets of the newest Visitor harassment, you could've talked to him all night. Well, we'll tell Julie as soon as we see her." He clapped the distressed Visitor on the shoulder. "Don't worry about it, Willie, we'll figure out something. Now, I want you to get out from behind that bar and start enjoying yourself. This is a party, remember? I'll try to find Julie."

* * *

Juliet Parrish sat huddled in a huge rattan chair, her legs curled beneath her. Her abdomen lurched queasily almost continually now, and within the last twenty-four hours she'd also begun to experience sharp little cramps from time to time. Not surprisingly, she wasn't really in the mood for a party. Julie was determined to put up a good appearance, though—especially in front of Mike Donovan.

He was sitting across the dining room from her on a low, overstuffed couch, his ex-wife beside him. Margie looked lovely, her hair softly curling over the shoulders of a light blue dress. Julie tugged at her indifferent ponytail and pushed her glasses up on her nose—she hadn't had the time or energy to put on makeup or do her hair. And after a day in heels and business suit at Science Frontiers, she couldn't bear to part with her T-shirt and old jeans.

"To the newest member of our team," Mike said, raising his glass as he looked at Margie. The faint pink flush across his nose and cheekbones told Julie he'd already had a couple of drinks before this one. "To Margie Donovan, the heroine of the power pack raid."

"Oh, Mike, it wasn't that big a deal," she said, blushing but obviously pleased by his praise.

"Are you kidding? Folks, you should have seen her." There was undisguised pride in his expression—and something else more subtle as he put his arm around her. "She was fantastic. She saved my life. Hell, she saved *all* our lives. It was her idea to hide out in the carwash until we lost them."

"I dunno, Gooder." Ham Tyler stared down into his Scotch and soda. "The whole thing struck me as being a little too easy somehow. I hope to hell they didn't manage to plant a bug on us or something."

"*Easy?* Tyler, you get hit in the head by one of 'em? We were damn lucky to get away at all, let alone with only one injury."

The main door of the Club Creole unlocked, everyone tensed a moment, then relaxed as Robin and Elizabeth Maxwell came in, followed by Kyle Bates, on crutches.

"Speak of the devil." Ham gestured with his glass. "Hey, hotshot, we're over here. So look who gets the hero's escort, Gooder."

Julie watched as Kyle eased himself into the offered seat,

grimacing a little at the attention. She was grateful that her friend and colleague, Dr. Joe Akers, worked at the nearby clinic and could patch up the resistance members as needed, and she was happy with her own work as a researcher. Still, there were times that she regretted not having completed her studies in medicine. "How are you, Kyle?" she asked.

"Just a wrenched knee, no big deal. Doc Akers said it'll be good as new in a week or so."

Miranda Juarez smiled, then drew her features into a mock frown. "Shouldn't you be home resting it?"

"Hey, you couldn't expect me to miss my own party!" Kyle protested.

Donovan looked over at him. "Sorry we had to leave you behind, buddy."

"You did the only thing you could." Shrugging, Kyle accepted a glass of champagne from Robin. "The only thing I'll expect is a featured heroic role in *Lizard Kill, Part II*, which I know they'll make once we get rid of them again—permanently, next time. Here's to it."

As glasses were raised and clinked, Julie saw Robin glancing over at her, frowning slightly. Julie sighed and shook her head a little, knowing the young woman would mentally translate her gesture to read: *No, I haven't started my period yet; no, I'm not feeling any better—worse, as a matter of fact—and no, I don't like what's going on between Mike and the former Mrs. Donovan.*

At the next table, Robin bit her lip, her expression pensive over her glass of champagne. Poor Julie, she looked awful, and Mike Donovan was acting like a real jerk.

"Mother." Elizabeth touched her arm. "What's wrong with Julie?"

"I'm not sure," Robin admitted, looking at her friend again. Julie had always been tiny; now she looked pale and haggard, her eyes surrounded by dark circles, her cheekbones accentuated by the weight she'd lost.

"There is something . . . wrong about her, inside." Elizabeth's blue eyes were cloudy and distant.

"Do you know what it is?" Robin found herself holding her breath as she leaned toward her daughter.

"No. Only that it troubles her and is causing her pain."

Elizabeth stared down at the tablecloth. "And . . . that there is nothing that we can do to help her."

Chris and Maggie strolled in from the back entrance a few minutes later. They looked casual and weren't holding hands, but Julie immediately picked up on the significance of the glances that passed between them. She smiled a little ruefully. She and Mike used to sneak sideways looks like that when they were together.

"Hey, Chris." Ham raised his glass. "How's it going?"

"Real good. Congratulations on swiping those lizard Duracells."

"Went down pretty smooth," Ham admitted modestly. "Even Gooder here managed to pick up his feet." Donovan flipped him the finger, and everyone laughed. "So, no dark glasses, Faber. That mean your sight's back to normal?"

Chris grinned and looked over at the bar across the room. "Anybody wanna hear me read off all the labels on the third row?"

"No, but we're sure glad you can," Mike said. "Congratulations on your recovery. It looks like maybe you got more than your sight back during your little vacation." Smiling, Donovan glanced at Julie, who hastily dropped her gaze.

"What I'm really lookin' for is champagne for the lady an' me," Chris said, expertly scooping up two glasses and a bottle from the table.

The lurching in Julie's stomach suddenly intensified, bringing with it a rush of nausea. She slipped out of her chair and hastened toward the kitchen—she wasn't sure she'd make it all the way downstairs to the ladies' room. But the spasm subsided as she pushed open the swinging doors. Standing on tiptoe, she was able to reach into the cabinet where Elias kept the first-aid supplies for the club's employees, and pulled out the bottle of Pepto-Bismol.

It was almost empty—Willie had been using the stuff in his nightly drink specials for the Visitors. Still, there was enough for one final swallow, and she upended the bottle, grimacing at the taste, then leaned against one of the huge refrigerators.

Her reflection was blurred and distorted in the shiny metal surface, but Julie could mentally sketch in the bruised-looking smudges under her eyes, her pallor. *I thought pregnancy was supposed to give you a healthy glow,* she mused bitterly. *I look like hell.*

She pressed her hands to her abdomen as a cramp awakened, making her catch her breath. *Am I getting my period?* she wondered. If she *was* pregnant, spasms like these, she knew from her medical training, could be an ominous symptom. And there was no doubt that she'd been heavily exposed to the original red dust in the weeks before V-Day. . . .

She'd seen the pictures taken after the Visitors had left that showed the frightening side of the toxin the humans had unleashed—mutations, gross birth defects. What might it have done to her? And there was the new Catalina variant. She'd been working with it, testing it daily. Who knew what effect *it* might have on a developing human fetus? Could she be carrying the beginnings of a monster inside her?

Julie swallowed, scrubbing fiercely at her eyes with her knuckles. She would *not* cry, especially not with Mike out there in the next room, sitting cozily next to Margie. She remembered seeing a picture Donovan had shown her of Margie holding a month-old Sean. If she *had* to have a baby at this, of all times, please, God, let it be normal, let it be cute and healthy like Sean, with its father's thick dark hair.

The scrape of a footstep sounded close by, on the other side of the refrigerator. Julie whirled around to see Margie stepping back from the massive door leading to the club's cold storage area and the hidden entrance to resistance headquarters.

"Excuse me," Margie said. Weaving a little, she hiccupped, then she giggled. "Champagne goes straight to my head; it always did. You can ask Mike. Uh, anyway, I was trying to find the ladies', and I got completely turned around. This is the kitchen, isn't it?"

"You can use the employees' bathroom over there," Julie said, pointing to the small door in the side wall.

"Thanks." Steadying herself along the counters, Margie made her way to it.

Julie waited for her, her mind in almost as much turmoil as her stomach. The rest rooms were on the other side of the club and downstairs. Heading into the kitchen was a pretty radical mistake for someone to make, even if she was a little tipsy.

Could it be that Margie was looking for something—something like their secret headquarters? And had she found it?

* * *

Robin had seen Julie get up and walk quickly to the kitchen, her expression queasy. For a moment, it looked as though Mike might get up and follow her, but then Margie leaned over and said something to him, and he laughed.

With sudden resolve, Robin stood. Her friend Julie was hurting, and it was time Michael Donovan was reminded that there was more to life than having a good time. God knows, *she* had had to learn that lesson.

"Where are you going?" Elizabeth asked, looking up at her.

"I'm going to talk to Mike. It's okay, honey. You wait here."

Her daughter looked solemn. "Be careful, Mother."

"Well . . . sure. We're just going outside the door. Be right back." Bending down, she gave Elizabeth a quick kiss on the forehead and marched over to the next table.

Mike Donovan found himself wishing the world weren't so complicated. Champagne in sufficient quantities tended to soften the edges of reality, turn them gentle and water-colored, but underneath, he was still a little uncomfortable about the way Margie was pressing against him and the fact that she felt good next to him.

He also felt awkward about Julie. Several times, he'd tried to catch her eye, give her a reassuring wink, but she wouldn't look at him. She appeared tired and pale and was uncharacteristically quiet. Julie was usually the life of the party.

He saw her get up and head toward the kitchen and was wondering whether he should follow, see if she was okay, but then Margie started to relate the story of the mouse in their honeymoon suite, and he had to laugh and embellish the tale.

"Hey, Mike."

He squinted up through the haze at Robin Maxwell. Hands hooked into her belt, the slight young woman was looking down at him, her expression grim.

"Hey, Robin. What's up?"

"Can you take a little walk outside with me? We need to talk."

"Uh . . . yeah, sure. Excuse me." He got up too quickly, causing the room to lurch a little.

Without a backward glance, Robin led the way outside. The air was cool, fresh, and smelled good after the smoky closeness of the club. He inhaled deeply. "What's on your mind?"

"You and your ex-wife seem to be getting along really good," Robin blurted, turning to face him, and he saw with surprise that she was furious.

"Yeah, well, it's been a long time, and a lot of things have happened since Margie and I last saw one another. Life seems too short and precious these days to hang on to a lot of old bitterness, I guess."

"You ought to be more aware of what your apparent reconciliation with her is doing to Julie."

Donovan felt his mouth tighten. Mingled with his resentment at this eighteen-year-old lecturing him on his love life was the deeper, more honest realization that she had struck a nerve of his own guilt. "Just because Margie and I are talking to one another in civilized tones again doesn't mean we're reconciling."

"Come *on*, Mike. Do you have any idea what Julie must be thinking, seeing you two together all the time?"

"Julie knows how much I care about her."

"Does she? Your timing really stinks, Mike. Julie needs you now more than she ever has." Robin stopped suddenly, her expression under the lamplight that of someone who has said more than she had intended.

Donovan's comfortable glow vanished in a wave of concern. Reaching out, he grasped Robin by the arms, turning her to face him. "*Why?* What's wrong? Julie's not sick, is she?"

"She's . . ." Drawing a deep breath, Robin looked at him, then down at the ground. "I think you need to have a long talk with her. Soon."

"Hey, if you know something I—"

Something metallic clattered to the sidewalk behind him, and Mike whirled around. Two Visitors in guards' uniforms staggered back from an overturned chair belonging to the Club Creole's sidewalk café. One belched, then muffled a laugh under his gloved hand. "Excuse *me*," he said loudly.

"Hey, the lights are on, but the door's locked." The other continued to pull irritably at the door handle as though he could force it open by willing it.

"The sign says 'closed,' friend," Mike said, jerking a thumb at the window.

"We want a drink," the other said, turning aggressively. "We want it *now*."

The first one nodded and turned from the door. "We had a

rotten day, and we intend to get drunk and stay that way all night."

"Sounds to me like you've had enough already. Why don't you go home, sleep it off?"

"I've heard that human's voice before, Harry," the first one said, fumbling for his sidearm.

"Yeah . . ."

Mike suddenly recognized their voices, too. These two were the same guards he and Ham had decked earlier that day when they'd stolen the van!

"Oh, shit," he muttered, diving outside the reach of the lights haloing the club's entrance. "Robin, get outa here!"

Her scream shattered the night's quiet behind him as a brilliant streak of light slashed the darkness just above his head and sent chunks of paint, brick, and mortar flying out of the wall.

Hitting the sidewalk, Donovan rolled as more brilliance scored the pavement where his head had been an instant earlier. Mike heard the club's door open, and Kyle hurtled out. His swinging crutch caught one alien in the arm, sending his lasergun spinning into the darkness. Jumping to his feet, Donovan used the diversion to tackle the second Visitor, and they staggered and went down in a tangle of flailing arms and legs.

Wrenching his arm loose, the Visitor slammed his gun against Mike's head. Light and sound scrambled together in Donovan's awareness for an instant as pain cut a laser bolt across his vision. Groping for the other's hand, he pounded it on the pavement until the weapon clattered out of the alien's fingers.

Dimly Mike heard Robin shout, "Kyle, look out!" and he saw her lift a piece of two-by-four to clobber the Visitor who had pulled Kyle to the ground.

Then the Visitor under Mike heaved up, throwing him off balance, and the alien was reaching for the lasergun—

Donovan felt heat high up on his thigh; the Visitor screamed and writhed, clutching his stomach as it glowed then charred, and a burning-chicken smell filled the air. The Visitor convulsed again, then lay still.

Shakily, Mike pulled himself to his feet as Ham Tyler stepped down from the doorway of the Club Creole. "Stand back, honey," he said to Robin, sighting along the barrel of his newly charged laser pistol, then he coolly french-fried the other Visitor.

"Nice of you to drop by," Donovan said. His voice sounded weak and tinny in his own ears.

"It was getting stuffy in there anyway." Ham's glance flicked laconically past the two Visitor bodies. "You all right?"

"Yeah, I think so." He felt experimentally around the wet place in his hair, where the lasergun butt had hit him. Then he felt real regret when he noticed the torn and dirty elbows of his new sports jacket and the singed spot high on the leg of his new slacks. "Next time, Tyler, watch where you're aiming. Just because your sex life's lousy doesn't mean you have to try to end mine."

"If I wanted to do the world a favor, Gooder, I'd aim for your mouth. Let's go dump the bodies."

Chapter 11

Turnabouts

Robin's heart pounded, her mouth was cottony, and her stomach felt like a popped balloon. She stumbled a little as she walked slowly back into the Club Creole, her legs weak and trembling. She was halfway to her table before she realized her numb fingers were still clutching the broken two-by-four.

Miranda took one look at her face and set a margarita in front of her moments later. It was a double, and Robin gulped it gratefully, letting the fiery tequila replace the coldness inside her with warmth.

"Take it easy," Miranda said. "You don't want to get sick."

"Mother, what happened outside?" Elizabeth's eyes were large and watchful in the dim lighting of the club.

Trying to steady her breathing, Robin set down her glass, knocking some salt onto the tablecloth. "There . . . was some trouble outside. A couple of Visitors . . . they were drunk, and they picked a fight with Mike."

"Is he all right?"

"Yeah, he seemed okay. The Visitors aren't, though. Ham killed them. Just shot them, right in front of me."

Miranda made a sympathetic noise. "*Pobrecito*, no wonder you look shook up."

Robin nodded mutely, sipping her drink. They sat in silence for several minutes, then Elizabeth spoke.

"Mother, do you think the humans and the Visitors will ever be able to exist together in peace?" Elizabeth looked at her, her blue eyes troubled.

144

Robin looked up at the tone in her voice, sensing the anguish her daughter was feeling. "Honey, I don't know. I like to think that maybe, someday, it'll be possible, but there's so much anger between us now."

"Father Andrew once called me a symbol of peace." Elizabeth stared down at the candle flickering on the table between them, her voice low and flat. "But the longer I live, the more I end up feeling like a symbol for war—something inhuman, a living mistake between two cultures that should never have met, that are too different to ever really understand one another. Or even want to try."

Robin wanted to reach over and hold her, but something in her daughter's posture kept her seated. "Elizabeth, honey, what is it?"

"Mother, I had another of the dreams last night. The red dust was thicker this time, but I could still see the man's face through it. He was a young man, very handsome, and he was holding out his hand to you. Then I saw you, and your face was a stranger's, full of hate. He screamed and pulled off his face, and he was really a Visitor. Why are you in the dream, and why do you have that look on your face?"

Robin took a deep breath, realizing she would have to face memories that she'd spent the last eighteen months doing her best to forget. Guilt awoke once again, mixed with the terrible anger of betrayal, but she fought it down, forcing her voice to stay low and steady. "The young man was your father, Elizabeth. And, yes, I did kill him, just about the way that you saw it in your dreams. He had hurt me, betrayed me, and I . . . wasn't really responsible for my actions. It was weeks before I could even realize what had happened, what I'd done, and then it seemed as if somebody else had tossed that red dust in with him."

"How can you love me if you hated him so much?"

Robin stared at her bleakly. Desperately she searched for words, special words that she could say to her daughter, the words that would make everything okay, soothe the restless demon that lurked deep within her. But they stuck in her throat as a soft, formless sound. Then Kyle came limping slowly through the door, and Elizabeth rose and ran over to him.

The moment was lost, and Robin was left alone with her tears and her margarita.

* * *

"Exactly what did you learn from Bernard, Willie?" Julie asked, absently stirring her half-finished Coke with a straw.

"Well, he is a scientist, he does not like working directly for Diana, and he does not grasp his liquor at all well. He was becoming intoxicated after only two of my drinks."

"What else?" Elias asked.

Willie's features wrinkled in concentration, and Julie found herself idly admiring the exquisite skill that had gone into creating the life masks that could mimic even subtle human expressions. The Visitors might have taught Earth doctors a few things, given new meaning to the profession of plastic surgery, if they had ever kept their promises of sharing their vast scientific achievements.

"He says Diana has been working him over lately," Willie answered after some thought.

"What?" Julie looked at him blankly, then at Elias.

"You mean she's *overworking* him," Elias corrected automatically. "That he's working a lot of hours."

"Yes, that is it." Willie nodded. "Bernard is overworking on a special project that they are calling Operation Red Dust."

Julie felt the muscles in her abdomen tighten and hoped she wasn't going to be sick again. "Do you know what they are doing?"

"They are creating a decaffeinated—no, no, a defector? A . . . defecation?" He waved his hands in frustration. "My English is so small."

"Describe it," Julie coaxed. "Take your time, Willie."

"It is a substance to kill all the kelp and sea plants in the ocean surrounding California."

"Oh, my God," she said softly. "A *defoliant*."

"Yes, that is it!" Willie brightened.

"Aw, man!" Elias grinned in relief. "Just something that kills seaweed? I was thinking this could be really serious."

"It *is* serious!" Julie said, banging her hands down on the bar. Her agitated gesture sent the partially full glass of Coke cascading down the bar in a brown puddle as she turned to face him. "Don't you know what this means? The ecology of the whole California coastline is in terrible danger! If the seaweed dies out, so will the plankton, which the smaller fish feed on, then there won't be any larger fish, and—"

"Biology wasn't my best subject in school," Elias admitted. "As a matter of fact, *school* wasn't my best subject in life."

"This is most serious." Willie nodded, his expression solemn, even haunted. "This is how it began on our home world. We did not take care of our own plants or our small animals, and now our world is dying. We must stop—"

"Is there a doctor in the house?" Ham asked. Kyle Bates was leaning on his shoulder, holding a broken crutch and grimacing as his injured leg bumped into one of the barstools. Mike Donovan was behind them, looking similarly dirty and rumpled, with a smear of blood near his left temple.

"No," Julie said, sliding off her barstool, "but I guess Miranda and I'll have to do. Miranda!"

"Actually, I was thinkin' of something tall, cold, and definitely medicinal." Ham glanced over at Willie. "Like a double Scotch."

Julie took a step toward Donovan, her eyes fixed on the cut. "Mike, are you . . . ?"

"Oh, Mike!" Margie ran in from the other room, her expression stricken as she reached for his face.

"Aw, it's nothing," he said, pulling away from her in embarrassment.

"Let me see." Briskly assuming her best "impersonal physician" demeanor, Julie stepped past the other woman and ran expert fingers into Mike's hair, checking the scalp wound. It wasn't serious, so she bent to examine Kyle's swollen knee. Miranda, wiping her hands on a dishcloth as she came in from the kitchen, took one look and went right back for the first-aid kit and a bucket of ice.

"You should've seen what the other guys looked like." Donovan grinned weakly as he accepted the brandy Willie put in front of him.

"You didn't exactly help this along," Julie said, unwrapping the Ace bandage around Kyle's knee. "What the hell happened?"

As Mike briefly related the incident outside the club, Ham drank most of his Scotch, reached into his jacket, and pulled out two crumpled wads of cloth. Staring at them for a moment with a look of profound disgust, he threw them into Elias's face—two Club Creole shirts. "The damn scalies had them on under their uniforms. *Now* are you satisfied, Taylor?"

"I'm glad nobody was seriously hurt," Elias said, yanking the shirts off his head and glaring at Ham.

"*This* time." Julie looked at him wearily, wondering for the thousandth time when all this was going to end.

"Are you listening to me?" Ham was up and standing in front of Elias in the next instant, his barely controlled fury turning his body rigid. "We just got jumped outside by two of your regular customers, although I'm afraid you won't be seein' *them* around anymore."

Elias shrugged and attempted a smile. "Hey, be cool. At least they already paid for their shirts."

"Oh, no, Taylor." Ham pushed his face inches from Elias so that the younger man stepped back a pace. "You're not fobbing us off with cute remarks or sanctimonious statements about you being king of the club, running the show up here—not this time. Far as I can tell, the lizards are running things around here now anyway. I want to know what you're going to do about it."

"It was just one of those things. They happen around any place that serves liquor where people—or lizards—drink too much."

"Except this is more than a place that serves liquor, and a lot more's at stake here," Julie said, holding Kyle's leg while Miranda gently rigged an ice pack. "Like people's lives and what we're trying to do to make this a better world for humans and a lot poorer one for Visitors—most of them anyway," she amended, looking at Willie.

"What do you want?" Elias spread his arms. "You got the power packs you needed to defend yourselves, and—"

"—And another giant-sized crisis is brewing," Julie pointed out. "We've got to put a stop to the Visitor's Operation Red Dust."

Under her hands, Donovan flinched as she dabbed the cut above his hairline with Betadyne. "Ow, that hurt!"

Not as much as you and your little Margie sitting together all cozy on the couch hurt me, she thought, resisting the urge to swab harder. "Donovan, you're always such a pain in the ass to patch up," she said aloud, daubing at the excess. "Hold still, you big chicken."

Mike grimaced again but remained in his seat.

"Ham's right, Elias," she said. "We've got to step up activities. Which means we'll be running in and out of here more often—and some of us appear on wanted posters."

"You want me to declare the club off limits to Visitors, don't you?" Elias asked sullenly.

"Either that, or we find a new clubhouse for our little games," Ham said. "It's that simple."

Elias looked as though he was going to say something else for a moment. Instead, he shrugged and reached over the bar for a bottle of beer. "Okay, Ham, you win. But *only* until this crisis is over. The Visitors account for almost forty percent of my gross receipts, and I can't take that kind of loss forever."

"Your patriotism and willingness to sacrifice for the cause are duly noted and appreciated," said Ham, clinking his glass against Elias's bottle with exaggerated solemnity.

"Thank you, Elias," Julie said, stretching up to kiss him on the cheek.

Elias's grin flashed. "Hey, do that again and I'll think of something else I can be noble about."

Willie's start-up of the blender drowned out all possibility of conversation around the bar for several seconds. He looked around apologetically as he poured himself a drink. "How can we learn more of this Operation Red Dust?" he asked.

"Well, I have an idea," Elias said, leaning back against the bar. "Willie, do you still have your old uniform?"

Julie's attention was drawn to Margie, who had started putting on her jacket and was moving toward the door. Donovan was standing beside his ex-wife, and Julie strained to hear their conversation.

". . . walk you to your car?" Mike was saying, helping Margie with her coat.

"No thanks, Mike." She smiled.

"It could still be dangerous out there."

"I'll be fine. Don't worry so much." Reaching up, she pulled his head down to hers and kissed him, harder and longer than could be considered just sisterly.

Julie bit her lip and took a sudden, intense interest in the ice fragments at the bottom of her Coke glass. Her stomach felt taut and uneasy again, and she doubted that it was entirely due to whatever was wrong with her. *Hey, grow up!* she scolded herself fiercely. *Mike's an adult, and you're supposed to be one too. People can change, move in and out of relationships. If it's over, it's over. The best thing you can do is let it go, be as gracious as—*

"Hey." He was suddenly standing beside her, and his hand

on her shoulder made her jump. "I've been wanting to get a little time with you all evening."

"Hail the conquering hero," she said. "Obviously, you've been busy."

"Aw, that was no big deal." He absently touched his temple. "A couple of drunks, except they were carrying laser pistols. Makes me want to be back in New York City, where the most dangerous thing there is the ordinary, garden-variety mugger."

"*Margie* thought it was a big deal." She heard herself sounding bitchy and petulant, but she didn't care. She was tired, her stomach hurt, and as far as she was concerned, Donovan had behaved like a jerk most of the evening.

"Julie, *are* you jealous of Margie?" He looked as though the idea had never occurred to him before—not seriously, at least.

"I don't know, Mike. Should I be? You two have been spending a lot of time together, you have a lot in common again, it seems, and there's obviously a lot of mutual admiration going on."

"Yeah," he said, his mouth tightening in the way that told Julie he was angry. "I *like* her again. Probably for the first time in ten years or more. And, yeah, we have something in common. She's the mother of my son, my missing son. We both miss him, and she's the only person who shares the way I feel about that, because he's *her* son also. You don't just throw that away, whatever happens."

Julie's stomach lurched queasily, and she thought, *Maybe I'm carrying your next child, Mike. What would you say if I told you that?* But aloud she said only, "Mike you don't owe me any explanations."

"Yeah, I do." His expression turned gentle and earnest, making him look suddenly much younger. "Because *you're* the—"

"You mean I missed out on the action again?" Chris Faber's expression was genuinely amazed as he strolled up to shake Mike's hand.

"It was over almost before it started, thanks to Ham." Donovan smiled, his eyes still on Julie.

"It would have been over 'fore it started if I'd been there," Chris said matter-of-factly.

Beside him, Maggie Blodgett, looking flushed and pretty—and slightly lit—laughed. "C'mon, Mr. Macho-man. About the only thing you're ready to tackle tonight is your pint-size pooch, then your king-size bed."

He put an arm around her, and the new tenderness in his expression made Julie's throat contract. "You're getting bossier than The Fixer over there, woman."

Giggling, she pushed him away. "Julie, in your considered medical opinion, is it true that large men actually hold their liquor worse than smaller ones?"

"I don't know, Maggie. Maybe I should do some lab tests on it." Juliet tried to smile, but the cramp which caught her then almost made her gasp instead. She took a swallow of her mostly melted ice, trying to cover her discomfort and wishing Nathan hadn't scheduled that damned shutdown today. If she'd been able to see Joe Akers, by now she'd know one way or another what was wrong.

"Well, anyway I look at it, he's a handful." Maggie squeezed Chris's arm affectionately. "G'night, everybody. Great party, Elias."

The party was drawing to a close as people reached for coats and purses. Her nausea intensifying, Julie thought that visiting the bathroom might be a good idea, and it would get her away from Mike a few moments, give her a chance to sort through her jumbled emotions. "Excuse me," she murmured, standing.

"Are you okay?" Mike's green eyes were narrowed in concern as he looked at her. "Robin and I had a talk earlier. She said you and I had something to discuss."

For an instant, Julie wanted to fling her arms around him, hold him tight in the way she had so often up until recently, and tell him her hopes and fears as to what might be happening to her. But was this the right time and place?

Was there a right time and place?

"I . . . I'll be right back, Mike." Almost running, she burst through the kitchen doors.

Washing her face with cold water and swallowing a couple of spoonfuls of antacid helped. Eyes closed, she leaned heavily against the cupboard. She knew he cared about her, he really did, and she cared about him, enough not to give him something else to worry about. At least not until she was sure.

She knew he was suspicious now, though. How long could she keep up the feeble excuses about a virus or being "just tired"? He wasn't stupid; he would—

Her gaze fell on the door to the linen closet. The handle was tilted at an odd angle, as though it hadn't quite caught.

Julie frowned. The members of the resistance lived with a constant low-grade paranoia; they were all very careful about security measures. Slowly, she approached the door. Maybe someone with just a little too much champagne in him or her had left it open by mistake.

She opened the door and went into the dark closet. Her eyes scanned the neat, ordinary-looking shelves, especially the ones in back, which concealed the secret door. Everything seemed as it should be—all the linens, toilet paper, and other supplies were in place and appeared undisturbed.

Smiling a little at her own jumpiness, she was about to turn around and go back when she distinctly heard the scrape of a footstep on the stair below.

Julie looked around frantically for something, anything she could use as a weapon, her heart pounding loudly in her ears. An aerosol bottle of ammonia-based glass cleaner was the best she could find. Making herself small in the darkness of the closet near the outer door, she tensed, holding the bottle ready.

A thin rectangle of light appeared at the back of the closet as the door panel slid sideways; the opening grew larger, briefly framing the shape of someone. Then darkness swallowed the figure again, who stepped forward—

"Mike!" Julie shouted, ducking as she squirted the intruder full in the face.

Gasping sharply, the intruder staggered back against the shelves, arms flailing. Julie dashed for the outer door and jerked it open just as Ham, Mike, and Elias ran into the kitchen. "Someone broke into headquarters!" she panted. She fumbled for the light switch, flooding the closet with brightness.

Rubbing at her eyes, Marjorie Donovan slowly rose to her feet. In her hand was a small, unmistakably Visitor device.

"It neutralized all of our security systems, alarms, everything." Elias turned the object they had taken from Margie over in his hands.

"It also probably located the hidden entrance and activated the lock," Julie said, pushing her glasses up to rub her forehead.

At almost five in the morning, gray predawn light was trying to filter through the drawn venetian blinds of the Club Creole. Dishes and condiments on the still-uncleared tables looked like small ghosts in the dimness of the farther corners. Elias had sent Miranda and Willie home two hours ago.

Margie sat in a straight-backed chair in one corner, her expression vacant, staring down at nothing. For several hours they had been trying everything short of physical abuse to get her to talk, to answer even their simplest questions. She had remained silent and unresponsive, almost catatonic as she sat in the chair.

"Let's try it again," Ham Tyler said, draining his beer bottle and rising to his feet.

"I'm going to make some more coffee," Elias said, and went toward the kitchen.

Mike Donovan heard the words, saw the people he knew and cared about—especially the one he'd once been married to. But nothing seemed quite real anymore. Everyone moved, spoke, and looked as though each was part of an elaborately staged play that Mike was watching. In ten minutes the curtain would fall, and the applause could start because it would be all over . . .

"I'm getting real tired of this." Ham Tyler paced like a barely restrained panther, hungry for a kill. "You listening, bitch?"

His sudden shout as he leaned over her made Margie flinch, but she didn't raise her head or respond.

"I'm not known as a patient man, Mrs. Donovan. Ask your ex-husband over there. He'll tell you how ugly I can get. Or maybe you wouldn't believe him. Maybe it's best if I just show you."

Reaching for his empty beer bottle, he slammed it down on the table's edge with a twisting motion. He grabbed Margie by the hair and jerked her head back, holding the bottle's broken end close to her face. "You're a nice-looking woman, Margie. I'd sure hate to ruin such a pretty face, but I've done a lot worse for—"

"For God's sake, Ham!" Julie started forward.

Margie whimpered a little, her terrified eyes focused on the jagged shards, but she made no other sound.

"Lay off, Tyler." Anger pushed its way through Donovan's numbed sense of reality, and he moved toward the shorter man.

"I'm tired of talking to myself," Ham said, holding his ground. "First time we've gotten a little rise outa her—"

"I said, lay *off*!" Careful of his approach, Mike clamped a hand on Ham's arm. "Can't you see what's going on? Diana must have converted her. She's probably been conditioned so she *can't* talk if she's been captured."

"Mike's right, Ham," Julie said more softly. Her face and voice grew strained with the memory of old horrors. "I . . . personally know what it's like to be caught in the grip of that special kind of hell. After Diana's finished with you, you lose control, you feel like a stranger to yourself, and even though you know what's going on around you, you're absolutely powerless to stop it. So leave her alone, okay?"

Tyler looked at her for many seconds, then slowly he lowered the bottle. "Only for you, Doc," he said. "Otherwise she'd be worm food by now."

Mike looked at his ex-wife and felt a sharp pang of grief. First he had lost his son, Sean, to the Visitors, then he had gotten him back briefly—much too briefly—but soon Diana and her damned mind manipulation had stolen him away again. Now the pattern was repeating itself with Margie.

He sensed himself skating toward some thin-iced edge, toward a dark morass of defeat and hopelessness as profound and final as any he'd every experienced since the Visitors had first arrived. What was the point of fighting so hard all the time, when they were going to get you in the end anyway?

As though reading his thoughts, Julie touched his arm for a moment, then she went over to Margie. "Margie, I know what you're feeling." Kneeling by the older woman, she brushed the hair back from her forehead. "Diana converted me once, almost two years ago, and I've never forgotten how horrible it was. You have to understand, Diana will kill you when she's finished with you. You have to keep in mind that she's *not* your friend, that all her words are lies. But we're your friends, we want to *help* you. You have to trust us."

Something seemed to soften in Margie's expression, and she lifted her head and actually looked at Julie.

"But you have to trust us," Julie repeated.

Margie appeared as though she might say something. Her mouth worked soundlessly for a moment, but then her eyes turned dull and her head lowered again.

"It's no good," Ham said, moving back to the table.

Julie sighed and straightened, shaking her head. "There are a number of psychiatrists specializing in PVSS—Post-Visitor Stress Syndrome—these days. Maybe Dr. Akers can recommend someone who's worked with conversion victims."

"Yeah," Donovan said. "Sean's doctor was—"

Margie suddenly leaped out of the chair, knocking the shocked Julie and Mike aside. Julie slipped and fell. Before anyone could react, Marjorie had snatched the small Visitor device left on a nearby table, then shoved the table over at Ham, catching him in the legs.

Moving at almost superhuman speed, she grabbed a half-full pitcher of beer from another table near the door and flung it in their faces; Elias yelped in surprise and dropped the carafe of fresh-brewed coffee, narrowly missing Julie at his feet.

Mike wasn't so lucky. Some of the steaming liquid sloshed onto his right hand and arm, sending white-hot agony blistering through his skin, and he screamed.

As Margie aimed the Visitor device on the front entrance, they heard the locks snap back audibly. As she snatched the door open, Ham Tyler calmly pulled out his lasergun and sighted on her back, his finger tightening on the trigger—

"No—!" Donovan leaped at him, slamming his shoulder and knocking his aim off so that a black, charred-looking rose suddenly bloomed in the wall beside the door. They heard the bang of the outer wrought-iron gate and knew she was gone.

"You stupid son of a bitch!" Ham muttered, pushing past him to go after her, but Mike grabbed his arm.

"Don't hurt her," he said, his voice soft and final.

Jerking his arm free, Ham glared at him, his expression suggesting that he would just as soon use the laser on Donovan as his ex-wife. "You disgust me. You and your half-baked selfish actions under the guise of—"

"I mean it, Ham. Anything happens to her, and I'll come looking for you."

Tyler smiled slightly. On him, the expression looked cold and out of place. "See you around, Gooder."

Chapter 12

Contingency Plans

At ten the following morning, Nathan Bates was an unhappy man. Julie could hear his shouting even in the outer office.

"I don't understand it, Diana. This was supposed to be a routine delivery. You assured me the route was a safe one and that there was nothing to worry about!"

"Dear Nathan. Unforeseen events happen in everyone's life. Surely you, of all people, can appreciate that."

Even through the electronic distortions of the telecommunications system, Diana's voice dripped oiliness. Julie's mouth twisted downward as she poured two cups of coffee, dumping cream and sugar into one. Diana was hard to take at the best of times, but after less than two hours' sleep, Julie found the Visitors' commander of Earth-based forces damn near impossible to stomach.

She could feel the strains from last night around her eyes and in her throat, and the demon in her abdomen had been twisting and coiling restlessly since she had dragged herself out of bed and down to Science Frontiers.

She wished Mike could have stayed with her, even for a couple of hours. But his arm, although not badly burned, was painful, and the codeine he'd taken had made him so drowsy that Elias had taken him home. Besides, Julie knew he probably needed time to think things through.

". . . already paid for them, too," Bates was saying, pounding his desktop for emphasis as she put the black coffee down in front of him. Acknowledging her with a quick glance, he leaned forward toward the screen. "And since Science Frontiers had not accepted delivery on them, their loss would seem to be *your* problem, not ours."

"If you could control that annoying resistance of yours, then neither of us would have these problems," Diana said.

"We're working on that," Bates said tightly. Julie had seldom seen the head of Science Frontiers and Los Angeles's provisional government look so angry, his dour mouth compressed into a thin line, knuckles whitening on the handle of his coffee cup as he took a couple of slow, deliberate swallows. "In the meantime, Diana, I need those power packs."

"Yes, I know. I have already contacted our ship over Buenos Aires and directed them to release the power packs from their own reserve stock rather than subject you to additional delays while we manufacture them here."

Diana's voice was soothing sweetness itself—the voice of the old woman who lured Hansel and Gretel into her gingerbread house, or the evil witch who made Snow White eat the poisoned apple. Julie had to press a hand over her mouth to suppress the sudden, insane urge to giggle.

"And when can we expect them?" Bates asked, slightly mollified.

"Tomorrow afternoon. I will send an escorted shuttlecraft directly to the helipad on the roof of your main building."

"Thank you, Diana. We'll look forward to that. I wish you a good day—"

"Ah, Nathan . . . there is one small thing. Hardly worth mentioning, but I wanted to inform you that there will be a little oceanfront testing tonight. Our troops and vehicles will be moving in and around the coast. It's really nothing to worry about, but you might want to notify the local residents. Humans are so excitable, after all."

Tonight! Julie had to work to keep her expression unchanged as the implications hit her.

Frowning, Bates gestured to Julie to come closer. "Is this what's been rumored to be a wide-scale experiment conducted in local waters?" he asked.

"Hardly 'wide-scale,' Nathan. This is a small . . . water purification project that will no doubt benefit humanity as well as our people. And as you know, those things that are mutually beneficial to our two races can also be highly profitable to Science Frontiers."

"Would you care to enlighten me further concerning this?"

"That would be premature, I think." Julie didn't have to see Diana's face to picture her smug, patronizing expression. "Nathan, don't look so suspicious. I thought you humans loved surprises. Believe me, this one, if it works out, will be worth waiting for. I must run. Give my love to Julie."

Bates stared at the screen for some moments after Diana's image had faded from the screen, his expression thoughtful as he re-formed a paper clip. "Did you hear that?" he asked.

"Yeah." Julie stifled a yawn and feigned indifference. "I wish she'd choke on a mouse and die."

"You look terrible," he said.

"I was at a . . . birthday party last night." She smiled ruefully. "I know I'm moving a little slowly this morning. Guess I drank too much champagne."

"You should take better care of yourself. Of course, I dimly remember what it's like to be young. I used to be that way myself." Bates leaned back in his leather chair, idly twisting the paper clip in his fingers. "So what do you think of this 'little water purification project'?"

"I don't like it—the sound of it, I mean," Julie said. "Do you think they may be onto us? Onto the fact that Science Frontiers is behind the ocean-based red dust experiments?"

"They're onto something." Bates pressed a button on his console. "Mr. Chiang, have some of your men down by the beaches tonight. Check any unusual Visitor activities and report back to me."

Julie bit her lip and pushed her glasses back onto her nose. Once in a very great while, she wished that the resistance and Science Frontiers could work together. Having the resources of Nathan Bates's vast conglomerate at their disposal would have been extremely helpful on several occasions—and this might well be one of them. She couldn't tell Bates what she knew without risking his discovery of her own connection to the hated resistance, however, and her position of trust was too valuable to risk.

Meantime, she had to get to a phone as fast as possible. . . .

*   *   *

"The warehouse operation is proceeding, uh, smoothly and on schedule, Diana." In her laboratory complex aboard the Mother Ship that morning, Bernard fidgeted with the hem of his uniform sleeve. "We, uh, will have sufficient quantities of our red dust by ten o'clock this evening. The distribution in coastal waters can occur anytime after that."

"Excellent, Bernard! I am most appreciative of the efforts you have made on our behalf. I know our Great Leader will also be very pleased."

"Thank you, Diana." He pulled himself up a little straighter, a smile lifting the turned-down corners of his mouth for an instant.

Diana smiled at the botanist and thought he looked tired and in need of some diversion. Perhaps, when this was over, she could express her gratitude in a more personal way.

He was shy and rather thin, but she had certainly had worse. And for him, it would no doubt be the most thrilling—

Barely pausing to knock, Lydia strode into the lab, a folder under one arm. "Security division reports that they have troops standing by to assist with Operation Red Dust this evening, Diana," she said.

"Thank you, Lydia."

"Should we anticipate any trouble from the humans?"

"None. Nathan Bates is a fool, and far more concerned about his profits and losses than anything we might be doing. He doesn't suspect a thing."

Lydia's blue eyes narrowed. "What about the resistance?"

"Dear Lydia, have you forgotten about the little bird I let out of our cage to fly and find their nest and then come chirping back to me? I expect to hear from Marjorie Donovan sometime today. In the meantime, no doubt Mike Donovan and his playmates are so busy plotting uses for the other presents that I sent them, that they will never realize what has happened— until they open the door to their secret hiding place and we are there."

"I must admit, Diana, these little operations of yours have gone much more smoothly than I would have anticipated." Lydia's smile looked plastered to her face.

"Yes, there is a certain elegance about them, isn't there?"

"Certainly more than some of your recent endeavors."

Diana's smile faded, and she felt her crest prickle as venom rose in her mouth. "And certainly better than some of *your* schemes, darling, which proved very costly." She glanced at Bernard, who was tugging furiously at his sleeve, obviously wishing he were somewhere else.

It really was poor form for senior officers to air their personal grievances in front of junior personnel, and she would not lower herself to respond in kind to Lydia's unprofessional remarks.

"Let us return to tonight's operation." Swallowing her venom, Diana smoothed her features into a smile again and moved over to a nearby worktable. A map of Los Angeles and the coastline was spread out on its surface. Various red-marked lines curved through the blue of the Pacific Ocean, whose coastal islands jostled against marked-in Visitorese comments.

"I have studied the local currents and have plotted, in order of preference, the most auspicious spots in which to dump our red dust so that it will diffuse quickly. You will note that the warehouse itself, where we are manufacturing it, is located on one of the possible sites. At worst, we could simply push it off the pier there, although it would spread more slowly than at these other areas." Diana pointed to several spots highlighted in green.

"And how do you intend to transport the dust to those other places?" Lydia asked. "It is highly volatile outside of the water, Bernard said. I hope you aren't planning to use our own vehicles—"

"Of course not, Lydia. Especially when there are always humans who are willing to do things in exchange for money. Small boats can be used to reach the desired distribution points, provided the cargo is loaded and unloaded very carefully. Of course, the risks are great. . . ." She shrugged. "That's why I have asked Bernard to make extra quantities."

Actually, she hadn't, and the botanist blinked at her. "We, uh, were only planning to have a ton or so in reserve, Diana," he said, reaching for his sleeve again.

"That may not be sufficient. Bernard, you should return to the warehouse at once to personally oversee the final operations and the manufacture of additional quantities, which we will hold as needed. We will join you later this evening."

Bernard had to suppress a sigh. "Yes, Diana. At once."

Moving slowly, Willie pulled the old and hated uniform out of the back corner of his closet, where he had stuffed it over a year ago. He had wanted to throw it away then, but Elias had stopped him, saying, "It might come in handy someday. You never know."

It still fit, although it was a bit snug around the waist—that was the fault of Miranda and her cheese enchiladas, and Henri, the Club Creole's wonderful French chef, who knew how to prepare some fine vegetable meals.

He had to sit on his narrow bed to wrestle on the stiff black boots, then he fastened the belt and placed the cap on his head. His shoulders unconsciously straightened as he faced the mirror. Gazing at his reflection, he remembered the combined excitement and dread he'd felt when he had learned he'd been chosen to be among the enlisted personnel accompanying the first ships to Earth.

Even though he'd been drafted, there had still been good moments for him while wearing this uniform—the parades, the honors, children coming up to rub his crest, then later gaze wide-eyed at his human appearance. The Great Leader himself had come to wish them well, giving a stirring, emotional speech about how they were all ambassadors for their world, going forth to meet and make new friends across the stars.

How real it had seemed then, and how false it had turned out to be, when he'd discovered the real reason behind their visit to Earth.

Willie turned away from the mirror, his expression grim as he headed for the door.

"You look real official, Willie," Elias said, leaning back against the bar in the Club Creole. In front of him, the early afternoon lunch crowd laughed, talked, and clinked silverware against china—a smaller group than usual, since the Visitors had been banned from the club. He was wearing his "jive 'n' slide" suit, as he called it, the one he put on to impress bankers, creditors, and an occasional young woman.

"You look . . . most elegant, Elias," Willie said, tugging self-consciously at his belt.

"Thanks. I hope this works. Come on." Picking up several large paper-wrapped bundles, Elias led the way to the front and his waiting car.

"What did Julie say when she called?" Willie asked, trying to see over the packages he was also balancing in his arms.

"Diana's apparently going to move on her Operation Red

Dust sometime *tonight*. Which is why we've got to get down to the legation to see if we can find anything more specific about the when and where."

Miranda helped them load the bundles into the trunk of Elias's car. "You two be careful," she said, giving each of them a quick kiss. "I'll hold the fort until you return."

"There is no armed encampment here, Miranda." Willie looked about in confusion. "And how would you pick one up?"

Elias grinned. "Come on, Willie. It's just another one of our quaint human expressions. I'll explain it to you in the car."

Willie could feel excitement as tiny spasms moved up and down his spine and crest. Not particularly athletic nor skilled in the use of weapons, he had seldom been included in any actual resistance operations. Here was his chance to do something more than hunt for bandages or pour coffee or cognac following a raid.

"Let me do most of the talking," Elias advised as they swung into the wide horseshoe drive of the Visitor legation fifteen minutes later.

"Good afternoon," said the guard in Visitor's uniform, stepping out of the gatehouse. "May I help you?"

"I'm Elias Taylor, owner of the Club Creole, and this is . . . Benjamin. I wanted to make my personal apologies to Diana and my many fine Visitor friends from the legation who patronize my humble establishment for the unfortunate incident that occurred outside the club last night."

"I'm afraid Diana will not be available to receive guests this afternoon. Perhaps if you come back tomorrow . . ."

"Oh, but surely I could speak to someone. I feel terrible about having to close my club to the Visitors, and I'm anxious to make some amends. You see, I have small gifts, humble tokens of my goodwill, to give all my friends here." Slowly, Elias reached into the bundle beside him on the seat and held up a blue Club Creole shirt.

As they had hoped, the Visitor's eyes lit up hungrily. The shirts had become real status items among humans and Visitors alike. "Why, I think this one would fit you just fine."

"I'll see whether someone else might be able to see you," the guard said, reaching for the shirt with one hand and a phone with the other. "You can park your car in the lot over there."

" 'Benjamin'?" Willie asked as they got out and retrieved the rest of the packages.

"It was my brother's name. Don't do anything to disgrace it."

"May I see your passes, please?" The Visitor guard at the desk inside the entrance was the picture of politeness but hardly warmth.

"Oh, this is a very informal visit. I'm Elias Taylor. . . ."

Thirty seconds later, Elias was winking and dropping a yellow shirt on the guard's desk. Grinning, the Visitor held it up to his chest as they walked past. "Check with Malcolm at the security office for your pass," he called after them. "Tell him George at the front desk okayed it."

"Thanks a lot, my man."

Outside Malcolm's office, a near riot ensued as legation employees clustered eagerly around Elias, seeking his apologies—and his shirts.

"Yes, step right up here, folks, for your free Club Creole sport shirts." Placing his and Willie's packages on a nearby desk, Elias began pulling the shirts out one at a time. "Two of my best customers got shot the other night right outside the club door. So to protect all of you, my friends, I'm declaring the place off limits until Nathan Bates can clean up the area and it'll be safe again. I sure miss my favorite customers. . . . Here you are, sir. A blue one, goes with your eyes. . . . No, I think you're an extra-large. . . ."

Amid the commotion of Visitors grabbing for and exclaiming over the shirts, Willie sidled away and slipped around a corner.

The nearest office was deserted—no doubt its occupants had run down the hallway to get their own shirts—but the computer terminal screen glowed ready.

Seating himself, Willie frowned behind his dark Visitor glasses as he tried to recall the general-entry sequence. His nervous fingers touched a couple of wrong controls, and he had to try several times before he managed to complete a successful log-in to the system.

Then the screen was flashing the symbols in Visitorese requesting his personal identification code.

Depending on the level of security for this particular terminal, a mistake here could set off alarms. Holding his breath, Willie carefully tapped in Bernard's name, position title, and access codes—the things he'd drunkenly babbled the other night at the Club Creole.

To Willie's vast relief, the screen flashed a series of questions about the area of inquiry and whether he wanted a new or existing file. Finally he tapped in the Visitorese translation for Operation Red Dust, and figures began scrolling before his eager eyes. The secret operation was a definite go. Two units of ground personnel and twelve armored vehicles were to be deployed at 0100 hours that night, and the location was a warehouse and dock near the—

"Hey!" A pink sport shirt in one hand, a Visitor in officer's insignia was pushing the door open with the other and striding toward him, expression grim. "Who the hell are you and what are you doing here?"

Chapter 13

Win Some, Lose Some

Willie sagged forward, thumping his head on the control console at the same instant as his thumb sent the information on the screen into electronic oblivion. In his year as a bartender, he had observed a number of drunken humans and Visitors. Now he hoped desperately that he could pull off a creditable imitation of a drunk himself.

"I said, who are you?" Grabbing the collar of his uniform, the officer roughly jerked him upright.

Willie belched gently, then grinned widely up at the man, making no attempt to straighten his glasses, which had been knocked askew. "Bernar'," he said, adding the title and codes he'd entered into the computer and slurring the words. "I've been working on special 'signment for Diana, an' I've been workin' *so* hard, have t' check our progress ev'ry minute. . . ."

"Back to your quarters and sober up, Bernard," the officer ordered, shoving him toward the door. "Or else you'll find yourself with a special assignment in a detention cell. Now get out."

"Yessir." Saluting sloppily, Willie staggered out the door and down the hallway, hearing the officer follow him.

"Oh, Benjamin, there you are." Hastily, Elias grabbed up his few remaining shirts and took Willie's arm. "Come on. Honestly," he rolled his eyes at the Visitor officer, "I keep telling him to lay off the stuff. He can't hold it worth shit."

The Visitor officer frowned, suddenly alert. "He said his name was Bernard."

"Even *he* can't remember sometimes, once he's been hitting the bottle. His assigned name's the first thing to go. It's really sad. He was a decent fellow, then he started hanging around the club all the time. Tell you what. I'll take him back with me for the afternoon and let him sober up. Least I can do, seeing it was my place got him this way." As he spoke, Elias herded Willie through the lobby and out into the hot afternoon sunshine. He turned at the last moment. "And thank you so much for your understanding, sir. Here's one for you—mint green, just your size."

"I . . . am afraid I had to unhonor your brother's name, Elias," Willie said, staring unhappily at the dashboard once they were in the car and pulling away from the legation. "He was most certainly not a drunk." He sighed. His one most important assignment, and he had not been able to complete it. He deserved to die in parched solitude for his incompetence.

"Willie, my man, you were brilliant!" Elias clapped a hand on his shoulder as he eased the car onto Fourth Street, heading back toward the club. "My brother, Benjamin, would have laughed, and he would've been proud of you, too. After all, you did it in the name of the resistance."

"So we know everything about this defoliation operation tonight, except exactly where it's going to be." From his perch on the edge of one of the desks downstairs in the Club Creole, Mike Donovan looked across the room. "Is that right, Willie?"

"That is correct." Still wearing his Visitor uniform, Willie nodded.

"And that knowledge cost plenty." Elias made a face over his ledger and adding machine. "All out of the goodness of my heart, not to mention the goodness of my wallet. Let's see . . . forty-three shirts at fifteen ninety-five each. My God, I've sacrificed all but the shirt off my own back to this resistance. I've probably depressed the market for a while, too. Maybe I can declare it as a business loss."

"We all appreciate what you've done, Elias," Julie said a little impatiently. It was almost five in the afternoon, and she had had a terrible day working on the computer shutdown procedures. She hadn't had time for lunch—even if her stomach would have allowed her any—and even had trouble getting away from Science Frontiers and Nathan Bates long enough to make the quick phone call which had sent Elias and Willie to the legation. Finally she'd announced bluntly that she was taking sick leave and going home—only she'd come straight here, even though she felt the only proper place for her was bed.

"The thing is, now how do we find out exactly where the drop-off point is?" Donovan asked. "There are a lot of piers and warehouses out there, and—"

"No luck finding the former Mrs. Donovan," Ham Tyler said tersely as he strode in from the back entrance. "Even my own underground contacts, which are a hell of a lot better than yours, report no sign of her. It's like the ground swallowed her up whole."

"Or the Visitors did," Robin muttered from the couch, glancing quickly away from Mike's pained look and Elizabeth's more shadowed one.

"We should be so lucky." Dropping his jacket and holster over the sagging easy chair, Ham poured himself a cup of the thick sludge that passed for coffee in the resistance. "Because if she's gotten to Madam Chief Scaly alive and with the location of this place, then we can all kiss our Mickey Mouse clubhouse here good-bye, thanks to Gooder and his misplaced loyalties."

"You're out of line, Tyler." Donovan's voice was suddenly low and dangerous.

"Not as much as you were. Because your ex can also blow Julie's cover to hell and gone. I bet Nathan Bates'd be real interested in her moonlighting, wouldn't he? But of course Julie was the last thing on your mind when you came charging to the rescue."

Mike stood, fists clenched at his sides. "I said that's *enough*. Maybe *you* think wholesale slaughter is a great way to solve problems, but—"

"Tell me, Gooder, was she worth it?"

Mike's face darkened. "You're gonna be sorry you—"

"Stop it," Julie snapped, stepping between them. "We don't have time for this playground macho crap. There's a lot more at stake here, like the lives of all the people along the West Coast. So shut up, Tyler, and Mike, sit down."

Mike and Ham locked glares for a few moments longer, then reluctantly sat down.

"Why are people's lives in danger, Julie?" Robin asked.

"The Visitors' red dust is supposed to kill all the seaweed. That'll wreck the food chain, killing all the fish, and eventually the stuff might filter through to our drinking water. We don't know whether it's also poisonous to human beings, and I'll bet Diana hasn't spent a lot of time worrying about that."

"So we have to find out where the dumping site is going to be, and fast." Kyle, silent up to this time, raised his head, shifting his position to favor his still-bandaged knee.

"Can we get hold of the resistance network reports of Visitor movements up and down the coastline, maybe analyze the patterns over the past ten days or so?" Mike asked.

"Within the next six hours?" Ham shook his head. "No way."

Elizabeth, seated next to her mother on the couch, mentally withdrew from the argument as it escalated. It was a simple trick, one she'd taught herself from her days on the Mother Ship when Diana had been tutoring her and trying to fill her with violent, hating notions. There had always been so many arguments in her life. Didn't people ever get tired of shouting, being angry with one another all the time?

She stole a glance at Robin, who was leaning forward, listening intently to the words being exchanged. Things had been awkward and strained between them since last night, when Elizabeth had realized she was a living symbol of hate for her own mother. It wasn't her fault, of course, but that didn't make it any less true.

She could sense the emotional climate among the people present growing heated again and tinged with desperation. She bit her lip as she got a sudden, sharp image of the red dust of her dreams, of these same people clutching their throats, dying as the red wave washed over them, drowning them—

Stifling a gasp, Elizabeth blinked furiously, her gaze seeking something soothing, real. On the wall above Mike's head, there was a faded picture of an old sailing schooner riding high and proud on the sunlit sea, and she fixed on the image gratefully, enjoying the cool blueness of sea and sky.

She could almost feel the warmth of the sun, the salt-tangy breezes whipping her hair back as she gazed at the ship's prow, watching it turn leeward; and then California's coastline came into view. The air was turning pink with twilight, then dark as lights were blinking on around the suddenly modern shoreline.

And she was closer, a tiny ship herself, or a bird skimming low over the night waters toward the waterfront area, where fishing and other commercial boats jostled one another next to piers and low, weather-beaten buildings of various sizes.

She saw two Visitors come out of a warehouse bearing the legend "PRENTISS & LONG SHIPPING LTD." in large, fading white letters along its side. They were carrying what looked like a barrel between them. Then Diana stepped out, following from a safe distance, directing them to move with care as they carried their container down nearby steps to a small powerboat bobbing in the tide. . . .

. . . and a crack in the barrel opened up, spilling a little red dust onto the wooden stairs and pilings, and the dust swirled, grew into a red cloud that turned larger, darker, and she screamed—

"Elizabeth!" Her mother had grasped her shoulders, and her eyes were wide and frightened. "Honey, are you all right?"

Bewildered, she glanced around to see that everyone was silent, staring at her with concerned expressions. "I . . . I saw where they are," she said softly. "Or where they're *going* to be." Feeling small and drained of energy, she described her vision.

"Sounds like Pier Number Nine near Long Beach," Ham muttered almost to himself. "But maybe she remembers it from passing by."

"We've been on a lot of motorcycle rides together," Kyle said, looking over at her. "But I've never taken her around *that* part of town."

"I'm glad to hear that," said Robin, giving him a look.

"She could've seen it on TV or in a movie somewhere."

"It's real, Mr. Tyler," Elizabeth insisted, annoyed at his brusque, patronizing attitude. "And we've got to stop it. It's a horrible poison—it holds death for thousands of people."

Ham shook his head, his expression doubtful. "I can't put much stock in this hocus-pocus of yours, honey. It's all very well for card tricks and parlor games with Ouija boards, but we're talking a serious operation with a lot at stake. If you're imagining this whole thing, then—"

"I'm not." The firmness in her tone surprised everyone.

"I believe you, Elizabeth." Julie smiled.

"Seems to me we don't have much choice," Mike said.

"Certainly no better alternative, and Elizabeth's, uh, track record has been pretty impressive about other things."

"Do we put it to a vote?" Elias asked, looking around. "I'm with Elizabeth."

"I don't think it's necessary," Julie said, rising. "How about you, Ham?"

"Sentiment always wins over logic in this group." Tyler shrugged. "ESP is just the next step, I guess. Okay, let's mobilize. We meet at ten P.M. in the Safeway parking lot—you all know the one. Standard night gear and masks. Those of you with scaly weapons make sure you get a fresh power pack."

"Everybody try to get some rest, okay?" Julie said as people got up to leave.

Jacket collar up around her neck and wearing sunglasses, Marjorie Donovan slumped into the park bench in Griffith Park, exhausted. It was nearly eight-thirty in the evening, and shadows were growing very long and blue along the walkway, but she felt better behind the sunglasses, safer somehow, as though she could hide from the realities of her situation—and herself.

Her head ached dully, and her stomach spasmed from lack of food. Frowning, she tried to remember her last meal. Absently, she ran a hand along her grimy cheek, her fingertips tracing the haggard lines she knew were there from conflict and lack of sleep.

She was aware that she had been converted. That was one of Diana's cruel little touches, to ensure that her victims remained fully alert and aware of what was happening to them. ("Why, it makes you much more believable in your role, my dear," she had said. "Who would trust a Marjorie Donovan with a glassy look in her eyes, or saliva drooling down her chin?")

But how infinitely better it would be to be ignorant, or unconscious, when your body started to act in ways independent of your will, your mouth to say things you didn't feel . . . presenting a perfect, traitorous appearance while you watched, a mere spectator, trapped and helpless within your own body.

Earlier, in one of the public rest rooms at the observatory, Margie had attempted suicide. Her wrist still ached from the small, deep cut she'd managed to inflict on herself, but Diana had anticipated that, too. "Darling, don't think suicide is the answer—it isn't," she had warned. Sure enough, as the initial pain had hit her, Marjorie's right hand had trembled uncontrollably, causing her to drop the small penknife onto the floor beside the sink, then making attempts to retrieve it impossible.

So here she sat in the cooling evening, hunched into herself, trying not to think about the people in the L.A. resistance whom she had met and come to care for—whom she had also been conditioned to seek out, betray, and thus destroy.

Especially Mike Donovan.

A lump filled her throat, and the nearby street lamp blurred as tears welled up behind her half-closed eyes. She had fallen in love with Mike all over again, and this time they weren't starry-eyed twenty-year-olds still trying to find themselves, as well as knowledge, on the UCLA campus. He had changed, grown more thoughtful, understanding, considerate.

She had picked up from Diana and Lydia's conversations that the conversion process *wasn't* totally infallible. And Julie had told her that you could fight it if you had sufficient willpower. Certainly she had managed so far, wandering the L.A. streets and sidewalks throughout this unending day, trying to sort through the confusion of her feelings rather than going straight to Diana with her knowledge of the resistance headquarters and its activities. Maybe if she just sat here long enough, then she could regain herself. . . .

Slouching deeper into the park bench, she shoved her hands into the pockets of her jacket—and her fingers brushed against the Visitor device that she had used to locate and enter the secret room in the Club Creole. A tingling shiver ran up her arm, and she jerked her left hand back as though stung.

Then, resolutely, she closed her fingers over it again and drew it out, turning it over to examine it under the streetlight's glow. It was rather plain, really—a small gray box with a few pressure points on it marked with red Visitorese characters across its surface—and she didn't know how it worked, only that it did. What she did know was that it was also a symbol for the bondage of her spirit.

Her mouth tightening, Margie stood and raised her hand over her head to fling the device into the darkness—and then she spotted the Visitor ground vehicle parked on the roadway, perhaps fifty feet in front of her. Two guards were lounging against the side of the vehicle. One of them was smoking a cigarette, and its tiny red light as he gestured seemed to become a lantern beckoning her to safety.

She clamped a hand over her mouth to stifle the small groan that erupted from her throat. Backing away a few steps, she sought something, anything that she could focus on besides that small, fatal light. She slammed the device in her hand into the side of her leg, once, twice, but even pain couldn't keep her from looking at the Visitors nor stop her body from slowly turning, her legs from making the steps toward them.

"Yes?" The smoker glanced up indifferently at her approach.

"I'm Mrs. Marjorie Donovan. The former wife of Mike Donovan, the resistance leader."

"Is that so?" The other laughed shortly and pushed his cap back on his head. "Well, I'm Kermit the Frog, the beloved Muppet leader. Pleased to meet you. Now, why don't you—?"

"I'm working for Diana on a special top-secret mission," Marjorie said, holding the device out to them. "I need to be taken to her at once."

"This is all fun, lady, but—"

"Look, Keith!" The other touched his arm and pointed at the symbols scrawled across it. "It's genuine. See, there's Diana's special priority self-code inscribed right there."

The one called Keith swallowed, crushed his cigarette under the heel of his boot, then snapped to attention. "Right this way, please, Mrs. Donovan," he said, helping her into the ground vehicle's cab.

As the vehicle cut a tight U-turn in the deserted park street and whispered away, Marjorie sat between the two Visitors, her face impassive, except for the single tear which escaped to trickle down her cheek.

Chapter 14

Battle Readiness

That evening in Kyle's living room, Robin glanced over at Elizabeth and knew her daughter was close to tears.

That is, as close as she could get, since Elizabeth did not have tear ducts. The tight set of her mouth and the large, hurt look in her eyes spoke eloquently enough of her unhappiness, however.

"I want to come, Mother," she repeated.

"And we appreciate your willingness to help, honey, we really do." Robin pushed impatiently at a strand of hair that refused to go under her dark blue ski mask. "But we need you here to help . . . when we get back."

She almost said what she was thinking: ". . . to help Miranda with the wounded." It wouldn't be the first time that Kyle's house had been used as a makeshift hospital for members of the resistance.

"You're always leaving me behind," Elizabeth said. "To wait . . . and worry."

"This isn't a trip to the beach," Kyle said shortly, limping slightly as he carried several laserguns and rifles over to the pile of supplies on the couch. "You could be hurt."

"We've discussed all this before. Being alive means you take risks of being hurt sometimes." Elizabeth turned her wide, intense blue eyes on him. "Or else you're not truly alive—just a china doll put on a shelf somewhere to be admired but never touched."

"Wait a minute." He turned around to gently grasp her by

173

the shoulders. "There's the difference between 'risk' and 'foolhardiness,' which maybe we haven't discussed. Your mother and I know how to use those weapons over there on the couch—you don't. This will be dangerous any way you slice it; without a gun, well, it's craziness to even consider it."

"I . . . have ways of protecting myself."

Robin frowned. She knew her daughter hated calling attention to her differences. "Honey, you know that you don't have a lot of control over your abilities yet. And sometimes they don't work at all. You can't count on that to keep you safe."

"Your knee is still hurt," Elizabeth said, looking up at Kyle again. "That makes it craziness for *you* to be involved."

"It's not that bad." Kyle's mouth twitched in irritation as he released her and shrugged into his black sweater.

"You don't understand. Mother, I *have* to go."

"The answer is no, Elizabeth." Robin found it hard to put maternal firmness in her voice when speaking to this young woman who looked her own age, but Elizabeth was her daughter, in need of her best guidance. Remembering how her mother used to address her and her sisters, she made her tone and expression as severe as possible. "Period. End of discussion."

Elizabeth bit her lip, her expression tragic. Without another word, she turned and fled toward her bedroom.

"Eighteen going on eight." Robin sighed and sat down in the easy chair. "Honestly, I do the best I can, but I don't understand her sometimes."

Kyle smiled and laid a sympathetic arm on her shoulder, a gesture which sent a warm, tingly feeling though her. "You sound like every parent who ever walked this earth. It's easy to forget how special she is—and in some ways, very different. She's only eighteen *months* old, after all."

"You're right." Reluctantly, she drew away from him. "I'd better talk to her before we go."

Elizabeth was lying on her bed, her gaze fixed on a trigonometry book.

"I'm glad one of us will pass her GED," Robin said, attempting a smile as she sat down on the bed.

"It is the only thing I guess I'm good for." Her daughter continued working on a problem and wouldn't look at her.

"Elizabeth, you know that's not so." Robin reached out to

brush her hair back, but Elizabeth jerked out of her reach. "It's just that you're so special to us—to me. I don't want anything to happen to you."

"Because I am the Starchild? The bridge linking Visitors and humans, the hope for peace between the two species?" The cold resignation in her voice made Robin wince.

"Because you're all I've got left." Robin swallowed against the pain of still-raw memories. "My mother and father were killed by the Visitors, my sisters had to be sent away. . . ."

"Yes, and every time you look at me, I'm a constant reminder of what my father did to you—and what you did to him."

There was no reply to that, nor to the alien remoteness that had settled into Elizabeth's eyes. "I'll . . . see you later," Robin said, feeling very tired as she rose and moved toward the door.

"Mother—be careful." Elizabeth's voice was low, almost a whisper.

"Dammit!" Maggie Blodgett jerked her hand away as hot coffee sloshed over her shaking fingers. The mug slipped from her grasp and smashed onto the linoleum, sending clay fragments and brown puddles everywhere.

Druid began yapping and dancing around her feet. "Shut up, you," she muttered, pushing him away as she bent to pick up the pieces and search for a sponge in the lower cabinet.

"You destroying my kitchen, woman?" Chris Faber called from the bedroom.

She scowled in his general direction. Damn him anyway! He sounded positively cheerful about this whole operation—more like a kid looking forward to a trip to Disneyland or Knott's Berry Farm than somebody facing what could well be the end of the line for him and/or the others he cared about.

Hell, she thought, dragging out paper towels to mop furiously at the mess after giving up on finding a sponge. *The end of the line—buying the farm—the Big One. We can't even name death directly, let alone face it without a lot of cute euphemisms to cover how scared shitless we are by its prospect.*

"Mag, did we do a load of underwear? I can't find any clean shorts."

She bit her lip, hoping the sharp little pain would drive back the tears suddenly threatening behind her eyelashes. "For God's sake, Chris, you're not helpless. Look in your bureau drawer."

"Ain't none in there."

"Then it's all in the laundry hamper."

"No clean drawers?" Big, naked, and glistening from his shower, Chris appeared in the doorway, his face a study in put-on tragedy. "Hon, a man can't die or go to the hospital in dirty underwear! My grandma, God rest her soul, used to tell me—"

"Faber, *screw* you and your grandma!" Maggie's pent-up feelings of anger and frustration wouldn't be ignored any longer; they boiled up in her like a geyser, and she felt as though she were drowning as she viciously shoved the coffee-stained paper towels into the trash can.

Chris felt as though he'd been slapped in the face, scarcely feeling the cool night air on his wet skin as he stood there, staring at the tall woman with the honey-gold hair as she rushed around like a madwoman, cleaning furiously, scrubbing everything within reach. "Maggie, what's wrong?" he finally managed.

"Everything. You, the world."

"What is this? Nerves? Want to trade some jokes?"

"Oh, sure! Here we go again with the jokes. You cracking one-liners about being hurt or dying, as if it's no big deal, like we're going on a Sunday school picnic. When you know damn well that *this* time you may run into something worse than temporary blindness."

He sighed. "Maggie, I laugh to keep from crying—or from thinking about it a whole lot."

"Well, I can't *help* but think about it. About how I'm going to have to watch you charging down the hill tonight, lasergun blasting, playing hero once again." She looked down at the floor. "I care about you, Chris, and I might be starting to care too much. Loving like that scares me, because I also cared for a couple of other heroes not so long ago, and they're dead now."

Her words caught him hard and sharp in his throat, and he stood looking at her, blinking. Nobody had ever said they cared about him, not since his grandmother had died when he was nine years old—not his mother, who had somehow lost her way on a trip to the grocery store when Chris was three and had never come back, not his father, who had subsequently lost himself in another way, in bottles of cheap gin, and not the older sister who'd run away at sixteen with a Marine—no one.

Through his brief enlistment in the Navy, to his years involved in covert operations with Ham Tyler, there had been good times and bad, some laughs, a few women, but no one who had really *cared*.

"How about you?" He had to clear his throat to get past the sudden roughness in his voice. "You march around slinging bombs and rifles to make lizard meat out of those scaly bastards too, and I'll get to watch *you* put it on the line again tonight. Don't think," he took a deep breath, "that you've got any exclusive rights to words like 'caring' and 'love'."

"Oh, Chris . . ." Turning, she buried her face in his massive chest. "What a screwed-up world this is now."

"Yeah, I remember when the biggest threat to life and limb around here was the freeways." He held her tightly for several minutes, resting his cheek on the top of her head.

Finally she stirred and moved away, plucked a paper napkin out of the holder on the kitchen table and blew her nose. "I think maybe the worst thing the Visitors took away from us is time, a sense of the future beyond the next day or two. It's hard to think ahead anymore. It's hard to let yourself feel."

He turned her face up to his, his big hand cupping her chin firmly. "Maggie, I'm new at all of this. But I've seen some places in the world, even before the lizards came, where all people had to make their lives even remotely worth living was how much they cared for each other. No matter how hard it is, we can't let them make us forget that we're human, or then they've really won."

She took a long, shaky breath. "You're pretty smart, Faber, and don't let anybody tell you you're not. So what are we going to do? Just keep telling Visitor jokes and ducking, I guess."

"And spend as much time as we can making up for any time we don't have together." He grinned. "Like tonight—*after* this little cleanup campaign."

"Ever the optimist," she said, and pulled his head down to kiss him. "You're on."

Mike Donovan stared gloomily at the black turtleneck, jeans, and ski mask laid out on his bed. How many times did this make now that he had put on these or similar clothes in preparation for anti-Visitor action? Forty? Fifty?

Moving like an old, tired ghost, he picked up his jeans, remembering how he used to feel when getting ready to cover a hot news story—excited, eager, practically throwing on his clothes to race out in time to catch a taxi or plane, whatever would get him to the best vantage point quickly. Once his best friend and soundman, Tony Leonetti, had had to hiss at him to zip his fly as they trotted after the latest Nobel Peace Prize winner.

Now he dressed slowly, reluctantly. Tony had been dead for over two years now, killed by the Visitors, and these days his life was always the same—more surveillance, more skulking, more weary raids. Maybe Denise Daltrey was right, maybe it *was* someone else's turn to carry on. He was growing convinced that he did deserve a rest from the unending circus of death and destruction. With the Visitors, there were never any winners and losers, only which side lost less in a particular round. And you couldn't always tell who was on your side these days. . . .

Worst of all, lately there hadn't been anyone he could talk to, share his frustrations about the resistance with. Julie seemed so far away, almost as though there had never been anything between them. It had been weeks since he'd held her, felt her small body smooth against his own, heard her softly whispered endearments as he loved her.

But even more than a sexual impulse, right at this moment he wanted to hear her cheerful, calm voice, to give and receive some reassurance that everything would be okay between them—there probably wouldn't be time later. Pulling on his sweater, he leaned over the bed to pick up the phone, punching up her number.

A busy signal pulsed maddeningly against his ear.

Angrily, Mike slammed the receiver back in its cradle again. She was probably talking to Nathan Bates again—Mr. Slick himself, the richest and most powerful man in L.A. Donovan knew her boss had started making a habit of calling Julie at home, even late into the evening—she was, after all, very important to the "Science" part of Science Frontiers. Mike only hoped that science was the extent of Bates's interest—but he knew, from the times he'd watched Bates with Julie, that it wasn't. . . .

The hell with it, he thought, reaching for his gun.

* * *

Julie frowned into the phone as though she could will the busy signal away. "Damn," she muttered, going into the kitchen for a Coke. When she returned, she redialed, brightening a bit when it rang, but after seven rings, she had to admit he wasn't there and hung up slowly.

Maybe Majorie Donovan had been calling her ex-husband to say she'd thought it over, was going to turn herself in and get help to conquer the effects of her conversion, but only if he would agree to another try at marriage again, because that was the only thing worth living for, to her.

Biting her lip, Julie turned away from the phone and went slowly back to her closet to rummage for the old black sweat shirt she'd stuffed somewhere way in back. Her imagination was much too active for her own good tonight—along with her stomach. Her spasms were in rare form this evening, beating a soundless rhythm in her belly, almost like an inner metronome. She was glad that she had finally made an appointment at the clinic to see Doc Akers. For better or worse, she should know by tomorrow afternoon what was wrong with her.

Julie allowed herself a rueful smile at the optimism implied in her calm anticipation of a visit to the doctor tomorrow, following tonight's operation. But sometimes hope was all she had to go on, especially when the evidence tended to favor the opposite viewpoint.

Such as, how much hope did she still have for her relationship with Michael Donovan?

The question nagged at her as she shrugged into her sweat shirt and pinned her blond hair back into a bun.

Willie cast a longing glance at the blender behind the Club Creole's bar, but made no move toward it. Nervous excitement made his crest twitch beneath his wig, and he wished he could tear it off to scratch his head directly. Instead, he rubbed the spot as best he could and watched as Ham came in through the kitchen doors with an armful of weapons.

"Okay, kids, choose your favorite toys," he said, dumping the laserguns, Uzis, and ammunition onto the bar.

"Hey, watch it! That's real inlaid oak you're gouging dents in!" Elias scowled as he jammed a ski cap onto his head. He was already in a bad mood, Willie knew, from having to shut down the club early this morning under the guise of "electrical problems"—or so said the small sign hung on the door next to the one that said CLOSED.

Willie pushed at the sleeve of the dark-colored sweater Elias had lent him—it was too long in the arms. Once again, he was being included in a special resistance mission (Elias had said they needed everyone they could spare), and, he had to admit, once again he was scared.

Not of dying. To die—that was not such a terrible thing. Assuming a good and worthwhile life—and Willie had done his best, especially under the circumstances here on Earth—his life-essence would be pulled back to the Place of Beginnings on his home world. There it would lie to bask in the blue-white warmth of Sirius while absorbing all the wisdom of the sands in the state of *preta-na-ma*—peace—forever. . . .

No, death was not the worst thing. Rather, it was the fear that he might fail in his responsibility for the lives of others, that he might live to know that people who were important to him had died because of his mistakes.

"Here, Willie, I will help you." Miranda was suddenly at his side, rolling up his sleeves with quick, efficient motions. "There . . . now you are a fine-looking member of the resistance."

She would be leaving after them to join Elizabeth at Kyle's house. Although she was good with an Uzi or M-16, her skills as a nurse might prove even more useful later on, she had said. Willie managed only a weak smile at her before Elias and Ham began picking up their weapons and commando jackets. "Come on, Willie, let's go," Ham said. "You can kiss the lady when you get back."

Picking up his lasergun, Willie stuck it in his belt the way he had seen a TV star do it, and followed the others out to the waiting car.

From the front porch of Kyle's house, Elizabeth heard the engine of the Yamaha rev up several times, then saw the motorcycle roar out of the garage and down the driveway. Robin, perched on the seat behind Kyle, lifted her hand in a quick wave, then they were out of sight, the cool evening fading into silence again.

Slowly, Elizabeth walked down the steps, the toe of her sneaker kicking irritably at a dried leaf. Fear, deep and disquieting, lurked within her and was growing. When she had retreated to her room to study, as her mother and Kyle completed their preparations for tonight's operation, she found she hadn't been able to concentrate. The diagrams and equations of her trigonometry book had kept fading before her eyes, turning into a dull-red, dusty curtain of death. . . .

Reluctantly, she reached up to close the garage door, and her glance caught a small gleam way in one corner. The outside light was reflecting off the handlebars of Kyle's old Kawasaki.

She walked slowly toward it, her heartbeat quickening. The sleek black motorcycle was clean and well oiled since Kyle had worked on it last week. This was the bike he had used to teach her to ride, and she could almost feel the powerful little engine vibrating under her arms and legs again, the wind tearing at her hair and face as she rode, daring the night to catch her.

She looked down at the bike, and the knowledge, the certainty that tonight she *had* to be with her mother and the others she loved grew until it pushed all lesser realities aside.

She needed the ignition key. But Kyle kept all his keys in a big metal clip fastened to his belt.

Straddling the saddle, she stared down at the ignition slot, focusing her mind, her energies, imagining a tiny hand made of electricity that could reach in, just so—

The lock turned, she pressed the starter button, and the motorcycle coughed and then rumbled into life. Releasing the kickstand, she put the Kawasaki in gear, eased the throttle open, and went speeding out into the darkness.

Chapter 15

Night Moves

Shifting the lasergun at his side to a more comfortable position, Mike Donovan crouched behind the rusted trash barrel. He glanced back to count the dark shapes of Ham, Robin, Chris, Julie, Elias, Willie, Maggie, and Kyle as they skulked, one by one, along the wall of the waterfront warehouse to come up silently behind him.

From this vantage point, he could see the sprawling piers, derricks, and buildings that curved along this section of the waterfront not too far from Los Angeles harbor. The three-quarters moon was high and bright over the Pacific, casting its pale gleam down on the outlines of ships and cranes.

As the sea-fresh air caught in his nostrils and tugged at his ski cap, Donovan thought briefly about San Pedro less than a mile behind him, about the nice little house he, Margie, and Sean used to share. . . .

With an effort, he dragged his gaze and thoughts back to the present. Over at the next pier, fierce incandescent lights pushed back the darkness, revealing a virtual lizard hive of activity. He leaned forward as far as he dared, past the concealing barrel, to adjust the small pair of binoculars he was carrying.

Uniformed Visitors, forty or fifty at least, moved purposefully around the warehouse near the end of the pier, where light spilled out in a harsh rectangle from the open door onto the weather-beaten boards. In groups of two, many of them were carefully carrying what looked like old-fashioned wooden barrels between them out of the building to a conveyor belt next to it. In a neat and well-spaced row, the barrels moved slowly along to more Visitors waiting near the end of the belt, which actually protruded well out over the water. There, the barrels were gingerly lifted off and set down.

Periodically, someone at the end nearest the water would blow a whistle, the belt would stop, and the barrels accumulated at the end of the pier would be carried down some steps and out of sight—probably to a lower dock and one or more waiting boats, Mike reflected.

"Let me take a look, Gooder," Ham said, reaching for the binoculars. After a couple of seconds, he grunted in surprise. "Huh. Chris, how's your night vision?"

"Better'n ever."

"Then take a look at this, will ya?"

Shifting his ever-present gum in his mouth, the heavyset man took the binoculars, and then his own eyes widened in surprise behind the eyepieces. "That shit must be touchier'n nitro."

"That's what I was thinking." Ham nodded.

"How can you tell?" Mike whispered.

Chris looked as though he had been asked to explain table manners to a five-year-old. "Look at the way they're handling it, gentle as baby lizard eggs. And wooden barrels, to reduce the possibility of sparks."

"Uh-oh." Ham adjusted the eyepiece as everyone looked over at the next pier again.

One of the barrels, placed too close to the next one, rolled into it, sending it wobbling perilously close to the edge of the conveyor belts. The Visitor who was loading them dashed over to it, saving it just in time from teetering over the edge.

"That was a close one," Mike said, letting his breath out.

"Hey, lookit there, Gooder. Ms. Primo Leather-ass herself."

A slight, dark-haired woman strode out, flanked by two officers—Mike didn't need the binoculars to recognize Diana's imperious movements as she gestured angrily. One of the Visitors with her pulled out a lasergun, and the hapless loader screamed, then crumpled to the dock. Turning, she marched back into the building; a moment later, the body was efficiently tossed over the edge of the pier into the Pacific, then the conveyor started up again with someone else in charge.

"One down, forty-nine to go," Ham muttered, showing his teeth in what passed for his smile. "This may be easier than I thought. If one of us gets close enough to get off a clear shot at one of those barrels, it might be enough to send the whole works up like the Fourth of July. Wouldn't even need your own well-made explosives, partner.''

Chris shrugged philosophically. "They can be recycled."

"Wait a minute," Mike said. "We don't know how much of that stuff's in there, or even how volatile it is. We could take out the whole harbor, including us."

"That's the chance we'll have to take," Julie said grimly. "Whatever happens, we've got to stop them from contaminating the ocean with that stuff."

Mike nodded. "But first we go check out the warehouse. Then we rendezvous and decide the best way to blow it up."

"Okay," Ham said, rising. "Time we split up. Gooder, you, me, Robin, Maggie, and Willie will try and get a look inside from the right side of the building. Chris, you take the others around to the left. Unless you're jumped, no shooting. We'll meet back in ten minutes."

As Ham moved down to repeat the marching orders to the rest, Mike saw Robin smiling at Kyle and squeezing his hand, Willie and Elias giving one another "five," Chris leaning over to give Maggie a quick but firm kiss. He glanced over at Julie and winked; she smiled wanly in return.

"Good luck," Ham said.

"Or to paraphrase my old Navy CPO," Chris said, checking his rifle, "let's go out, kick ass, and make luggage."

As they made their way to the next pier, dodging between mooring posts, parked vehicles, and the shadows, Mike glanced over between the piers to his right. Down here, he could see the flotilla of small boats—powerboats, sailboats, even a catamaran—bobbing quietly in the black waters close to the concrete pylons, waiting. From snatches of conversation and laughter drifting over from one of the closest vessels, he surmised that they were all waiting to receive the barrels for transport and dumping in deeper waters—for a lot of money.

Mike's mouth thinned. Some people would do anything for money, but from this perspective, it was doubtful any of them had seen much of the little byplay on the pier, and Diana wouldn't be inclined to tell them that their cargo was dangerous.

The warehouse was a long, gray wooden building stretching almost the entire length of the pier. Careful of the ropes, lumber, and other objects scattered along the wharf, they moved silently to the back of the building, the apparent site of the red dust's manufacture.

Lights glowed through the dirty windows, but this end was obviously deserted. Chris gave a quick thumbs-up and disappeared around the left corner, followed by his team. Mike inched forward, flattening himself against the rough boards, his eyes straining in the darkness for any movement.

They were halfway around the right side of the warehouse when Mike spotted the darker-gray outlines of a slightly recessed door. He reached for it—and was knocked backward as it burst open and ten Visitor shock troopers spilled out.

"Shit!" Tyler muttered with as much emotion as Donovan had ever heard him express as the gun was knocked from the ex-CIA man's hands. Mike struggled to get up, raising his own gun as Robin and Willie were grabbed, his mind swirling with vague, heroic notions of going down in a blaze of glory. But then something exploded behind his left ear, and the darkness of the sky and the water rose, mingled, then swallowed him whole. . . .

Water, cold and salty, splashed into Donovan's face, making his ski mask crawl against his skin. Groggily, he tried to pull away only to discover he was being firmly held by two Visitors in guard helmets, his arms pinned behind him.

He raised his head, which ached sharply along the left side, trying to blink the water out of his eyes to see where he was. Then his head was roughly jerked back as the ski mask was yanked off his face. "Hey, pal, watch it!" he muttered as an artificial fingernail scraped his chin. "My face doesn't come off the way yours does."

Mike had to narrow his eyes against the sudden brightness, but after a second he could see that Robin, Ham, Maggie, and Willie were receiving similar treatment. He was inside the warehouse, which seemed very warm and stifling after the ocean air outside. Here, an acrid, sour smell permeated everything, making his nostrils sting, and even the Visitors coughed occasionally as they moved around the stacks of barrels.

"Why, Mr. Donovan!" Diana turned from a discussion with several officers and strode forward to stand in front of him, resplendent in her white dress uniform, the one she reserved

for special occasions. Looking at her, Mike found it hard to
believe that she was reptilian under that tight-fitting, curva-
ceous outfit and flawless skin—until he looked at the expression in her eyes.

"Well, well." Ham shook his head. "The queen scaly got
lucky again."

"And the ever-charming Mr. Tyler—and Maggie Blodgett.
And dear, dear Robin. I am especially glad to see *you*. Have
you met any handsome . . . males lately?" Diana reached
out to stroke her cheek; Robin jerked away and, glaring, tried
to spit at her. The guard holding her saw the movement of her
jaw and cuffed her warningly.

Diana turned to the others. "What an *unexpected* pleasure to
have you all drop in like this."

"It was not in our plans either," Willie mumbled honestly
from Mike's right.

"If I had known you were coming, I would have arranged
for a more formal reception." The Visitor commander smiled.
"As it is, you can be special"—she looked suddenly very
reptilian—"*guests* at my victory feast later, when we return to
the Mother Ship to celebrate the removal of your poisonous
bacteria from our ocean."

"*Your* ocean, huh?" Maggie said stonily. "Fat chance, you
leathery bitch."

Deliberately ignoring the gibe, the dark-haired Visitor
gestured to her guards. "But no doubt the real reason you came
was to personally thank me for my little gift to your
resistance." Donovan saw Margie escorted up to stand beside
her. "Lovely, isn't she? And perfectly loyal to me."

A pain worse than the physical one in his head stabbed
through Mike as he gazed into the lovely, impassive face of his
ex-wife. For just an instant, he thought he saw something
flicker deep within her eyes, although her deadened features
never changed.

Then Diana was strutting in front of him again, blocking his
vision. "Marjorie just arrived a few minutes ahead of you,"
she said, clasping her hands together in front of her. "It would
have been sooner, but a couple of overzealous security people
aboard the Mother Ship detained her until they could verify her
relationship to me. But it was worth the wait. I do so love
family reunions—they're so touching. Don't you agree, Mr.
Donovan?"

Refusing to answer her taunt, Mike pushed against the arms of his captors, straining to catch Margie's glance again. She stared at the floor, refusing to look up.

Diana's mouth turned down in annoyance, and she went over to the blond woman, lifting Margie's chin with her fingers. "She was just about to tell me the location of the resistance headquarters when you arrived." She smiled. "And now, my dear—"

"First, I . . . want to know where my son is," Margie said, making a visible effort to get the words out.

Diana's smile turned fixed. "Why, darling, I've told you he's safe and sound."

"I want to know . . . exactly *where*. And I want him returned to me." Sweat beaded her forehead as she locked gazes with Diana. "I want us to be sent somewhere where it's . . . safe."

"Of course, Marjorie. I always reward loyalty. One moment, while I confer with my senior aide on that subject." Donovan saw Diana step across the room to a tall, dark-haired Visitor, then overheard her say, "Our subject seems to be getting ideas of her own. A dose of procorb may be in order when we return. See to it, Captain."

Procorb was the Visitor drug that stole the human mind and will, turned its victims into pliable zombies capable of almost anything. Mike had seen his son, Sean, under its influence.

Returning to Margie's side, Diana smiled again. "He is in the Visitor youth camp near Carmel-Monterey. And tomorrow, you will be reunited with him and given tickets to anyplace you choose, plus a generous cash settlement. I will see to it personally. Now, if you please, tell me where the resistance headquarters is located."

Margie lowered her head as though all the fight had drained out of her. "They meet in—"

"Margie, she's *lying*, she'll *kill*—" Donovan's shouted protest was cut off as a heavy gloved hand slapped his face, sending lances of pain shooting around the blurred edges of his vision.

"Mr. Donovan, it is impolite to interrupt." Diana's face smoothed into pleased anticipation again. "As you were starting to—"

A commotion erupted outside; there were shouts, the sound of scuffles and grunts, and the crack of a lasergun being fired.

A moment later, a side door to Mike's right opened, and a large group of Visitor troopers entered, bearing the struggling, still-masked members of the other resistance team.

And one other person. Tight in the grip of a burly Visitor shock trooper, looking like a trapped doe, was Elizabeth Maxwell.

"Oh, no," Robin whispered, her eyes filling with tears.

"Mother!" Elizabeth tried to struggle out of the hands of her captor.

"Why did you come here?" Robin moaned, her shoulders slumping. "Oh, honey . . ."

"I knew I had to come," she said, looking at her.

"This *is* cozy! I wish Lydia were here to enjoy this instead of minding things back on the Mother Ship. Come here, my dear." Diana gestured to the guard holding Elizabeth, and she was released.

She ran first to Kyle, who was closer, his face still covered by the ski mask, then to Robin. Mother and daughter shared something deep and wordless for a moment as Elizabeth gently wiped away the blood at the corner of Robin's mouth where the guard had hit her.

"Come, come." Diana's beckoning gesture was impatient this time.

Slowly Elizabeth turned, her eyes large and filled with an emotion Mike had never seen in her beautiful features before.

Hate.

Smiling warmly, Diana embraced her. "I believe the human expression remains, 'My, how you've grown.' You must be so glad to be back with your own true people again."

"Diana, we are ready. Uh . . ." The thin, nervous-looking Visitor who had hurried in from the front of the building stammered to a halt as he caught sight of the prisoners. "Oh. Excuse me. I didn't realize you were, uh, occupied."

"That's all right, Bernard. These are all . . . old friends of mine. What is it?"

"We are ready to begin the dispersion of the red dust at your command."

"Excellent, Bernard! Even a little ahead of schedule." Laying a protective arm around Elizabeth's shoulders, Diana gestured. "All of you must step outside so that you may personally witness my triumph."

* * *

As she was dragged outside the warehouse, Elizabeth struggled again in the arms of the guard holding her but soon discovered she might as well be fighting against steel manacles. Bruised and breathless, she finally subsided, gasping in the sea-cooled night air. On either side of her marched the heavily guarded members of the resistance.

She had gotten to the waterfront before any of them, guided by the sense she knew but didn't understand. Concealing Kyle's bike behind an old garage, she had remained out of sight herself for almost an hour, slipping from building to barrel, watching as humans and Visitors moved past her hiding places.

Watching and waiting, although she didn't know for what.

Then she had seen the shadow-forms of Julie, her mother, and the rest slip by. She had wanted to join them then, but the deeper wisdom inside her directed her to remain silent, to follow at a distance.

She had just gotten up to the wharf when she heard her mother scream and then saw them all captured. At that point, fear had taken over from wisdom's caution, and she had bolted blindly forward, screaming, "Mother!" One of the troopers started for her, and she had run, twisting and turning, and almost gotten away. Then another trooper had stepped out into her path, laser rifle ready. The next instant, heavy hands had clamped on her shoulders, and she had been brought into the warehouse.

Now her fear had mostly vanished, leaving only an eerie, icy calm—and her hate, a bright, sharp thing which burned away innocence and ignorance inside her.

The Visitors were gathering around her, hushed and expectant as Diana stepped up onto a makeshift platform of piled wood-slatted pallets near the conveyor belt and faced them. "Ladies and gentlemen, you have all worked very hard and are to be commended for your efforts in this, our own Operation Red Dust. Our Great Leader will hear of your contributions, and I know he will be very pleased. Most especially, I would like to personally thank Bernard, our senior botanist, for his expertise in developing the dust and leading your teams to success. Bernard, please come up here. *Bernard . . .*"

As the gangly Visitor reluctantly joined her amid the sound of polite applause, Elizabeth looked over at the barrels lined up neatly near the end of the pier, others in a row along the conveyor belt, which protruded out past the edge of the pier over the night-dark water.

And the water seemed to start churning and boiling, turning red for an instant—

She stared, blinked, then the ocean was black and still again.

Bewildered, Elizabeth glanced at her mother and the others, then at Diana, who was saying, ". . . know, we have some humans who are waiting to transport the dust to their designated areas, and I do not wish to delay them. But, Bernard, I wish for you to have the honor of releasing the first barrels, right off the end of this pier. . . ."

Taking the device Diana held out to him, Bernard stepped over to face the conveyor and pressed a control. The belt started up again.

To Elizabeth, it seemed as though the barrel on the end was poised on the edge of infinity, then it tipped slowly over. The loosened lid came off, and a dull red dust puffed out, turning fiery and golden in the incandescent glare of the loading dock lights, surrounding the barrel with a weird, glowing halo as it splashed into the water.

Her mind slipped sideways, and she was back in her dream again. Before her terrified, unseeing gaze, she envisioned the dust growing and expanding, turning everything red, the water into a hell-colored, bubbling poison, the whole ocean, the sky, everything turning a dull red, the color of drying blood—

—and all the people in the world, including all the ones she loved, were clutching at their throats, clawing at their faces, writhing in agony as they died. Kyle—Julie—Mike—Willie . . .

Her mother . . .

"No!" Elizabeth screamed, her mind going white-blank as she thrust out her hands in a pushing-away motion, an impulse echoed within her by the abilities buried deep in her consciousness. *"No!!"*

Chapter 16

The Tide Turns

Everything in Juliet Parrish's awareness seemed to turn slow motion and surreal. She heard Elizabeth scream, saw her throw up her hands, and then barrels went *flying* off the conveyor belt. As they clattered to the ground, they exploded, sending a fiery mixture of dust and splintered wood into the air.

One barrel crashed into the midst of those waiting to be delivered, setting off a chain reaction which sent light and sound roaring into the night. Julie suddenly felt her arms freed as her captor turned and went running for his life. Diana and Bernard leaped off the platform only an instant before it lifted into the air and ignited, sending flaming showers down on the hapless, screaming Visitors who hadn't moved fast enough.

Throwing her arms over her head, Julie sprinted with the others toward the right outside wall of the warehouse, which looked like the safest route to take. Another violent eruption of flame scattered shrapnel around her; she felt a sudden, sharp stinging in her right calf and arm.

Something shoved her violently to the right, and Julie saw that it was the Visitor named Bernard who had thrust her out of his way. Then, as she staggered, trying to keep her feet, he stiffened, half turned, agony contorting his face. In seeming slow motion, he toppled forward, a splintered metal fragment from the conveyor belt blossoming like a grotesque parody of a cornstalk out of his back.

The screams of injured and dying Visitors, plus those of the humans in the boats below, mingled in a hideous chorus all around Julie as she ran, limping now. Acrid smoke from the fires springing up everywhere made her eyes water as it tore at her lungs. She could barely see.

Another explosion sent heat pushing against her back like a demon hand, then the pier rocked beneath her, throwing her off balance. She fell to her knees, painfully dragged herself up again as two Visitors behind her were pitched into the ocean, flaming now like an oil slick. *Run,* she told herself, *just . . . keep running. . . .*

Ahead of her, she glimpsed long-legged jeans and a black jacket running hell-bent-for-leather beside the wall. For an instant, she experienced a sharp, bright stab of relief that Mike was okay. Then getting closer, she saw it was Elias instead. Willie, Robin, and Elizabeth were close beside him.

At least *they* were still safe. But Mike—?

As she glanced over her shoulder, she saw another barrel go up, sending debris in a flaming arc through the wall of the warehouse. Almost instantly, sheets of fire were visible through the windows, licking up the old wooden scaffolding within, reaching for the huge stack of barrels in the back, the ones that hadn't yet been loaded onto the conveyor belt—and the vats of red dust that hadn't been packed. . . .

Julie put on a burst of speed, dragging it up from a reservoir she didn't know she had, and she was passing the far corner of the building. She saw most of the others ahead of her as wraiths through the smoke, running for the shore and safety.

"It's gonna blow!" Ham Tyler yelled from somewhere ahead of her. "*Move* it!"

A fountain of flame sprang from the building's roof, along with the thunderclaps of more explosions. Julie felt as though her feet had left the ground. She was no longer running—she was *flying* to get away from the ticking bomb that was now the warehouse.

Then it went up, and even facing away from the explosion, she was blinded. The warehouse had become a sun-bright ball of light. The heat and noise hit her a second later—hit her with a terrible, final concussion, sending her forward and down into dark, dark, dark. . . .

Robin Maxwell's universe had shrunk down, narrowing to one person—her daughter, Elizabeth—and nothing, not even death itself, seemed as important to her.

Immediately after Elizabeth's powers had pushed the barrel off the conveyor, starting the chain reaction of explosions, a glazed look of horror had stamped itself into her daughter's features as she stared at the escalating destruction she had begun. Elizabeth had even taken a step forward toward the fire at the end of the pier, like a moth drawn to flame, and Robin had had to grab her by the hand and forcibly drag her away toward the outside wall of the warehouse.

Eighteen years old, going on eight . . . or eighteen months. Snatches of words from her conversation with Kyle earlier that evening came drifting into her head as she ran for the safety of the shore. In so many ways, Elizabeth *was* only a child. They all tended to forget that and expected so much of her sometimes—but she had so much potential.

And Robin loved her so much.

When the big explosions came behind them, sending first a column of fire into the sky, then a fireball that swallowed the world in impossible noise and brightness, Robin did the only thing she could. Pushing Elizabeth to the ground, she fell on top of her, shielding her with her body. She would gladly die, if her daughter could live. . . .

It wasn't supposed to happen like this. Elizabeth stared numbly at the barrels as they tumbled into one another and blew up, sending Visitors running for their lives or jumping into the flame-infested waters. *It really wasn't supposed to.*

Over and over, the litany sounded in her head. She wanted to stay back to fix things somehow, make it all better, but her mother grabbed her hand, pulling her along with a grip strong as metal, away from the death screams which followed her accusingly.

They all had been right—she didn't know how to use or control her powers, and now she had endangered everyone she loved. But she had had to stop the red dust from contaminating the water. That was the biggest certainty of all. Otherwise, her nightmare world of red dust growing, expanding to destroy hundreds, thousands of people, would have turned terrifyingly real.

Elizabeth sensed the final explosion building behind them an instant before the blast. She began a formless thought of protection, then her mother pushed her down and sprawled on top her, slamming them onto the old wooden planks near the end of the pier just as the building blew up behind them, sending heat and a rush of wind past them.

An instant later, it was over, the building crumpling into ruin as debris rained down into the water, the fires now burning steadily all over the damaged pier.

"Elizabeth . . . Elizabeth, honey, are you all right?" Her mother's voice finally got past the ringing in her ears and the crackle-burning sounds of the fire. Rising to her elbows, Elizabeth looked up into her mother's face, then reached out a hand to brush at the tears that streaked down her dirty face.

"Are . . . *you* all right, Mother?"

"Oh, fine, baby, fine." Robin hugged her hard, and Elizabeth realized that her mother had been willing to die to save her and that she really did love her—for herself.

"I love you, Mother," she whispered fiercely, returning the hug with all her strength.

When the first explosion occurred, a jagged barrel stave gouged out most of his Visitor guard's throat, and suddenly freed, Mike Donovan went sprawling onto the pier's wooden beams as they shuddered under him.

As the night sky blazed in a grim parody of Fort McHenry, he saw his friends duck and scatter away from their own helpless captors while fiery debris rained down like napalm. Chris Faber grabbed Maggie, and Ham Tyler dropped, rolled, coming up with his dead guard's laser pistol, then calmly proceeded to snap off a couple of quick shots at Diana, who hit the wharf and rolled just as her platform blew up behind her.

Then Mike was up and hurtling toward safety, seeing Robin on his right dragging a dazed Elizabeth along. In front of him were Kyle and Elias leading the escape along the side of the warehouse as the Pacific suddenly erupted from the explosion of a small powerboat that had been hit by one of the barrels.

Suddenly a figure appeared from out of the smoke on his left, and Mike saw it was Margie, her expression that of a woman just waking up from a dream, and the cameraman lurking forever inside him noted the striking picture she made, a pale, hollow-eyed beauty with flames reflecting off her eyes, the water, the night.

But Willie was nowhere in sight as the smoke thickened— and neither was Julie.

If anything had happened to *her* . . .

Mike slowed, looking over his shoulder for her, only to see another explosion send a fireball through the roof of the warehouse less than fifty feet behind him. The next instant, the pier directly beneath the building sagged and crumpled, sending rubble, wood, and flames into the blood-colored waters.

He coughed, his chest on fire from the fumes, but conscious only of the agony within his mind and heart.

Julie, he thought. *Julie, no* . . .

Then he saw her, a petite phoenix in sneakers, bolting out of the smoke, the ragged knot of her blond hair bobbing like a beacon in the hellish darkness as she pulled off her ski mask.

She hadn't seen him; she was running past. Unable to force sound past his smoke-filled throat, he reached for her—and the world ended behind him as the warehouse went up.

Mike threw himself on top of Juliet, heat white on his back, invading his closed eyelids. He was suddenly, calmly certain that he was going to die, and that it didn't matter as long as he could save her.

He grunted as something slammed on top of him, driving him down. Jagged shards of light leaped before his vision like negative images of the debris rocketing past, then Donovan felt himself sucked down into a whirling cauldron of thunderous sound and darkness.

Moments or an eternity later, ears still ringing, he cautiously lifted his head. Julie lay beneath his body, face pressed into the crook of her arm . . . so still. . . .

Then she stirred, lifting her head. "Huh . . . who . . . ?"

"Oh, God, I love you," he whispered into the back of her sweatshirt.

"Mike?" she struggled feebly, trying to move his weight off her.

He couldn't move and wondered vaguely if he had been paralyzed by the explosion, but then his scrambled senses sorted themselves out, and he realized he was pinioned by someone else lying on top of him.

Levering himself up by his arms, he felt the sudden absence of weight as the other tumbled off. He turned his head and with horror recognized Margie's slack face and blood-streaked blond hair as she lay sprawled on her side, facing him, like a grotesque parody of the way she used to lie beside him each night in sleep. "Oh, God!" he sobbed, crawling toward her, trying, without moving her, to examine her wounds.

There was a horrible, dark, wet-looking place in the back of her head, and another, larger place on her back, where twisted fragments of flesh and fabric parted around the shattered remnants of her backbone.

Mike had seen the victims of war before, the dead, the dying—even children—their bodies charred, maimed, and mutilated as they croaked their last pitiful sounds in Spanish or Vietnamese.

But nothing had ever seemed half as obscene as those splintered white fragments in Margie's back, exposed to the night, poking out from the bubbling, darker well of her blood.

"Let's go!" Ham Tyler was shouting from a thousand miles away. "We ain't out of the woods yet, especially if there's more of that red dust crap around. Some of the scalies still have guns."

"I will help, Mike," said a quiet voice, and Donovan looked up to see Willie.

The Visitor was covered with soot. Flying glass had slashed his right arm even through the borrowed sweater and jacket, where green ooze was congealing at the spot near his shoulder, but he gazed steadily at Donovan.

Mike looked at him for a moment, then nodded wordlessly. As carefully as they could, they picked up Marjorie and carried her up to the road a block or so away, Julie staggering beside them, racked by spells of coughing. When they were safely above the fires and the scattered Visitor troops, although still within the hellish glare from the burning pier, they laid Margie gently down on the narrow dirt shoulder, Mike cradling her head in his lap. His hands had turned sticky and dark red from the blood on her back.

She looked steadily up at him, recognition in her eyes, her mouth moving to form words, but no sounds came out, only a soft gurgling.

"Don't, Margie," Mike whispered, caressing her cheek. "Just . . . lie still."

She let out a small sigh, shuddered convulsively, then her gaze turned fixed and glassy. He watched with horror as her pupils widened. . . .

No, it couldn't be, she wasn't— Mike stared wildly around, focusing on Julie kneeling beside him, fingers touching

Margie's throat. She looked at him, then down, shaking her head as she coughed again.

For an instant he was furious with her. How could she just sit there, doing nothing, while Margie was . . . "Aren't you going to do something?"

She raised a sooty, blood-streaked face. "There's nothing I can—"

"What do you mean, nothing? Start CPR, mouth-to-mouth resusci—"

"Mike, she's gone. I'm sorry." Tears gathered, cutting through the filth in ivory streaks.

After a long, long while, the words reached him, and he understood. Slowly Mike reached down with a hand that trembled a little to close the staring, dead eyes.

Chapter 17

Afterwords

"Get away from me, you beast!" Groaning, Maggie Blodgett covered her head with the sheet as Druid, yipping happily, dove for her tousled hair once again. "God, I ache everywhere and want to sleep for the next twenty hours straight, and King Konglet here wants to play kissy with my head again."

"Can't say as I blame him," Chris Faber said, leaning back against the pillows. "Kinda like playing with your hair myself." For emphasis, he reached over to tug on a curl.

Sunlight was high and bright on the carpet of his bedroom, and he supposed it was twelve or one. Actually, it didn't matter. He had no place he had to be, and surely no place he'd rather be, than here beside the woman he loved.

The little Shih Tzu saw his hand movements as a further invitation to play, and jumped again, causing Maggie to squeal. "Faber, control your animal!"

"Druid, get down," Chris said in the tone he reserved for no-more-nonsense commands. The small, hairy face turned a look of disappointment in his direction, then bounded off the bed in search of other amusements.

"Well, we made it through another one." Maggie sighed as she inched herself up from under the sheets.

"Small doggy attack?" he asked, deadpan.

"You know what I mean."

"Yup." He stared up at the ceiling. "You were really great, blastin' away at those scalies like you were twice their size."

"You weren't too shabby yourself. For a big guy, you sure can move fast when you have to." Her eyes turned thoughtful. "We were lucky last night. Think our luck will hold out, Faber?"

"We have to keep believing that it will."

"Yeah," she sighed, then turned over to rest her chin on his chest. "I have to admit, living on the edge like this does make our time together even more special somehow, you know?" She kissed his shoulder.

"You bet your sweet ass." He grinned lazily. "Suppose we try out your luck right now, and see if you can come up with a Visitor joke I haven't heard."

"Oh, God, I'll never . . ." She thought for a moment, then her grin turned sly at the corners. "Okay. Why did the Visitor eat the punk-rock biker?"

Chris lay silent and perplexed for several moments. Finally he admitted, "Hon, you've got me for once. Why?"

"Roughage," she deadpanned, then began to laugh aloud at his expression.

"Hey, that's all right," he said after he'd stopped laughing. "Where in hell did you hear that one?"

"Nowhere."

"What do you mean, nowhere?"

"I made it up." She bit him playfully. "I figured it was the only way I'd ever get one by you."

" 'Roughage,' eh?" he said, mock-growling as he reached for her. "I'll show you roughage. . . ."

Willie was explaining the recipe for his blender drink to his new friend Claire when Mike Donovan walked into the Club Creole.

This was Willie's favorite time of day. At three o'clock in the afternoon, the lunchtime diners were almost gone, yet it was a little early for the happy-hour group. This was a good time to take care of small but necessary chores—especially with someone nice to talk with across the bar.

Someone very, very nice . . .

Wearing a cheerful blue dress, the young woman with soft red-gold hair and brown eyes had come into the bar two hours ago and ordered a Coke innocently enough. But her voice resonance and a couple of seemingly offhand remarks—actually carefully coded—had revealed her as one of his own kind *and* a member of the fifth column, the resistance group aboard the Mother Ships that was secretly opposed to the policies of the Leader.

She had heard that a Visitor worked as a bartender at the Club Creole and had been very anxious to meet him. Claire was especially impressed to hear of the successful action on the waterfront, and she had been suitably solicitous about his bandaged arm.

"Hi, Willie," Donovan said, sliding onto a barstool and waving away the offer of a Coors. "No, just coffee."

"Hello, Mike," the bartender said, turning his attention away from Claire to peer concernedly at his friend's face.

Donovan's bruises were dramatic but not serious; what really troubled Willie was his expression. Willie was not yet really skilled in reading the subtle movements of skin over flesh and bone that denoted human emotions. Something in the tautness around Mike's eyes, however, and the position of his mouth said that his friend was very disturbed about something more than grief from Margie's death, although he was trying to hide it, perhaps even from himself.

"Is anything the mutter, Mike?" he ventured, placing the coffee in front of him.

"That's '*matter*,' Willie," Elias corrected automatically, coming behind him with a tray of silverware.

"Have you seen Julie today?" Mike asked. "I've been trying to get hold of her, but they said she called in sick at work, and she hasn't answered her phone all day."

Willie frowned, trying to recall her exact words. "She said that she had an appointment with the doctor this morning, and she did not know how much time he would take from her."

"Oh." Donovan managed to look both reassured and worried at the same moment. "Did she say why she was going to—?"

"Hey, Taylor, when did you let the lizards back in?"

Willie felt his crest prickle in indignation as Ham Tyler sauntered into the room. "This is Claire," he said. "She is not a lizard, but one of my own kind, a member of our fifth column—and she is my friend, so you—"

"And any friend of Willie's is welcome at the Club Creole," Elias added, looking directly into the flat brown eyes of the former intelligence agent. From across the room, Miranda Juarez smiled and winked.

Shrugging, Ham took the seat next to Donovan. "How you doing, Gooder?"

"I'm okay," Mike said, finishing his coffee. "Heading on over to Julie's."

"Good idea," Tyler said.

"Well, see you all later," Mike said, slipping off the barstool. "Thanks for the coffee, Willie."

"You are welcome, Mike," the bartender said, smiling, then he turned back to the young woman across the bar from him. "Tell me about your cover. It sounds vacillating."

"Fascinating," Mike said over his shoulder as he pulled the door open. He stepped out into the summer heat and stood blinking for a moment in the brightness before he slipped on his dark glasses and pulled his cap down. Hard to believe that this was the same world as the one that had encompassed that hellish inferno down at the dockyards last night.

He sighed, feeling the tightness in his chest again as he thought about the phone call he'd made at noontime to Margie's sister so she could claim the body. He didn't even dare go to the funeral; the Visitors wouldn't miss the opportunity to stake it out, just waiting for him to show up.

Donovan turned as the door opened behind him. "Hey, Gooder," Ham Tyler said, stepping out. "Hang on a second."

"Sure. What's up?"

"I just . . ." Tyler hesitated for a second, then looked up. "I wanted to tell you I was sorry about Mrs. Donovan. During the fireworks last night, I didn't get the chance."

Donovan nodded, genuinely touched. "Thanks, Ham. I appreciate it."

Tyler sighed, looking up at the Mother Ship hanging over Los Angeles. "Hell of a world, eh, Gooder? And it ain't even all ours anymore, since the day those snakes parked up there. Speaking of scalies, I wonder how the Lizard Queen herself is doing?"

"Diana?" Mike frowned. "I was kind of hoping that she'd bought it, along with her red dust."

"No such luck." Tyler shook his head as he stared upward at the gargantuan vessel. "She's still around to continue making a pain in the ass of herself—I'd bet on it. She's got more lives than a cat."

* * *

Lifting her wavy dark hair back from her forehead, Diana stared into the mirror in her private quarters, checking the repairs to her pseudo skin and hair.

The places that had been torn looked smooth and seamless again. With a sigh, she turned and headed for the door.

The whole experience had turned into such a humiliation. First to have triumph at her fingertips and the members of the hateful human resistance falling right into her lap besides, only to have the whole thing go up in literal smoke, thanks to the Starchild.

Poor little misguided creature—she had obviously been too young to absorb many of the lessons Diana had tried to teach her before her second molt. But such splendid power. If only it could be turned to a larger good.

As she strode the corridor toward the science division, Diana frowned, remembering how angry and frightened she had been when the pallets had heaved up from under her, sending her sprawling onto the dirty pier. She had watched the fire rise, her troops scatter, until she had been forced to dive into the water to narrowly miss destruction from the shrapnel and the flames.

Probably the worst moment of all had been when the rescue shuttlecraft had swooped low over the water, throwing out a line. Diana had been hauled up ignominiously dripping and sputtering, her wig torn partly off from a piece of flying shrapnel and flopping down her back, exposing her crest, her lovely white dress uniform stained and utterly ruined. Scrambling soggily into the vehicle, she had turned to thank the pilot—and looked right into the smug, hateful face of Lydia.

As she turned the corner into her lab, Diana wondered briefly whether she would rather have died.

"Greetings, Diana." Lydia's smile was sickeningly wide as she strode into the lab behind her superior officer. "I *do* hope you are making a speedy recovery from your terrible ordeal, dear."

"Yes, thank you," Diana felt her own mouth tightening into a thin line. "You left a message that you wished to see me about the records Bernard left behind."

"Yes. Or, rather, those he *didn't* leave us." Lydia folded her hands over her stomach and shook her head in exaggerated regret. She was obviously enjoying this moment almost as much as last night's rescue. "It seems that Bernard may have been anxious about his work and the possibility that he could be replaced. He left very incomplete notes. I'm afraid his red dust defoliant can't be duplicated because we can't reconstruct his formula.''

Diana flicked her fingers dismissingly. "Well, it hardly matters. I just spoke to Bashir on the Iranian Mother Ship. He has already begun obtaining and processing water from the Persian Gulf. Our Leader will have the supply he needs, and it will only be a few days later than originally anticipated."

Lydia's expression turned scornful. "And how many of our people will die because of this delay? Did he also tell you that, Diana?"

"The unexpected is the hallmark of wartime, Lydia." Diana waved a nonchalant hand at her security officer. "I would always keep that in mind, if I were you."

Nodding curtly, Lydia turned and left.

"Damn her!" Alone in her private quarters a few minutes later, Diana finally allowed herself the small luxury of balling her hands into fists and savoring the hot rush of venom in her mouth for a moment. She thought about Bashir, how pleased, even smug he had sounded when he had assured her that the water procurement and desalinization could be handled aboard *his* ship without any problem. He would personally oversee the operation, he said, and then accompany the shipment back to Sirius—where, no doubt, he would be received with the full honors and recognition due a hero returning from the battlefield in triumph.

The honors that were rightfully hers . . .

Diana sighed. It would be a long time before she would be taking a vacation back home, it seemed. Lydia was about as trustworthy as a crivit in season, always positioning herself, waiting for the moment when she could strike. And then there was the damned resistance, which seemed capable of foiling her at every turn.

She frowned a little, and her mirror reflected an unaccustomed emotion for her—doubt. Alone in the solitude of her quarters, Diana considered the notion that maybe the humans weren't as mindless as she had always assumed. Perhaps they even had the capacity for the higher functions marking a truly intelligent mind, such as—

Alarmed, she cut that thought off. Otherwise she was straying perilously close to the path that those wretched followers of Zon believed, that all life, even human, should be preserved, not destroyed. The humans were food, their world the only viable source of nourishment for her people, and she had to keep thinking of them that way.

Especially that hateful Mike Donovan. She looked forward to the day when she would snack on his fingers one by one—and he would remain alive just long enough to watch.

Smiling at the image, Diana left her quarters, turning off the light, and her mirror glimmered into darkness.

"Who is it?"

It wasn't Juliet Parrish's voice behind her apartment door, and Mike Donovan frowned as he realized Robin was there. "It's Jabba the Hutt, who eats Visitors and people who don't answer the phone all day."

He had deliberately paraphrased one of their passwords from the old days, back when the resistance had been brand-new and his and Julie's feelings for each other had seemed fresh and forever. More than anything, he needed to see her alone, be with her tonight. He needed to know whether she still cared. His call to Denise Daltrey was overdue by now, and he couldn't escape the growing conviction that if Julie and he were through, getting away to New York might be the only answer. He wouldn't be able to stand seeing her, knowing she didn't care.

Robin opened the door. "Hi, Mike. She's in the bedroom."

"Is she okay?" Mike asked, seeing Elizabeth behind her mother in the living room.

"Yes," Robin answered, giving him a guarded look. "She'll be all right. The doctor told her to rest for a couple of days."

Julie was propped up on a pillow, sipping something from a mug. Mike stood in the doorway and gave Robin a worried glance as he saw how pale Julie was. She tried to smile, but even that seemed to take too much effort. "How's everyone doing?" he asked, dredging up a smile, although his eyes remained on Julie.

"Fine, Mike." Robin quickly crossed the living room to touch Elizabeth's shoulder. "We were just on our way out."

"No, we weren't, Moth—" Elizabeth's honest reply was stifled by an unsubtle finger to her mother's lips and Robin's quick head shake.

"I'll call you later, Julie, and see if you need anything," Robin said around the door, then it closed behind them.

Slowly, Mike walked into Julie's bedroom, decorated in shades of pale aqua and ivory, and sat down hesitantly on the chair by the bed. "Hi, honey. Are you all right?"

She nodded, not looking at him. Even her lips were pale. "I'm okay. Joe told me to stay home and rest for a few days, drink a lot of liquids. Get my strength back."

He scanned her face. "You're so pale. Were you wounded last night? I didn't notice—" He broke off, feeling like a heel.

"Just a few cuts on my leg," she said. "Really nothing. Don't worry about it, Mike. Nobody could have expected you to notice anything last night." She reached over to touch his hand. "I know how you must be feeling. I'm so sorry about Margie."

"I know I hurt you," he said. "I've been thinking about how it must have looked to you these past couple of weeks, and—" He leaned his forehead in his hands tiredly. "And I'm sorry, too. I was glad to see Margie, sure, and I won't pretend it didn't hurt like hell to lose her. But I'm here, walking around with some semblance of normalcy. If it had been *you*, Julie, I—" He swallowed. "I don't think I could make it."

"Mike . . ." He looked over to see that her eyes were brimming. "I don't know what to say."

"Just tell me what you're feeling. Whether it's . . . over."

"Over?" She sounded so startled that he glanced back up. "What's over? You don't mean—"

"You and Nathan? That's exactly what I'm asking. Is it over between us?"

Julie began an incredulous laugh, then stopped, her hands going to her stomach. "Ouch. Shouldn't have done that. Mike, are you crazy? I don't give a hell about that self-centered tycoon. Diana is the only person who deserves him. How can you credit me with such lousy taste?"

"You don't care about him?" He was startled. "Then why have you been so withdrawn? You've barely spoken to me, and you looked exhausted all the—"

He stopped suddenly, facts and observations clicking into place like the tumblers on a safe, unlocking the truth. "Pregnant?" His eyes searched her face. "Julie, are you?" He took a deep breath, looking at her hands as they rested on her abdomen, remembered her little cry of pain. "A miscarriage?" he asked hesitantly.

She nodded, biting her lip. "I think so. I began bleeding

early this morning. By the time I got to the clinic, all Joe could do was a D&C. He'll know for sure in a day or so, after he gets the tests."

Mike felt a profound sense of loss, remembering Sean as an infant, smiling up at him. "Julie, why didn't you tell me? God, I'm sorry." Memory struck him. "Was it when I jumped on you when the warehouse went up? Is that what—?"

She was already shaking her head. "No, Mike. You saved my life, remember? I'd been sick for a couple of weeks. I think it was something that would have happened no matter what. Probably because there was something wrong—" Her voice broke.

Donovan moved to hold her, gathering her slight frame into his arms as gently as he could. They stayed that way for a long time.

Finally Julie moved, looking up at him, seeing the pain in his eyes. "I'm sorry I didn't tell you. There wasn't time. Besides, I wasn't sure. At first I really thought it might have been the flu or a latent allergy to the red dust."

He nodded, his green eyes intent on hers. "You know, if things weren't so screwed up, there'd be nothing that I'd like better than you, me, and a couple of kids."

She nodded, her head moving against his shoulder. "I know. And it's funny, even though I was relieved, I felt such grief when I knew I was losing it."

"Are you in a lot of pain?"

"Some," she admitted. "Joe gave me something. But I'm supposed to take it pretty easy, at least until Wednesday."

He kissed her forehead, smoothing back her hair. "Can I stay? I'd like to be with you."

"All right," she answered after a moment. "Just don't answer the phone, in case Nathan calls with the last of the test results on the new red dust."

"Has it been worth all the hassles it ended up causing?"

She shook her head. "Even without the final tests, I'm afraid it's pretty conclusive. The variant should protect this part of the ocean, but it refuses to transfer to land-based vegetation. So we're back to square one in finding a solution for driving the Visitors off frost-free land areas."

Donovan was silent as he digested this piece of information. Finally he said, "What do you suppose Diana will do now?"

"Get the water from someplace else, I suppose." Julie wondered if she sounded as tired and discouraged as she felt. "Sometimes I wonder if it wouldn't be smarter just to give up. There doesn't seem to be any future worth living for. For us or anyone else."

Mike sighed. "I'd been doing a lot of thinking along those lines lately, too. But when I went over it all again this morning, I came out of it with the conviction that there *will* be a future, Julie. After all, *we're* part of a generation born from parents who spent nearly a decade wondering if the end of the world had come—who had a hard time hoping. *They* survived, they had us, and we have to hope there's hope for other generations."

Julie laced her fingers into his. "Other generations of other people's children at least. Maybe someday for *our* children as well. We've still got time."

"Yeah," he said. "We do. I love you, Julie."

"I love you, too."

They sat quietly looking at each other, the whisper of the air conditioning the only sound in the room. Finally Mike stirred. "Hey, it's time for dinner," he said. "I better fix you something."

"Just some soup will be fine," she said as he stood up. "What time *is* it?"

"Five," he said absently, then his gaze sharpened on his watch. "Hey, the telephone rates go down at five."

"Yeah, so?"

"So do you mind if I use your phone for a long-distance call?"

"No, go ahead." Julie watched him as he headed for the door. "You got a girlfriend, Donovan?"

He stopped halfway out of the room to grin at her. "Yeah. But I swear that as of tonight, I'm breaking it off. What time is it in New York?"

Julie smiled. "Eight. I'll even pay for the call."

Watch for

THE TEXAS RUN

next in the V series
from Pinnacle Books

coming in September!